BLOOD IS THICKER THAN WATER

Michael Christopher Carter

Golden Hill Publishing

ISBN-10 : 179097920X
ISBN-13 : 978-1790979202

Cover design by: MiblArt

CHAPTER ONE

Annabel Brimble didn't like the news. She made a point of not watching it. A big believer in your focus creating your reality, she saw no sense in filling her mind with detritus; the vast majority of which she could do nothing about.

People moaning and whining and tut-tutting in the streets cooing 'Oh, isn't it terrible,' and 'Whatever is the world coming to?', now repeated a thousand-fold; a million-fold, on social media boiling the world's problems down to one-hundred and forty characters or an amusing picture wouldn't do any good, Annabel was certain.

Then there was prayer. She hadn't always loathed it, and she wasn't sure she hated it now, appreciating the importance of giving responsibility to a higher power. Only, she'd never felt she had a choice.

"It's no use putting your head in the sand," her clergyman father had always criticised, and now she'd married the Reverend Bertie Brimble the condemnation continued.

She hadn't agreed it was such a bad idea. Her head in the sand seemed the perfect place to hide away from that which did nothing but bring her down. And who decided what was and what wasn't newsworthy anyway?

No, Annabel Brimble didn't like the news and she'd never regretted avoiding it… Until this happened…

"So, what do you think?" Bertie announced placing a brochure in his wife's lap. "Beautiful, isn't it?"

Annabel leafed through pages of picturesque beaches, brooding cliff tops, and mighty castles and agreed that, yes, it was beautiful. Was he springing a holiday on her? Because she couldn't be doing with that when she needed to be close for antenatal classes and getting the nursery ready. That was a joke. The two-bedroom flat was full to bursting with the two of them and Charlotte (the 'nursery' had been created with some plasterboard bisecting their bedroom.)

"Well? Do you like it?"

Annabel's head nodded up and down, slowly preparing to fend off his holiday plans.

"Look at that beach! Glorious, and not crowded like the ones in Spain."

"Where is it?" Annabel asked.

"Pembrokeshire."

"Where's that?"

Shaking his head at his wife's failure to know

every corner of the British Isles, he grinned. "Wales. South-West Wales to be precise."

"Well that'll be why then."

"Why what?"

"Why the beaches aren't full. It pisses with rain all the time in Wales."

Bertie sighed. "You know how I feel about profanities, Annie. And anyway, that's just on the mountains... Well, mainly. Tenby, which is where the house is, is one of the sunniest places in Britain, actually. Look."

He flipped to a particularly stunning golden crescent of sand accented by a castle-like fort on a little island just offshore. "The jewel in Pembrokeshire's crown... Tenby. Do you know what Tenby is in Welsh?" Annabel raised an eyebrow. "Dinbych y Pysgod. Do you know what that means?"

"You're being annoying. I've only just heard of the place and you expect me suddenly to understand Welsh?"

"*Little fort of fishes,*" Bertie announced undeterred. "The whole town cosies up on the cliff behind a mediaeval curtain wall. Stunning."

Flipping through more pages, colourful cottages and Georgian terraced houses encircled a picturesque harbour with turquoise sea fading to crystal clear pools at the shoreline. Determined to delay a holiday there until at least after she gave birth, she decided she would have to push him. "Why are you showing me brochures of

3

Tenby? Because if you're thinking about a break, I really don't think…"

"We're moving there!" Bertie beamed.

Air left Annabel's lungs as a flock of birds leaving a wire, the words echoing. *'We're moving there…'* Mouth gaping, nothing breached the silence which Bertie's exuberance filled like sand in a hole.

"Virtually no crime… Lowest crime statistics in Britain. Lovely people. Much better than around here." His arms spread and indicated the whole of Hartcliffe. "And I'm needed, Annie!" he hissed. "I can make a real difference there."

"If it's so wonderful, why do they need you?" Annabel forced the words through lips crinkled in disgust. How dare he ambush her with this? Not, 'what do you think about moving here?' but throwing it at her as an already decided fait a complis.

Bertie's eyes fell to the floor, when he looked up, his cheeks flushed with colour. "Well, the thing is, the vicar before me, Reverend Oliver Jones, has gone AWOL; left the parish in a right old pickle."

"And if you leave here, won't *our* church be in 'a right old pickle' too? You're such a hypocrite!"

A knock at the door punctuated the sourness and halted Annabel from flinging her cup of coffee at the wall.

The bible study group filtered in intermittently. "You're looking radiant," the first brave enough to try to penetrate Annabel's barrier of thorns clucked. She permitted only the briefest curve in her line-smile in concession. It wasn't this person's fault her husband was the most irresponsible fool.

Bertie shuffled chairs from around the dining table at one end of the room to form an ellipse of seats with him at the vertex ready to teach and field questions. All but one were filled and Annabel knew without asking who the latecomer would be.

Abi, a ditsy blonde, who on first being introduced to Annabel when she'd just become Bertie's fiancé, couldn't wait to add that her marrying Bertie herself had been 'on the cards' for a while. But she'd never seen herself as a vicar's wife, she had added, invalidating both Annabel's supremacy in her husband-to-be's affections and her choice of becoming *just* a vicar's wife. Abi always performed with such gushing charm that seemed to work far better on men than on the women of the group. Annabel detested her.

A rambling rap at the door preceded her chaotic entry. Shambling along the little hallway, she oozed into the lounge where she greeted everyone with air-kisses before her gaze fell on Annabel. With a long stare resting on her growing tummy, she smiled. "You're looking... flourishing," she settled on.

Annabel twitched her cheeks allowing them to

crash back to the blackness of her mood. If they did move home, at least she'd be away from this bitch.

"I thought we'd talk, this week, about *Colossians.* It can be difficult living as a Christian amongst non-Christians, can't it? But it's important we keep faith and set good examples..."

Annabel couldn't stand to listen. '*Good examples?*' Tearing your family away from their home without so much as a discussion was a good example, was it? She seethed in silence glaring out at the nodding congregation. Their living room couldn't hold many, but it was almost their entire church.

There were more mosques than churches in this part of the world, and whilst she admired Bertie's tolerance of other religions, she knew the lack of support bothered him.

Wales represented a far easier role, she assumed. The Welsh are known for their Christianity, Bertie would soon have them in the palm of his hand. And it did look nice in the brochures. Perhaps she was being silly. Who would choose a flat in an old terraced house where wheelie bins decorated the streets like square black Darleks ready to attack and take over the world at ground level?

And the crime here worried her, although she'd never had any trouble. She took a strange comfort in the multi-coloured faces she passed whenever she left the flat. Turbans and Burkas showing some of the different cultures which surrounded her were two fingers to the tyrannical religion of her childhood.

But was that reason enough to keep her little girl and her new baby away from what Bertie was offering? Imagine growing up going to the beach every day. It had to be better than here in Hartcliffe. Nature at its best, verses sprawling concrete. It was no competition, was it?

He'd probably assumed she'd be happy and it just came out wrong. She'd give him the benefit of the doubt, and of course talk with Charlotte. Would she have to learn Welsh at school? How would she feel about that?

Drifting back to the room, her thoughts having taken her away for longer than she'd realised as her husband was just wrapping up, Annabel held on.

"And before I bid you farewell tonight, I have an announcement to make." Bertie looked at everyone in turn before clearing his throat. "I've been asked to take a post in South-west Wales… Pembrokeshire, near Tenby. It's beautiful. A real opportunity for our family; especially important with Baby Brimble on the way." The hurt faces weren't convinced. "And they really need me there. They're… going through a rough time."

"What, in Tenby? I haven't heard anything. What sort of rough time? It looks like Paradise to me," an older member of the study group piped up.

"Well, it's not Tenby, as such, but a little village on the outskirts."

"Which village? I used to go there as a kid. St. Florence? That's nice. Saundersfoot? I used to love it there."

"Goreston," Bertie mumbled.

"Goreston?" Abi screeched. "*Goreston?* Isn't that where those two little girls were murdered?"

CHAPTER TWO

Once more Annabel crashed down at the mouth of that woman. Murdered? Colour drained from Bertie's face as he glanced at Annabel's glassy gaze. This wasn't how he wanted to tell her. As she looked up, her stare pierced through him, 'How *could* you?' it implored. He had no choice but to nod and confirm the facts, shrinking back as his wife's eyes shot to the floor. Tense shoulders showed her every breath, squeezing in and out of her tight throat. He mouthed sorry, but boring holes in the floor, she didn't see.

"Yes, Abi. Thank you. Goreston is indeed where those poor little girls in the news were abducted and murdered."

"And raped! Don't forget that!"

"Quite right. It's an awful business," Bertie wittered, the stiffening of Annabel's shoulders framing his unease. "That's why I've been called there. The community is understandably in turmoil. It's not what they've come to expect. The poor families are struggling more than most, I fear..."

"How can you say that? Losing a child is every parent's nightmare. They're not suffering more than I would if I lost my Suzie." Her dark skin paled with indignation.

She was angry. This was all going wrong. "No, Daphne, of course I'm not saying that. It's just, around here…"

"Around here you might expect as much… is that what you're saying? You preach so much tolerance and forgiveness, but all the while you're judging us all." The '*us*' a reference to a born and bred Bristolian, perhaps? Bertie wasn't sure but he wasn't thinking straight and he knew whatever he said next would make it worse.

"No, Daphne. That's not what I mean at all," he said, but he thought it probably was exactly what he meant and he felt ashamed. "It's just the parish there in Goreston have been abandoned by their vicar so I've been called in as an emergency in these troubled times."

"And what about us? You're just going to leave us…"

Bertie stared round at the nine people crowding his living room. Nine. One of whom was his own wife. How could they say their need compared to hundreds of good Christians suffering in Wales?

"Weighing it all up, yes. I'm afraid so. I am needed in Goreston. I know so, or it wouldn't have happened. God doesn't make mistakes, Daphne. When I got the calling to go to Wales, I *knew* it was the right thing."

"That's why you didn't bother running it by your wife and daughter, is it?" Annabel scoffed. "God said, so who gives a fuck what we think?" she swore deliberately and slowly. The shock reverberated around the room."

"Der is no need for dat sort of language, Mrs Brimble." Daphne admonished, falling straight back to the path of self-righteousness.

"Fuck off, Daphne. That goes for all of you!" she hissed.

"Annabel, please," Bertie cooed.

"Get AWAY from me!" she screeched. "Go on. Get out."

"Mrs Brimble; Annabel, we're here to help you. Let us help you," the kindly voice of one of the older members of the group soothed.

"Thank you, Mrs Morris, but I only found out about this proposed move hundreds of miles away to another country moments before you arrived. You see my husband didn't think to tell me or our daughter…"

"It's all very last minute, darling…" Bertie was silenced with a glare.

"If you don't mind, Mrs Morris, and the rest of you, I'd like the opportunity to talk to Bertie alone."

Chairs shuffled and watery faces mumbled their goodbyes as they passed in the hallway.

Abi paused and rested her palm on Bertie's chest. "If you need anything..?" Her simpering eyes filled in the gap. Annabel didn't care. If her clown of a husband wanted the final insult to be finding solace with that creature, that would make what she had to do very easy.

The door clicked and eight pairs of feet shuffled along the pavement outside the ground-floor flat, mumbling as they went.

"Annabel, darling…"

Annabel slumped on the sofa. Crumpling into her forearms leaning on her knees, she wept.

Bertie watched, hovering with the cuddle he knew would not be wanted. "Sorry," he hushed into the jagged air.

CHAPTER THREE

Twiddling his thumbs, Bertie opened his mouth and thought better of a number of attempts before he eventually spoke. "I had wanted to tell you... About the poor little girls, I mean. It's just that people started arriving early for Bible study and..."

"You found out about this 'opportunity,'" Annabel sneered, "in the last hour or so, did you? You couldn't possibly have mentioned it any other time than just before people came to our house? Not for a surprise visit even, but at the usual time they come every week." She was shaking her head. "No. I think you knew I wouldn't like the idea for a while and chickened out of telling me until you'd have to tell the study group." She frowned. "Why did you have to tell them tonight? When exactly is this planned move scheduled to take place?"

"Well, obviously there's a lot to organise, but I was hoping in the next two weeks."

Annabel banged the arms of her chair and snorted in a façade of strength disguising the anguish her moist eyes betrayed. Through the lump in her throat she squeezed the words through, "Safer than here, you said. You actually lied. I'd never have believed it of you, Bertie, I really wouldn't."

"I didn't lie. Statistically it is safer than here. What's happened recently is unprecedented."

"Oh, great, so we're joining the community just as it goes down the drain."

"They need me there. I'm not wanted here. You know that."

"No. I won't believe it. I refuse to consider that my husband would turn the rape and murder of two beautiful little girls into a job opportunity. Well? Tell me I'm wrong."

Bertie's face creased in puzzlement; wrong that she wouldn't believe it? Wrong that that was what he was doing? "There is opportunity in the situation, I won't deny it. But if you think that's the only reason, or even the main reason I agreed to take this job then you are seriously misjudging me. And okay, I decided without talking to you first, but you haven't been well in this pregnancy, you know? You've been… a little moody. I'm sorry, but a decision needed to be made quickly and I made it because I knew; I *know* it's the right one."

"And there's no arguing with that, is there? You've spoken to God Almighty, how can I say anything to compete?"

Bertie sighed. "If you really don't want to go,

then I'm sure I can sort it out."

"I don't want to go, so do sort it out!"

Bertie sighed again, caught out in his bluff. "But, honestly, Annie, it's such a great chance for us. Imagine Charlotte on the beach every day."

"All I can picture is our beautiful daughter being murdered like those other two."

"That won't happen. We won't let her out of our sight until he's caught. They've already arrested a suspect. We could be somebody there, Ann."

She noticed her name becoming ever-shorter as he tried to persuade her. She was in danger of being reduced to a grunt.

"We could get a puppy. Picture it. The vicarage is absolutely huge, and so charming. Views of the sea and an island with a monastery. And truly, love, it really is safer. Murders happen here every week, but it doesn't even make the news. It's the shock factor they want, isn't it. You're always saying as much. They're showing this with such dedication because it's somewhere so beautiful; so incongruous with the surroundings. I can make a difference for the people there, and we can make a difference to our lives at the same time.

"He's pretty clever, Him upstairs," he gave a reverential nod upwards. "We're doing His will by going, and he's rewarding us with a better life. Almost makes being selfless the most selfish thing you can do!" He chuckled at the well-prac-

15

tised phrase.

"Where do you want Baby Brimble to grow up? Here, where murders don't even reach the papers, or there," he pointed at the brochure, "where it's so beautiful and we can fulfil our rightful place?"

They'd dreamed of moving away, of a bigger home in the country. Maybe she was being foolish. It would be typical if she refused and then something terrible happened to Charlotte right here in Hartcliffe. *Ephesians 5:6 '... the wrath of God comes upon the sons of disobedience.'* Annabel couldn't bring herself to disobey to God. She didn't want to believe the angry jealous god of her father, preferring Bertie's loving friend of a deity. But what if her dad had been right? What if he did something to her baby because she didn't do as she was told? Babies had never fared well in the Bible. "Okay. I'm going to trust you."

Bertie rushed and hugged his wife who flinched at his touch. "I'm still mad at you, Bertie Brimble. I'm trusting you and your connection with God. Don't let me down."

"Of course not. It'll be great, you'll see."

"There're things to sort out, but I'm tired. Go and run me a bath."

"Of course, my angel. Of course."

CHAPTER FOUR

The bath had gone cold. Annabel shivered but was reluctant to leave the quiet sanctuary of their bathroom. Tears merged with the water trickling down her forehead from her wet hair. What had she agreed to?

Was it just the circumstances of their move to Pembrokeshire that was upsetting her? She could barely bring herself to think about that. But she wasn't sure she wanted to go anyway.

Her baby was due soon. She was familiar with the hospital and the community midwives, a couple of whom had been on the team delivering Charlotte ten years ago. What could she expect in Wales? Would they all talk about her in Welsh? It was a strange concern considering the variety of nationalities working in Bristol's NHS.

And her family were here. She didn't see them much, mainly because her father's judgement had never seemed favourable. Even marrying Bertie, whilst not attracting any derision, didn't achieve him saying he was proud of her. She thought she remembered him being pleased that a man of the cloth might keep her on the straight and narrow.

But she appreciated they were there… if she wanted them. Charlotte knew nothing of the proposal yet. What might she say? Obviously the big house and being near the sea would appeal, but what about leaving her mates?

It took a while as the images of Charlotte and her friends swam through her head to realise the implications. Little girls. Around ten years old. She sat bolt upright in the cold water and screamed. "Nooo!"

Bertie raced from the lounge to the bathroom. "What is it? Are you okay in there?" The silence that followed unnerved him. "Annabel. Are you alright?" Bang, bang, bang. Nothing.

With a shove of his hefty shoulder, the little bolt on the bathroom door sprang off and it flew open.

Open mouthed, sobs wracking her pale body shook droplets of water rippling the bathfull beneath. At the sight of Bertie, a creaking cry escaped and she squeezed the words from her lips. "I can't do it. I can't move. I can't take my baby *there!*"

"Okay, okay, hush, don't worry. I'll tell them we don't want to go. I'll tell them I don't want the job."

"What if something happened to Charlotte? What if she was the next victim?" She broke into more sobs.

Holding her wet head against him, Bertie soothed, "I know, I know. Don't worry. I'll never let anything happen to her... Or to you, or to any of us," he placed a hand on her belly. "My goodness. You're freezing! Here." He stood and trotted to the door where a dressing gown and towel hung.

"What are you going to do that the parents of the other girls couldn't do?"

Pausing with the towel poised, Bertie pursed his lips. "Don't forget, we're aware of the threat."

"Don't forget!? How could I? I'm going to have nightmares forever."

"I meant, if we know the risks, we can avoid them. The other poor families knew nothing."

"Surely the second family knew, Bertie? It must have been at the very front of their thoughts and they couldn't protect their little girl? Why are you so keen to plunge our daughter into the vilest of dangers? I just don't get it. And don't you dare say it's an opportunity. I can't accept that you're prepared to profit from other people's suffering."

"Okay, my love. Why not sleep on it tonight, and we'll talk frankly tomorrow. If you still don't want to move, we won't move?"

Annabel sniffled. "Promise?"

"I Promise," Bertie agreed.

Even though they were a hundred and fifty

miles from the murder scene in Pembrokeshire, it was with unease Annabel watched Charlotte disappear into school that morning. With Bristol's murder rate at a ten year high, she'd read last month that London had overtaken New York. Like Bertie had said, just because Pembrokeshire's tragedies were getting press coverage, didn't make Hartcliffe any safer.

She'd wandered home with frequent glances back to school. After a jittery meander, she arrived home to the flat. Perching on the sofa, one eye on the front door because she felt she might have to rush off somewhere any minute. She didn't want to move home, she was sure, but she didn't feel safe here either. What had Bertie done to her?

Turning on the BBC, it wasn't long before the murders were mentioned in the headlines, although Goreston itself wasn't named in favour of labelling it 'a small village in South Wales.' Annabel pressed her lips together. It was like the world conspired to keep her in the dark. She could thank Abi for that, at least. What happened, did they not credit the audience with knowing where it was? Or was it that Pembrokeshire Council somehow arrange for the news to be less specific so as to keep the tourists flooding in? She didn't have long to ponder as she winced when the two little faces smiled out from the screen. Hands flew to her trembling lips. Poor little angels. They could be Charlotte. If the killer had a type, Charlotte was it!

Dark hair and eyes, olive skin, a cheeky innocent grin. What might they have achieved with their lives if they hadn't been brutally stopped? They were beautiful and Annabel couldn't help but imagine fine-looking future offspring the world was also robbed of. Why were they always so delightful? All children were, she supposed.

Remembering it wasn't just their lives they'd lost, but their innocence too, Annabel's chest tightened into a knot as her eyes drew to the door where she'd leave to pick up Charlotte in the longest six hours' time.

When her gaze fell back on the television, the first victim, Chloe King's face shone from the screen, zoomed in until it appeared pixellated as the BBC told us how her parents were distraught and "would always remember Chloe."

You don't say. What a ridiculous statement. That's why she didn't like to watch it. That's not news. She didn't need Chloe's poor parents to be put through such ridiculous questions to be told they'd always remember her!

What were her last words, her last thoughts as the disgusting monster held her down and exposed himself to her and… She vomited. Why did they show this? Who was it helping? Chloe's family must have smashed their own television by now. Surely they couldn't endure the torture of the media showing their pride and joy; their lost reason for living, every five minutes?

Stabbing at the remote control, her finger threatened to pierce the plastic and shatter it into a million pieces. "Shut up! Shut UP!" she screeched.

Holding out her top prevented the congealing liquid from trickling to the floor. Hovering over the toilet, she let what she could drop into the water. Gawping at the mess still left behind, snarling, she ripped it from her body. Stretching it between her hands, she yanked until a satisfying rip reached her ears. Grasping the next seam, she tore at it until that too ripped apart. Tearing and ripping, the flowery blouse that had been one of her favourites, fell to the floor in strips.

Collapsing on top of the pile of fabric, she sobbed. How could anyone destroy something so perfect? How did that fit into God's plan?

CHAPTER FIVE

"What do you think?" Bertie asked the question as Annabel's eyes settled anywhere but her daughter's face. "You'd have to promise to do everything we say to keep safe. Do you hear me? Until the nasty man is out of harm's way."

Nasty man? Annabel slowly shook her head. What about murdering paedophile scum?

"A boy was murdered at the end of our street… Stabbed," Charlotte announced. "They told us in assembly. He went to our school. We were warned not to go out after dark."

Annabel's heart thumped. "End of our street?"

Charlotte nodded. "At the little shops. Outside the chippy, I think. They think it was to do with drugs, but I don't think the boy used drugs. They said it was… mistaken identity, or something. I don't know."

She took it all in her stride as only a ten-year-old can. But Annabel's cushion from the world had given up its last stich. Her stuffing flew about in chaos. Nowhere was safe. A boy. Murdered. Metres from her own home and she'd walked that way with Charlotte and, she cupped her tummy in her arms. No. No, no, no. "Okay. We'll go." Turning to Charlotte, she added, "If it's what you want, sweetheart?"

Charlotte nodded. The Brimbles were moving to Wales. And, into more danger than they ever imagined.

CHAPTER SIX

Removals had been organised in no time. Bertie had alluded that it had all happened so easily because it was God's will. Annabel wasn't so sure. They didn't have a lot of furniture, and most of what they did have they weren't taking with them. What suited a ground floor Bristol flat did not necessarily suit a large country vicarage.

They had also been fairly flexible on time because there was no chain; no contracts to sign, just a long drive they'd never come back from.

The firm they arranged came from Pembrokeshire and stayed overnight in Bristol before loading the beds and clothes and little else into a lorry that could have taken twice as much and still had room. As it pulled away, Annabel took her phone from her pocket and made the call she'd avoided for two weeks.

"Reverend Richards speaking."

"Dad? It's me."

There was silence from the other end until "Hello. What can I do for you?"

It was a reaction as though she only ever called to ask for something when in reality she'd never asked for anything in her life. She'd rather die first. "I just wanted to let you know we're moving; Bertie, Charlotte and I. To Wales."

Without inquiring where in Wales, a journey that could range anywhere from fifteen miles to two-hundred and fifteen miles depending on where in Wales they were headed, Reverend Richards sighed, "So I'll not be seeing you for Christmas, I suppose."

Why was that his first thought? Last Christmas he'd made such a fuss over the money they'd 'wasted' on Charlotte's presents, Annabel wasn't keen to see him in Bristol or Wales. "I'm sure you will," she chickened into saying. "It only takes two or three hours."

"Well that sounds terribly far to me."

Should she be glad he cared, or was this all about telling her off? "I have to go now, Dad. The removal lorry has just driven off and we'll need to be there to let them in."

"Okay. Well thanks for phoning," –at the very last possible minute, he managed to convey in his dark tone without saying.

"Alright. Well bye," Annabel ended, her throat too constricted for more. Her mum had tried to make things work between them before she passed away. Now there seemed little hope.

The lump in Annabel's throat remaining as

they hugged the few neighbours and members of the church who had come to wave them off confused her. Was she sad to leave this place? Certainly she loved the city, but the part of it they could afford existed a world away from the cosmopolitan centre. Pembrokeshire offered so much more. But the danger was also so much more poignant.

Abi hugged Bertie for an uncomfortable time. They'd never see her again, would they? Annabel smiled inwardly. When she finally released her husband, Annabel stepped forward and clasped her to her bosom. Face hidden over Abi's shoulder, she held on for dear life. She could feel her squirming in discomfort, but she clutched her firmer.

Abi wriggled free and made a show of air kisses. When they landed, Annabel grabbed her again and held her until she was in danger of being guilty of assault or from falling into fits of giggles. "Bye-bye, Abigail. Don't go changing, will you. Look after yourself." Turning away, Annabel opened the car door, eased her hugeness into the passenger seat and pulled the door shut, determined never to look at her again.

As Bertie pulled away with farewell toots of the horn, Annabel allowed a smile at her last resistance and stared through the front window never again to gaze back.

They left Hartcliffe and headed past the city. Bertie leaned over and squeezed his wife's knee affectionately between thumb and index finger. "Okay?" he inquired, her silence unnerved him. When she didn't respond, he glanced at their daughter in the rear view mirror, but whatever she was listening to in her large headphones had her full attention, so she too failed to reply to the same question and arched eyebrows.

"Goodbye shops," Annabel said to the passing scenery. She wasn't big on retail therapy, and even less so recently with her added bulk, but as they whizzed by it seemed as good a place as any to rest her discontent.

"They do have shops in Wales, you know," Bertie reproached, falling into the trap for which ten years of marriage should have prepared him.

"I don't think you want to be pointing out what Wales has got. I can barely keep my mind from that. I feel sick. How can we be sure to keep Charlotte safe?" Bertie's lips quivered like a fly trapped on the web of its executioner, with about as much hope of escape. But there was no sensible answer beyond the obvious so he was grateful when Annabel's expectation of a reply appeared short-lived. "We can't. You better know what you're doing, Bertie Brimble!"

But she knew the reality. Nowhere was truly safe, Pembrokeshire perhaps safer than most with the school's teachers, the police and of course, the public on high alert. And they already had a suspect. It was a lot of media-hype on top of two family's suffering.

And keeping Charlotte protected didn't have to be hard. She could miss school if necessary and they could not leave her side. keeping her away was against the law, but what were they going to do? It wasn't unreasonable under the circumstances.

The motorway that traversed Bristol and exited to more motorways heading north, south, east and west, was busy. Coming to a standstill as they crossed the river, Bertie had time to take in the scene. People bustled round the waterside shops and cafes as the River Avon glistened in the sunlight, water taxis casting their wake to the banks in white ripples. Idyllic, but this was never the Bristol they enjoyed. They never had the time or the money to venture into the city centre instead, imprisoned in the city's darkest corner knowing such a life was on their doorstep only underlined their desolation.

Charlotte was no fool and hid from the tension behind a wall of music. But Bertie believed everything happened for a reason so set about giving meaning to the virtually constant traffic jam which confronted them. Something which affected thousands of commuters every day now given divine-purpose by virtue of on this occasion inconveniencing Reverend Bertie Brimble... A chance to talk.

"This is a new start for us," he began. "It might be a good idea to air our grievances on the journey. That way, when we get there, we can begin as we mean to go on."

"Yes. Let's chat, and then the angelic faces won't loom at me every minute I close my eyes. I won't picture our daughter raped and left in a ditch somewhere, and we can have a jolly old time being the perfect couple for the church. Because that's what you care about. Your career."

"My career is helping others. If I care about it, it's just because I care about them!"

"…And the new house and beaches…"

"Well, I won't deny that is a good thing. It's God's reward for our hard work. You can't change the flow of Divinity, darling. You could try, but you wouldn't get far."

"And why are we so blessed when these poor parents are in a living hell? Hey?"

"Well," Bertie began his well-rehearsed sermon, "We don't always know what God's plan for us is. But if he tests us, he must know we are strong enough."

"Oh, make up your mind! Does he test those who are strong, or does he give them new opportunities in Pembrokeshire? Or are you not strong, Bertie? Are you weak and shallow?"

Where was all this venom coming from? His eyes fell to their little creation growing inside her.

"Don't you dare blame this on my bloody hormones!"

"You know how I dislike colourful language, sweetheart," he admonished.

Mumbling a few choice words under her breath, she knew was being unfair. Other occasions, hearing her husband's explanation of why bad things happened to good people, she remembered agreeing with most of it. Now it was too close to home, or soon-to-be home. And despite her outburst, she was sure hormones were playing their part.

When the silence built to an intolerable tension, Annabel reached out a hand and placed it on Bertie's thigh which was enough for Bertie's belief in everything being amazing to be topped up. She smiled. He was right. This could be a new start, and who better than the irrepressible Bertie Brimble to rebuild the crushed community?

Reaching the M4 motorway to 'Wales and The West' stoked the fire of change. After that, hills entered the scenery prompting eyes to gaze with a new joy. And by the time Britain's longest bridge loomed into view, a bubbling excitement breached the surface beyond the gloom; a high mountain top piercing the clouds of Annabel's torment.

The first rat-tat of tyres on the expansion joint clicked a switch in the Brimbles and they gazed in awe at the four miles of sea below. Towers soaring in the middle where the bridge was suspended on poles to allow for big ships to pass underneath to the Bristol Channel were like the gateway to a fresh world. Beyond them, the slow descent into the Principality of Wales. But the sign welcoming them to their destination brought a sudden pang of doubt in Annabel's chest. *'Croeso I Gymru – Welcome to Wales,'* it declared. How would Charlotte cope with learning a different language?

It had been discussed before the final decision had been made, and she'd assured her mother she would be fine… It couldn't be harder than Urdu that she'd begun to learn in the multicultural Hartcliffe. Bertie had filled her with useful facts to make it seem more exciting and she'd said she was keen to learn Europe's oldest language. Annabel sighed quashing her own fears. Baby Brimble would benefit too, apparently. Learning Welsh from nursery age left the brain susceptible to absorbing other languages later. And Welsh schools had an enviable reputation for language development and other aspects of academia too. Oh, yes. He had all the figures to craft a convincing case, and as the cities of Cardiff and Newport gave way to the dunes and glimpses of the sea, it was easy to let them persuade her.

She recognised the industry of the steelworks at Port Talbot from an old chemistry textbook. It looked both impressive and a blight on the landscape. It was hard to view the mountain backed bay without imagining how it must have looked without the embellishments of commerce and the M4 motorway.

As the journey progressed, she would come to

view it as perhaps the last sign of civilisation as the houses grew sparser and sparser and the motorway ceased and became an ever-narrowing trunk road.

A sign declared Tenby was but a few miles away. *'Little fort of fishes,'* she remembered Bertie saying and reading in one of his pamphlets. That's what the unpronounceable signpost translated to. *'Dinbych y Pysgod.'* Shaking her head, she wished Charlotte good luck with that under her breath.

Bristol was a lovely city full of history the world came to admire, but what she saw now was the most stunning vista she'd ever laid eyes upon. Jagged rocks punctuated the turquoise sea as it made gentle progress onto a crescent of golden sand to caress the colourful little boats bobbing in front of the equally vibrant houses encircling the harbour. Perched on top of the backdrop a large hill branched out into the sea with its lifeboat stations and was crowned with castle ruins and a statue of Prince Albert.

Passing the harbour, the castellated town walls directed them through narrow roads where timber-framed buildings leaned on one-another for support across cobbled streets. A larger expanse of golden sand filled their view now. "Beyond the rocks, opposite the island you can see offshore, that's our new home." The female Brimbles could only nod in wonder.

Cresting a hill after passing 'Wales's best holiday park' according to the sign, a sharp right took them through dense woodland. An archway of trees excluded the sea view for long enough that when it appeared again it burst into a vista making them gasp in unison.

With a grin as broad as his face, Bertie announced, "This is our new home!"

A steep gabled rambling house, as big as the entire terrace of houses their two-bedroom flat had resided, revealed itself before them as Bertie pulled onto the gravel drive through a five-bar gate.

"Wow. I bet Reverend Oliver Jones regrets leaving this place," Annabel declared with a slow whistle.

Bertie nodded solemnly. "I dread to think what he must have gone through to make him go. A crisis of faith, I suppose. I'm sure the church will find him another post somewhere else if he wants it. He's rather blacked his copy book here, though, I'm afraid."

Annabel snorted, but didn't bother saying, 'Afraid of what? Look at the house we get to call home now!' and then the word 'afraid' spun round her mind bouncing in jagged spikes wreaking guilt at their good-fortune in the face of other's misery. But then Charlotte raced around the garden squealing, "I love it, it's sooo cool!" and preceded to climb a tree for the first time in her life. Life goes on, and they were at least here to help.

CHAPTER SEVEN

I t wasn't necessarily their taste, but the décor certainly suited the house. It could be mistaken for a museum of Welsh life with the many original features.

Once the keys had been procured from the church warden, or rather, after they received a phone call detailing under which plant pot they were hidden, Charlotte happily leapt from her somewhat low tree climb (she'd chickened out when the branches grew more spaced apart) and bolting through the front door, she ran up the stairs to pick her bedroom.

There were four to choose from. Sensibly, the room with the en suite bathroom she left for her parents before taking one two doors down with the most glorious views over the church and trees towards the sea.

Sighing, she nodded to herself, she understood the challenges here. There were new friends to be made, as well as inviting some of her old friends for a holiday. She'd have to learn a new language, but she felt confident enough about that. And she had to be careful… Not only to avoid whoever was responsible for killing the other girls, but also not to do anything to make her mum and dad worry.

Snapping away with her phone, she took pictures of her new bedroom and its views. About to share them with online, she paused. An assembly about keeping safe on the internet made her nod. She swiped her screen and kept the photos to herself for now. That was the sort of considerate thinking that would keep her parents happy. She couldn't be accused of showing some weirdo exactly where he could find her bedroom!

"What do you think? Will it do?" Bertie stood in the doorway, grin only moderately misplaced by the act of speaking.

"It's amazing, Dad," she said, rushing to hug him. "We're so lucky."

Bertie nodded. "I want get my bearings and see the church for the first time. Want to come?"

She did want to see the church, but she hadn't seen everything here yet. "Can I come another time?"

Bertie chuckled. "Of course. Mummy's waiting for the removal van. Perhaps it is better if you stay here, anyway. You can tell the nice men where you want everything. See you later."

The furniture was soon in place and the men from Pembrokeshire Removals bid cheery goodbyes (or Hwyl Dda's, as they'd said), but the boxes of stuff took longer to sort out, particularly with so many spaces to put things. Annabel's nesting instinct knew no bounds in the vast farmhouse kitchen. Several times she had changed her mind about what cupboard should house what as more boxes were opened. Maybe she should wait until all the boxes were emptied, she considered, but she was enjoying herself too much.

A loud knock at the door disturbed her reverie. Dusting her hands off on her pinafore dress as she stepped into the hallway and walked to the front door, a ripple of excitement ran down her spine. She had no idea who to expect, but here she was, the lady of a fabulous house.

Fumbling with the old locks, she managed to prize the door which had swollen in its frame in the hours since air had circulated once more in the house, Annabel pulled it open.

Flinching back from the man standing before her, manners restrained the gasp threatening to leave her lips as eyes sunken into shadows either side of a small pert nose gazed at her with a laser intensity. Desperate to look away, to be free from their piercing, she forced herself to maintain his stare in a moment of pseudo assertiveness. It seemed important.

"New vicar?" the man said, pupils swiftly darting to every corner, falling back onto Annabel in time to witness her confirmatory nod. "Is he *here*?"

His unusual emphasis of *here* struck her as

odd. Suddenly unwilling to admit to being alone, she winced at the noise of Charlotte racing downstairs to greet their visitor. But she didn't want to allude to Bertie being here and have the man come in.

"Is that your little girl?" The man leaned around Annabel, craning his neck, his eyes shone. "Hello, little girl," he oozed.

Annabel's head shot round. "Go upstairs! Do as you're told," she snapped. Charlotte nodded and stepped back. Mouth open in halted greeting, she edged to the staircase and hid out of sight. She sensed danger. "We're very busy. I'm sorry, I'll have to ask you to leave."

"Well, is he here? Simple question."

"I… I…" Annabel couldn't decide what to say. Sending this man to meet her husband alone at the church made her uncomfortable, but would that be better than this? Bertie would think so. He was kind and gentle, but he was also large and a fierce protector of his family. She could phone him to warn him.

Plastering on her warmest fake smile, she made a face like she'd just recalled, "Sorry, I remember now. He went to check out the church while I supervised the removals. *Coming,*" she called behind her at an imaginary removal man.

"Who are you talking to?" the man frowned. "There's no-one here."

How did he know?

"I watched the van drive away. There wasn't

much stuff in it either, so I doubt they're coming back with a fresh load or to help you move it."

His eyes, never still, flicked from one window to the next. Why was he so interested? Annabel's brain seized as her mouth dried, rendering her mute.

"When's it due?" he pointed a prodding finger at her bump making her hug it in her arms instinctively.

Prizing her dry pallet apart, she hoped her mind might catch up with a plan of what to say. "Soon," she rasped through the tight gap. Wanting to declare, 'Well, thanks for calling by, I really must get on,' all she managed was incoherent mumbling as she attempted to push the door closed. She knew it would be easy for the man to intervene to stop her with it wide open so she surreptitiously moved it to a position she could slam it shut.

"I'll call again." The man shuffled away. "When you're settled in," he smirked, parting his lips for a moment. "Tell the vicar I was here, won't you?"

Who was here? Annabel didn't want to ask. As the stranger turned and walked down the path she closed the door and threw back the bolts. "Charlotte!" she hissed. "Lock any windows, there's a good girl."

"Who was that man, Mummy?"

Annabel shook her head. "I don't know, but I didn't like him, and I don't trust him. He might try to get in the house. Lock the doors and windows and I'll phone Daddy. Okay?"

Racing to the back door, Charlotte found it was already locked, but in this rambling old house, she didn't know where to head next. She hadn't even been in all the rooms yet.

The kitchen led to a small lobby with a stable door. There were bolts already in place, but the window was slightly ajar.

Grasping the handle, Charlotte pulled but the casement wouldn't budge, the hinges rusted and the wood swollen underneath the white paint. That's why it's been left open then, deduced Charlotte whilst calculating the modest opening's potential risk.

Deciding it was too slender for the man she'd seen to have any chance of gaining entry, she left to find other rooms with other windows.

Small three-stair cases led away from the central hall in three directions to compensate for the uneven floor. A washroom next to the kitchen had a similarly small casement in a similar state of perpetual openness. The next led to a room already filled with study furniture including a magnificent old desk. Charlotte didn't have time to admire it. Rushing past, she reached a large sliding sash window. She'd never seen one up close before. She didn't know if it was locked, but her attempts to open it were futile so she presumed it must be. A determined attacker could break it easily though, she thought, amazed the centuries old wood and thin glass were even intact.

The final staircase accessed a large room which they'd quickly allocated as the family living room. With a similar sizable window, she quickly ascertained that too appeared locked and fragile.

Back in the hallway, her mother was on the phone, "Damn! Why do you never have your phone on? Bertie, you have to come home. I hate talking to these things," she muttered. "A very odd man came to the door asking about you, staring at Charlotte. He made me very uncomfortable and I think he might still be hanging around." Covering the mouthpiece, she turned, "Have you locked the doors and windows, Charlotte?" she asked.

"Not upstairs yet."

"Hurry, Bertie."

The pair climbed the uneven staircase to the upstairs rooms. The windows all seemed fastened, and whilst just as fragile as the ones Charlotte examined in the lounge and study, they were probably too high up to be a real risk.

"Why are you so scared of that man, Mummy?"

Annabel glared. Did she really have to remind her? "I didn't like him, that's all."

"Why?"

Annabel's frown deepened. "He was rude. And he's been watching us… Waiting for the removal men to go away."

Charlotte wondered if that might have just been out of politeness, but she wanted to appear obedient and aware of danger. Her mother may keep her locked in her room for her own safety if she didn't seem like she could be trusted. "We should be safe now..."

The words had barely left her mouth when the unmistakable sound of the door rattling stopped her dead. "Mummy?" Charlotte cried, shuffling towards Annabel and throwing her arms round her.

"Wait there on the bed," Annabel instructed as she pushed herself up and crept to the window. Peeping through the musty curtains, she glimpsed a figure as it slunk along the side of the house out of sight from where moments before it had shaken their front door.

With a gasp, Annabel scrammed for the bedroom door and pushed it shut. Instinctively sliding a chair under the doorknob, she prayed it would be enough to stop an intruder while she got help.

'The mobile you are calling is switched off... Please leave a message after the tone...' "Shit. Not again. Why do you never have your phone on, Bertie Brimble?" Annabel dialled again. This time 999. She had no choice.

'Which service do you require?' the voice enquired.

"Police. Someone's trying to get into my house and I'm alone with my daughter!"

'Putting you through.'

Annabel listened as the operator passed her

call to the police and heard her mobile number read to them in case she was a hoax call.

"Someone's breaking into your house, madam?" the unmistakeable sound of police speak came through loud and clear. "Is that right?"

"Yes! Please hurry."

"Where are you? Where is your house?"

"I don't know the road. It's the Vicarage in Goreston. Next to the church. I've only moved in half-an-hour ago."

"A car is on its way. Stay on the line. Where are you in the house?"

"Upstairs. In my daughter's bedroom."

"Is she with you?"

"Yes."

"And is she okay? Is there anyone else in the house?"

"My husband is at the church not far away. The man who came to the door looked angry with him. I don't want him to hurt my husband."

"You spoke to the man?"

"Yes. He came to the door and was strange. Something wasn't right about him. He seemed... threatening. I watched him walk away, but now he's back and he's trying to get in the house."

"Stay in the bedroom. My colleagues will be with you shortly."

BANG! BANG! BANG!

The sound came from one of the doors downstairs, but it was impossible to tell from which direction behind the closed bedroom door. Breathing hard, she closed her eyes to calm herself for her daughter's sake.

"Is that the police?" Charlotte asked, still hugging her mother.

"They haven't quite reached you yet," the operator interjected, hearing Charlotte's question. That banging was the intruder, was it?"

Annabel nodded before realising she wouldn't be heard and whispering, "Yes!"

"Okay. Hold tight. They'll be there really soon."

The sirens wailed through the wooded valley. Moments later the tyres rumbled onto the driveway and doors slammed.

"They're here."

"Okay. Give them a chance to check out the situation, and they will call you on this number when they're happy it's safe. Okay. Good bye and good luck."

Craning against the window, it was impossible to see or hear what was happening.

"What is it, Mummy? Are the police here?"

Annabel nodded. Two squad cars, lights still blazing were evidence enough. Surely they were safe, but what had they found, she wondered, shallow breaths leaving her faint.

The trill ring and buzz of her phone as it vibrated made her jump. "Hello?" she whispered, clutching the phone to the side of her head.

"Hello, Madam. It's Police Constable Griffiths here. We've apprehended a male attempting entry to your property, but we'd like you to come down and help us with a couple of things, if that's okay?"

About to say 'Of course,' she stalled. What if the weird man suddenly had her number? What if he'd overpowered the police and knew phoning her is what they would do next?

"How do I know you're really the police?" She thought she heard a sigh.

"I'll come to your front door. You can see my ID. You can phone HQ for verification if you're still worried... I understand you've had a bit of a scare."

Reassured, but not enough to put Charlotte in danger, Annabel moved the chair to open the door with instructions for her to replace it as soon as she left. Waiting to hear it slide back into place, she moved.

Padding down the stairs, she could see the police uniform through the small rectangle of glass in the door. There was no chain so she decided it would be safest to talk through the thin glass. He did say he understood.

The officer smiled. He wasn't the man who had been before and his photo ID bore his resemblance. Doubting herself as soon as she decided he could be trusted and opened the door, she knew she was being irrational.

"Good afternoon, madam. PC Griffiths as you can see from my badge. As I said, we have apprehended a suspect, but he has an unusual story I'd like you to verify… You see, the thing is, the chap we've caught prizing open a side window claims he's your husband. We obviously want you to confirm he's telling the truth."

Colour drained and her knees buckled. Bertie! Coming back from church and finding all the doors and windows locked. He couldn't have just phoned, could he? His battery is never charged. Now she felt a fool.

Turning the corner with Constable Griffiths, her face was red as she saw a sheepish Bertie restrained and handcuffed by three other officers. She nodded. "Yes. That's my husband, Bertie Brimble; The Reverend Bertie Brimble. But there was a man who called round and he was aggressive. That's why I locked the doors and windows."

"Don't worry. You did the right thing. We wouldn't want you risking your safety because you're worried about wasting our time. And please don't hesitate to call us again if you're worried. But you're okay for now, yes?"

Annabel nodded, an apology weaving its way to her lips, but no. She had been scared. "What will you do?"

PC Griffiths tilted his head from side to side, pursing his lips. "I'm afraid there's nothing we really can do at the moment. He hasn't committed any sort of offence. Keep a diary. If he's persistent in calling unwanted, there may be something we can do; or if he makes any specific threats, maybe we can have a word with him. It sounds terrible. We'd love to stop crime before it's even happened, and there are lots of things we can do to that end, but this situation is difficult. Like I say: make a note of his frequency of visits, and what specifically he says. We'll do everything we can to make you feel safe." He crinkled his lips in a comforting smile and walked towards his car.

Bertie was de-arrested and un-cuffed and stood beside his wife as the squad cars manoeuvred in the drive exiting down the lane.

They'd been lovely, kind, and patient, but they must think I'm a neurotic nutter, Annabel sighed. They probably have a lot of those in the climate of fear the village trembled. Without a word, she turned and strode back inside. Bertie followed, every bit as calm, patient and patronising as the police.

Annabel sat at the kitchen table with her head in her hands. Bertie placed a hand on her shoulder but she shook it off. Pulling out the chair next to her, he faced her. "Tell me about the man who called round. Why did he scare you?"

"Oh, I don't know. I'm probably a neurotic freak."

"I doubt that. What did he say?"

"He wanted you. When I said we had just moved in, he said he'd been watching and asked if you were here in a really unfriendly way. When Charlotte came downstairs his eyes lit up. I didn't like it."

Bertie nodded. "You did the right thing. We have to be careful. It could be easy to forget why we're here." Eyes leaving hers to stare at the floor, he regained eye contact to tackle a difficult subject. "Charlotte needs to start school soon…"

"She's not going! No way. We have to keep her safe. You said they'd arrested someone. She can go to school when we know she'll be safe."

"But she'll miss out on the first days. We don't want her to feel uncomfortable. We can walk her to the door and meet her at the door at the end of the day. The school won't let any of the children leave the building. The little girls are on everyone's mind. Nothing can possibly happen to her there and she'll resent being kept at home."

"I just want to keep her close to me. Until I know she'll be safe," her voice cracked.

"You've had a scare. We'll talk about it another time."

Annabel's head fell back in her hands. Where was the safest place for her daughter? Could she keep her safer here with strange men and thinly glazed windows? Maybe school was the best place for her. She shook her head. They could discuss it later. "Come on. Help me finish unpacking."

CHAPTER EIGHT

Annabel had expected the strange man to call again over the weekend. When he didn't, she considered he'd been scared off by the presence of the police.

Saturday had been a trip into Tenby for school clothes after Charlotte joined the pincer movement with her father squeezing Annabel into letting her go to school. Annabel always hated school and would have grasped any opportunity to stay away. What was the matter with the child?

Charlotte and Bertie had been right though: starting in September along with everybody else was definitely the best way to make friends. And beginning wearing the same clothes as everyone else was also a good idea, hence the trip into town to a dubiously named 'Tees R us' which at first Annabel had assumed was something to do with golf, but now understood it to mean T-shirts are us; a name which didn't exactly scream 'school uniforms.'

As the bell tinkled in answer to the opening

door, Annabel wondered how many firms plagiarising the now defunct 'Toys R Us' regretted their moniker.

"How can I help you?" the man behind the counter asked.

"We need everything for Goreston School, please. PE kit, the lot."

"Okay," he said, looking Charlotte up and down. "How old are you, young lady?"

"Ten," Charlotte replied.

Nodding, the man selected a few items from the shelves. "Behind those boxes, there's a curtain. You can go behind there and try them on, if you like."

"Go on," Annabel agreed. You're starting on Tuesday. We won't have time to come back."

Moments later, Charlotte presented herself, fully attired in the Goreston bottle-green livery where she proceeded to give a twirl.

"Perfect," Annabel declared.

Paying the fifty-eight pounds for the various items, they popped the carrier bag into the car but didn't get in. "Come on. Let's go and get an ice-cream or something."

Tenby bustled along heedless of the torment the small neighbouring village was going through a couple of miles away. Most of the tourists would have booked their holidays months before and would soon have put the distasteful murders from their minds in the light of all the colourful houses and smells of the sea and of the delicious street food.

A horse and carriage at the corner promised tours of the mediaeval walled town, but Annabel and Charlotte walked on. Choosing which of the many ice-cream parlours to give their trade proved tricky with the sheer number to choose from. They opted for a mobile one in the street, closed to cars, café tables spread on the cobbles. Charlotte had a simple vanilla while Annabel went for a curious Bakewell tart flavour.

Licking their ice-creams as they walked, they passed dozens of café's whose patrons spilled out into the sunshine like a little town square in France or Italy, the huge tower of St Mary's church carefully casting its shadow behind the buildings so as not to spoil the fun.

Glimpses of turquoise sea between Tudor timber-framed shops hinted at the magnificence that opened onto the harbour where a brass band gathered in a marquee ready to perform before what posters publicised as the '*Tenby Spectacular.*'

There promised fireworks and funfair rides as darkness drew and Annabel felt suddenly uncomfortable. She hadn't intended to stay late, and even if she had, funfair and fireworks seemed just the place she might inadvertently forget herself and let her guard down.

Hoping Charlotte hadn't noticed, she grabbed her hand and yanked her in the opposite direction. "Come on. We need to get home." Charlotte pulled her hand away in shock, sending the remnants of both their ice-creams tumbling to the floor where they landed top down with a splat.

Gripping her daughter's hand hard, Annabel dragged her through the street, jaw clenched. Reaching the car, she growled, "Get in."

The short drive to the Vicarage was in silence. When they reached the sign informing them they'd arrived in Goreston and reminding them to please drive carefully, the holiday atmosphere of the jewel in Pembrokeshire's crown was tarnished.

As though the sky knew that sunshine would be inappropriate for the village in its misery, clouds gathered in darkening plumes in a reflection of a thousand occupant's moods.

Charlotte whimpered, "I'm sorry, Mummy."

Annabel shot her a look. "What for?"

"Dropping our ice-creams."

Leaning towards her, Annabel put her free arm around her shoulders and gave a gentle squeeze. "Don't be silly. That was my fault. I'm sorry. I got a bit panicky, that's all. You'll be a parent one day. Then you'll understand."

Relieved to be back in her mother's good books, when they pulled into the drive, Charlotte skipped out of the car. Running around the front door, she stopped dead and screamed. "Mummy! It's that man again."

Throwing open the door, Annabel reached her daughter as the man from yesterday edged towards her, arms outstretched.

"Chloe? It's not you is it?"

"No. I'm Charl…"

"Get away from her!" Annabel threw herself in front of her daughter. "Get away and leave my property now!"

"Is the vicar here?" the man asked?

"Just go away!"

Watching to make sure he left, with trembling fingers, she called the police. "He was here again… The man. He was here again and he wanted my daughter!"

Scurrying inside, it didn't take long for her thoughts to catch up with her and she was certain, 'Chloe' was the name of the first little girl to be murdered.

Convinced the weird man must be her killer, she clutched Charlotte to her as she waited, breathing heavily, for the police.

"Has he been here again?" Bertie asked, having walked in past the police car in his driveway. "Are you both okay?"

Annabel nodded and Bertie sat beside her as the lady police officer went through the details.

"The problem we still have, Mrs Brimble, is other than your suspicions, the gentleman hasn't done anything wrong. I know… I know," she answered to Annabel's snort, "We don't want to wait until something does happen. Of course we don't. But there is no law against knocking on someone's door. And you say he asked to see the vicar? Well that makes sense, doesn't it? I mean, your husband is a vicar, isn't he?"

"It might be a cover," chimed in Bertie. I mean, if he wanted to speak to me, why not come to the church? On both occasions he would have found me there. Everyone knows the vicar lives here… It's the Vicarage. I don't think Annabel would be afraid of him for no reason."

"Okay. So what exactly did he say, again," the police lady asked.

"He only asked for the vicar as he was leaving. And that was after I screamed at him to go. Before that, he was trying to talk to Charlotte. He reached out to her but I dived in-between… But he called her Chloe. The first little girl was Chloe, wasn't she?"

The WPC exchanged a glance with her colleague who stood behind her. He gave a cough to say he caught her drift.

"Can you describe him for me again, please?"

Annabel frowned. They'd been through all this. "Well. Like I said, he's quite tall…"

"How tall?"

"Not as tall as Bertie. So probably just under six foot, I suppose. Dishevelled. Matted dark hair and clothes he looked like he slept in. Just like I imagine someone on the run from the police might look. Because you let him go, didn't you? Your prime suspect? And now he's obsessed with Charlotte." Turning to Bertie, she hissed, "See!

We should never have come here."

"How old would you say he was, Mrs Brimble?"

"I don't know. Not old. Thirty? Maybe mid-twenties."

"Could he have been younger? Could he have been eighteen or nineteen, do you think?"

Annabel considered. His face wasn't lined, more gaunt. Haggard. She'd assumed his age because he looked troubled. But he could be younger than she'd reasoned. "Yes," she agreed. "He looks older, but it is possible."

"I might have an idea who's been bothering you, but I can't say anything at the moment. If it's who I think it is, you shouldn't have any more trouble."

"And if it isn't?"

"Obviously, keep us informed. But, the man we arrested, Terry, was much older. In his fifties."

Annabel slumped back in her seat. Of course. She'd seen his face almost as often as the two girls, "Why did you let him go? Is it because you didn't think he was guilty after all? Because if that's the case, this other chap might be the one."

"I can't really say anything about that, I'm afraid. I'm sure you understand. But I suspect he's long gone now. I wouldn't imagine he'd stick around in such a small community with his face plastered all over the news. Keep Charlotte safe, but try not to worry. We'll catch up with him."

"Before he rapes and murders another innocent child?"

"We're hopeful."

"Oh, well," Annabel scoffed. "I'm sure that will be a great comfort to the next victim's family. Unbelievable. Letting a killer back out onto the streets. You should be ashamed."

Standing to leave, the police lady smiled. "I understand your frustration, but believe me; we're doing everything we can. And do let us know if you're bothered by this man again, okay? Bye for now."

Walking to the door, the two officers stepped to their car and opened the doors. "Don't put yourself in danger, Mrs Brimble, but do try to be aware that people are going to come to see your husband, and they might be in quite a state. If I was seeking religious counsel, I'd probably look haggard too. Do you understand?"

'Please stop wasting police time.' Received loud and clear. But if Charlotte was in danger, she'd waste their time every day, if she had to.

CHAPTER NINE

Sunday was spent in rehearsal. No service was to be held until next week because no-one had been sure if and when a new vicar might be found, or if Reverend Oliver Jones might even make a reappearance. It was too late now if he did. Too late for him in Goreston at any rate.

So, the three Brimbles, and soon-to-be Brimble, went to the church together. Bertie was pleased with the support, but Annabel was at least partly motivated by not wanting to be without her husband back at the house.

"It's a lovely building. Is it older than the churches in Bristol, do you think?"

Bertie's mouth curved downwards as he contemplated. "It's pretty old. I don't know much about the history of the place. I suppose it would be fun to find out."

Fun. Annabel shook her head. "Yes. I would be interested," she agreed, imposing a more grown-up perspective.

"What do you think my sermon should be about? I mean, should I avoid the obvious, or plough straight into it?"

"I don't believe you have a choice. If the last vicar left due to stress, they don't want to sense the new one is unwilling to tackle how they're feeling. I expect some will be having a real crisis of faith. They knew these poor girls and their families. I'm struggling to cope. If someone already had doubts, they're going to need you. You can't brush it under the carpet, Bertie."

Nodding along, he pursed his lips to the side. "What about Oliver Jones deserting them? Should I mention that?"

"I don't know. Do you know why he left? Do you have any evidence?"

"The church warden said he'd acted most peculiarly for weeks before he finally did a moonlight flit. That's why they're so sure he's gone for good. He couldn't cope."

"I think he might be better left out of it."

"Apparently, there's an Alpha course starting soon as well. I normally like to run those with people I'm more familiar with."

"Let's be honest, Bertie. There weren't many takers in Hartcliffe were there. We were a bit of a lost cause."

Bertie smarted at the remark, fretting at how on earth he was going to manage a successful course introducing very beginners to Christianity if he'd never done it before. Sweating, he frowned. "I need to get through the sermon first, I suppose. I'd better start writing."

"Can we see more of the church first, Daddy?"

"I meant when we go home. And you shouldn't have been eavesdropping. I thought you were seeing what's up the tower."

"Bats! I saw one hanging upside down a few stairs up. The view from the top is amazing. I could see the whole of Goreston, plus the sea."

Charlotte had gone up alone as the only member of the family small enough to fit. Annabel was usually slim, but she was blooming nicely at the moment, and Bertie had allowed his fondness for everything sweet to take its toll on his waistline.

"I'll have to work on this," he said with a two-handed wobble of his ample belly.

"And I'll have to work on this," Annabel emulated the move, but the taut sphere didn't wobble at all. "He can't stay in here forever."

"I think he likes it," Charlotte smiled.

"Well you certainly did! You had a lovely fortnight holiday after your due date, didn't you!"

Charlotte grinned. Since Mummy had announced she was to have a little brother or sister (and more recently, brother as scans confirmed), she had been furnished with tales aplenty of when she was in Mummy's tummy. She had no doubt, but she still lapped up hearing what a fabulous big sister she was going to be. She couldn't wait.

"What about outside?"

"Better not. There's a pool or a well, or something. It's probably covered up, but I don't know. It might not be safe."

"A pool? Wow. That sounds amazing. I can't wait to see that. I'm coming every day after school."

For a while, Annabel had pushed aside the imminence of her daughter leaving her side for eight hours. A shudder shook her spine. "Mmm," was all she could agree.

"Let's get home. Daddy needs to write his sermon."

"You've got a week. I bet I won't have that long to do my homework."

"Maybe not. But I'm probably a much slower writer than you, little miss clever-clogs."

She smiled. She like it here.

CHAPTER TEN

The afternoons had been hot, but the clear skies gave chilly nights and chillier mornings. Annabel hadn't slept. She had allowed herself to be convinced that going to school was the best thing for Charlotte, but the thought of not being able to look at her and know she was safe at any time gnawed away at her.

She'd risen throughout the night, glugging glasses of milk and chewing chalk tablets to remedy the acid burning her stomach and throat. The little life inside her added to the problem, his wriggling sending spurts of sourness from her diaphragm.

As dawn crept over Caldey Island and illuminated the kitchen window, Annabel knew sleep had evaded her and she decided to send Charlotte off with a proper breakfast. Her favourite thing to eat was pancakes smothered in Nutella.

"Wow. Thanks, Mum!" she cried when she came downstairs to the delicious smell.

"Well, we can't have you going hungry on your

first day," Annabel grinned.

"Any for me?" a dishevelled Bertie inquired from the doorway.

"Of course! You know I can only make a big batch." Her recipe book gave instruction for 'serves six' and she'd never bothered to scale it down. The batter always kept fine in the fridge for the brief pauses in-between Charlotte eating her first and her sixth pancake, anyway.

Clearing away the plates, Annabel felt a tremble of nerves shake her, but she pushed it aside. Eyes scouring their surroundings as they left the house, Annabel expected the strange man to burst from the bushes but they made it all the way from front door to school gate without seeing him.

"Bye-bye, angel. I'll be here when you come out. Do not even think of leaving on your own, you hear? Even if you make friends and they think walking home with your mum isn't cool, don't go without me."

"You said you'd be here when I get out anyway? How could I leave without you?"

"Well, just in case. You never know. Wait for me, okay?"

Charlotte nodded, her brain racing behind her eyes.

"Promise? Say it."

"Yes. I promise. Can I go in now? This is embarrassing."

Annabel squeezed her shoulder. "You've got

your lunch?"

Charlotte nodded.

"Do you need any money? For tuck shop, or something at break time?"

"No, Mum. Let me go in. Okay?"

The pancakes hadn't been the best fuel to get Bertie off to a flying start with his sermon. He'd followed them up with some strong coffee but felt stodgy in stomach and mind.

Pacing round and round his study, he'd retreated to the kitchen where he forced in a bowl of fruit-topped granola hoping the vitamins and fibre might clear the way. And now he felt full and sick.

There was no point in just sitting at his desk writing nothing. His first sermon was important; too important. The mood in the village was dour, and the church, thanks to Oliver Jones, had failed to play its part. Now Bertie had to set them alight with no prior knowledge of any of them, or risk losing their trust before he'd even started.

"I'll go for a stroll," he said to himself, but if questioned, he might say he was in conversation with him upstairs. "Walk a bit of this food off. I can go to the church. Being there might be just the inspiration I need."

Squinting through the window, he tried to decide if he needed a coat. Opting for a thick cardigan, he pulled the front door to and walked out of the driveway. Looking back at the house, he smiled. It was a handsome old place, undoubtedly.

The morning sun began to warm the air and Bertie relaxed into his stroll in full swing, arms loosely at his side, a smile playing on his lips. Arriving, he paused at the gate and took it all in.

The grey church looked ancient. Its mighty stones worn with time, stubby tower crooked away from the sea, cowing from the stark wind that must batter it on stormy winter nights.

The graves were neat, but very old. The surrounding ground maintained insomuch as the grass was trimmed and the weeds and hedgerows strimmed. But flowers or other signs of recent tending was absent from the headstones suggesting it hadn't been used in a long time.

Walking past, he confirmed his hunch with dates on stones dating from 1696. Most seemed to be from the nineteenth century and he didn't spot one from later than the twentieth.

Some were very simple, but as he rounded the church, they appeared to become grander until the final grave impressed him in the form of a very large crypt. The engraving worn through the years, but Bertie thought he could make out the name Cawdor. Nodding to himself, he shuddered at the idea of the bones inside. Why? What bothered him? Was it the likely larger number of deceased within, being a family tomb, or was it the above ground nature of it? Shuddering again, that must be it, he thought. Not a believer in an afterlife, other than in Heaven, he couldn't imagine why it made him shiver. Reassuring himself with practical notions; he knew it had to be accessible because digging a fresh hole for each member of the family would be unpleasant.

It must have cost a fortune, he surmised, forcing a nonchalant hand to rest on the stone. Resisting turning away, at last he moved off towards a small back door of the church. That's when he saw it.

He'd been told about the Holy Well, and if he was being honest, he was a little disappointed. Not the cleanest of wells, the water had a reddish hue that on closer inspection, Bertie decided was due to the reflection of the foliage surrounding it.

Scallop shells lay round and about and Bertie imagined people dipping them into the water and drinking. He was both excited and appalled at the idea.

Kneeling beside it, he cupped some of the cold liquid in his hand and brought it to his nose. It smelt fine. Plucking a scallop from within reach, he scooped a shell-full and examined it. It looked clean, free of sediment. He'd heard that Victorians had frequented the Holy well and declared it to have great health benefits. Eyes narrowing, he drew it back to his nose then lowered it to his mouth where he allowed a drop to moisten his lips.

Smacking them together, he couldn't taste

much. With a shake of his head, he poured the rest of the water into his mouth and savoured it like wine connoisseurs he'd seen on foodie TV programmes.

Frowning, he struggled to identify the taste. Coins? Then nodding, he knew exactly what it was, and why the Victorians had prized it so. Iron! It was full of iron and that explained some of the colour too.

Shrinking his neck, he smiled to himself. He must be imagining it, but he felt good. Energised. Free. Dipping the scallop shell back into the water, he proceeded to drink giddily until he felt full. Laying back on the grass beside the pool, he remembered why he'd come to the church and searched for inspiration for his sermon. With a laugh, he thought he'd found it. But, he just didn't care. With a shrug, he realised he couldn't care less; about the sermon; about how his new parish reacted to him. And maybe that was the best lesson of all: for him and for them.

CHAPTER ELEVEN

He lay for quite a while before the Autumnal sun failed to keep him warm and he pushed himself up to standing. What should he do? Shrugging, he went to the back door of the church, more because he hadn't used it before and was curious than because he wanted to go inside.

Grabbing the ancient looking doorknob, he gave it a turn and pushed the door but it was locked. Frowning, he shook it back and forth. "Damn," he said, scowling now. Stretching back, he brought his full weight into the ancient oak with his shoulder, the centuries old wood absorbing the force without a murmur.

Furious, he pounded at it with clenched fists. Sweat dripped from his brow blurred his vision and he batted them away with the back of his hand a little too aggressively and it hurt.

Curling his hands into claws, he flexed his big arms and straightened his neck. With a growl, he turned swiftly, eyes hunting for something to match this door for strength. Shaking his head, he knew the strewn branches from a nearby tree would be no use.

A key! There must be a key. If it was locked, somebody locked it so there had to be a key. Jogging around the church to the front door, he giggled to himself that he had outwitted the door, or soon would have.

Shoving the iron studded oak slabs that formed a pair of formidable doors at the vestibule, Bertie entered the church. His gaze fell on the crucified Jesus above the altar and he looked away with a shudder. Pausing to take a breath, as a stranger, he padded the knave to where he estimated the back entrance to be.

Reaching it, he re-grabbed the knob and gave it another mighty shake as though it might suddenly work from inside. Scouring around the frame for a possible hanging key, he could sense the rage surging within him as one wasn't forthcoming.

Scanning eyes alighted on a doorway a few feet away. He recalled a small office lay beyond and he rushed to it defying it too to be locked or the glass and pine would succumb to his might.

It didn't dare and gave up instantly to his first turn of the handle. "Keys, keys, keys. Where are you?"

Joining the door in their desire to placate the madman rampaging through the church, the keys gleamed on their hook, willing him to find them. When he did, it was as a genius crying eureka at a scientific breakthrough.

Plucking them from their resting place, he scrammed back for the door and thrust the key into the hole, groaning with phallic satisfaction as he did, almost desiring to pull it out and re-enter just to relive the gratification.

Turning the key, the door sprung open and Bertie burst through. "Hah! Thought you could outsmart me, did you!" he cried, and then, standing breathless, the futility of what he'd achieved and how he'd gone about it struck him. "Calm down, Bertie. What's the matter with you?"

Chuckling to himself, surprised at the childish hedonism he'd had from something so simple, he forgot the fury—it was so unlike him—and walked back to his office; this time to sit. "You've got a sermon to write," he instructed, pulling out a pad and pen.

"Bore da, plant. Good morning, children. Did you all enjoy the holidays?"

The children had been asked this every return to school after every school break since they began four years ago. Usually, a rowdy hubbub would follow as each child raved about what their free time had given. Not today though. Their two classmates smiling lifeless into their homes every day throughout the summer had made term-time a day to make it all real.

"What's the matter, Sali Morgan?" the teacher asked the crying child. In response, she pushed back her chair and ran from the room. "Lauren, could you go after Sali, please? Check she's okay?" Eyes moist, Lauren followed her friend out of the class.

"Once I've called the register, we'll go to assembly where Mrs Davies will want to talk to you all about keeping safe. I'm sure you have heard about poor, poor Chloe King and Holly Jones?" It was miss's turn to lose her composure. "I never taught Chloe or Holly, but..." Her voice faded. Grabbing a handful of tissues she fluffed them in her face, shoulders shaking with the insufferable loss. This wasn't what she expected when she chose her path as a primary school teacher.

Calling the register seemed more than she could cope with but it was important, more so than ever, to know where the children were all of the time. Reading through the list of names and ticking each one off with a relieved sigh, she paused to re-welcome Sali and Lauren to their seats. Mouthing 'Are you okay?' she pursed her lips and offered a watery-eyed smile when the pair reluctantly nodded. Coming together with their classmates and facing what happened was an essential part of the grieving process. But it would be so hard.

Miss carried on with the calling of names. "Caitlyn Harries?"

"Here, miss."

"Charlotte Brimble?"

"Here, miss," Charlotte answered.

The room fell silent. A new girl. A girl who hadn't known Chloe or Holly. A girl who had no idea of the pain they were going through. A girl who sounded funny. A girl who could have some of the anger they felt at losing their friends. Why was *she* here when they weren't?

A sound broke the silence.

"Buzz buzz. Buzz, buzzzzz! Charlotte Bumblebee!" a boy from the back yelled. Laughter broke out and for the poor children dreading this day; children who had each been taken in tight hand grips to the school gate, it was a relief they never imagined for this terrible day. Even Miss Evans allowed a smile to play on her lips, grateful for something to break the tension.

It was respite for everyone except Charlotte. Each child in turn, through vocation or peer pressure, joined the buzzing. Glaring around at the taunting faces, Charlotte half expected the teacher to join in. Jumping up, she yelled, "It's Brimble, not Bumble. Don't be so childish."

"Don't be so childish!" a voice mocked.

"Sit down, please, Charlotte. And Caitlin? Charlotte's right. It's not big or clever to mock someone just because they've got a funny name or they sound different." The teacher smiled at Charlotte seemingly unaware she had reinforced the prejudice.

"My name is perfectly normal, thank you, miss," she said.

"Maybe where you come from!" another voice

chided.

"Where's that? A beehive!" someone else laughed, the whole class joining in.

"That's enough. Now let me carry on with the register or we'll be late for assembly."

As miss read out the Jones's and the Griffiths' and the Scourfields', a hissed insult reached the air un-checked by the teacher. "Bumblebee, bumblebee,' and everyone laughed again.

Sitting at his desk in his tiny church office, Bertie remained uninspired poring over the scribblings on his pad

'*Consider it all joy, my brethren, when you encounter various trials*.' James 1:2, seemed inappropriate, not striking the right note. Of course he believed everything, even the untimely demise of two beautiful little girls, was part of His plan, but he couldn't expect that message to be well-received. Not in such a brusque way. Not so early on in their relationship.

'*And we know that God causes all things to work together for good to those who love God, to those who are called according to His purpose,*' Romans *8:28*. Again, a sentiment to which Bertie adhered, but knew was not what was needed to help this community right now.

'*Be strong and courageous, do not be afraid or tremble at them, for the LORD your God is the one who goes with you He will not fail you or forsake you.*' Deuteronomy *31:6*. But did he really want to focus on Oliver Jones leaving them? Perhaps something about a new start, something from the New Testament, Matthew or John? But it wasn't a joyous resurrection, was it. He replaced a vicar who abandoned his flock when it was suffering terrible loss. Okay, he wanted them to feel free from the burden, but how?

Pushing back his chair, he tapped his lips with his pen. The cool water called to him. He'd felt so calm and unbothered when he'd drunk from the well. It couldn't be the water, of course. His body might need iron, but it had to be the relaxing surroundings. Sitting by a pool in a forest, enveloped by views of the ocean, a mediaeval church as a backdrop, who wouldn't relax?

Standing decisively, he strode to the back door and out. Kneeling beside the Holy Well, he cupped his hands and splashed the water over his face. With a joy far greater than this simple pleasure dictated, he plunged one of the scallop shells beneath the surface. With trembling fingers, he brought the reddish liquid to his mouth and poured it past his quivering lips. "Ahhh," he sighed, scooping and scooping until, giddy, he fell back against the grass.

"Bzzzzz bzzzz," they ran around her flapping their arms manically. Why did they persist with Bumblebee even though they knew her name was Brimble, and why was Bumblebee an insult anyway? Swiping at a scrawny girl as she passed,

Charlotte missed and tumbled forward.

"Look out, she's trying to sting you!" one screeched in a fit of laughter.

"She doesn't wanna do that, mun. Everyone knows what happens to a Bumblebee what stings you…" stepping forward, she shoved Charlotte who in combination with her already unstable balance, crashed to the floor. The girl leered over her. "It DIES!"

The crowd fell silent. Mention of death took all the fun out of it. From the sneers and head-shaking it was Charlotte taking the brunt of the sudden drop in mood. Leaving her humiliated on the floor, the girls walked away, "Buzzz bzzzzzzz," one of them began, but it had lost its shine now.

Eyes stinging, Charlotte pushed up on grazed hands. Wiping grit from a surface cut onto her skirt, she hobbled away to a corner where she could hide until the bell went for class to restart.

CHAPTER TWELVE

Annabel had got to the school gate early and she wasn't the only one. Staring at the entrance, her eyes watered with the strain. The muffled timbre of the home time bell filtered through the stone walls of the old school and the door finally swung open.

Children ranging in height from tiny to youth followed teachers in orderly lines. Reaching the gate, parents were called forward one at a time to claim their child. If there was any doubt, the child was questioned until the teacher could be satisfied this was a safe person to hand responsibility over. A timely exercise but vital to protect them. Annabel felt reassured.

Being unknown, she was one of the last to be beckoned. "Charlotte, is that someone to collect you?"

"Yes. That's my mum."

The teacher smiled. "Hello, Mrs Bumble," she erred, "May I have a word?" Shuffling away from the few remaining children, she spoke in a hush.

"Charlotte's had rather a tough time of it today. You'll know the school has had tragic news over the summer?" she paused for Annabel to confirm she understood. "I think being new, and probably not being…" she hovered on 'Welsh' but decided on, "Local, has meant she's borne the brunt of some of her classmates frustration. Talk to her. See if she's okay. And if the teasing continues, she must tell me. We want Charlotte to be as happy here as the next little girl," the phrase brought back memories of the little girls lost and her face burned as tears spilled. "I'm sorry."

Annabel's distaste at her daughter being bullied on her first day faded in the insignificance of what teasing amounted to compared to what this village had suffered. She'd make sure Charlotte understood it wasn't personal and they'd come up with a plan. "Okay. I'll talk to her. Thank you."

Stroking Charlotte's hair, she turned to leave the school ground. Trees lined the street every ten yard or so making the building fall in and out of view. Opening her mouth to begin her chat with her daughter, instead Annabel screamed.

Leaning against the fourth tree from the school the man from the house stared straight at them. His gaze trained on Charlotte, Annabel pushed her behind herself. Thrusting her hand into her pocket, she fumbled out her phone. Holding it in clear sight, she yelled, "I'm calling the police. You leave my daughter alone, you hear!" shaking fingers struggled to unlock the screen.

The man looked away from for the first time roaring, "No! Don't," then sprinted across the road out of view.

Unwilling to remain outside, she grabbed Charlotte's hand and marched her as fast as her burdened bulk allowed, back to the Vicarage, tears streaming down her face. This was too much. There could be no doubt in her mind Charlotte was his objective. Why else would he wait by the school? By the time they left there had been no-one besides them were around.

Slamming the front door, Annabel walked to the kitchen and leaned against the worktop. Running fingers of both hands through her hair, they fell to the nape of her neck and hung, limp, dragging her to the depth of her despair.

A broken breath fuelled her voice enough to say, "Don't go outside, Charlotte. I want you where I can see you."

Her phone rested in her hand, her sweaty finger struggled to swipe it open. She wanted to call the police, she knew they were tiring of her. While feeling foolish was of little concern, she didn't want them to ignore her call if she really needed them. What could she say he'd done wrong? He was outside the school. Annabel knew why, but he hadn't broken the law. He must be so smug knowing the police arrested the wrong man.

And what would 'really needing them' look like anyway?

At what point is it correct procedure to tell the police the murdering paedophile who has been demonstrating his interest in your daughter has finally made his move and done something illegal? Undoubtedly a point too far.

Bertie could add credibility. They could phone them together. She knew he wasn't home. He always bounded out like an oversized puppy when his girls walked through the door whenever he was. Shaking her head she recalled his obsession with finishing his debut sermon before Sunday. He must be at the church to get in the mood. Twisting her wedding ring, she forced her gaze away from the front door. A watched kettle never boils.

She ought to make dinner preparations but she felt too stressed. Opening the freezer, she longed for a ready-meal to present itself, but as they never bought any, it wasn't going to be. A takeaway, perhaps? Tenby must boast plenty of those. Good old British fish and chips. If she knew when Bertie was due home, she could pop off in the car and get some. Should she ring and risk disturbing his creativity? She decided she could wait a while longer. It was still early and he might even be walking back right now.

Sitting at the kitchen table, she pulled out her crochet and hoped the concentration would take her away from her constant cogitating. Ambition for a blanket had been downscaled to a scarf which may well become a little T-shirt if she could make the arms. At least it created a distraction.

Baby Brimble wriggled around. He knew when his mummy was distressed.

Placing the crochet in her bag, Annabel paced to the window. Staring out, there was no sign of her husband. It was getting late, so she decided she had no choice but to phone. Answerphone, as usual. "Bertie, call me. That man was outside the school. He was waiting for Charlotte. You have to help me tell the police. Make them listen... Oh, and I'm too stressed to cook. I was going to get fish and chips so let me know when you're expecting to come home... Bye."

Pressing her lips together, Annabel pushed her phone back into her pocket and picked her crochet back from her bag. Why did he never have his phone on? Infuriating.

She was making headway with the scarf-shirt when the front door finally fell open. Bertie stumbled down the hallway. When he reached the kitchen, instead of a warm greeting, he sniffed the air, "I can't smell anything cooking. Where's my dinner?"

Not hello. Not, how was Charlotte's first day. She'd let it go. He'd finish this sermon soon and things would return to normal. "I did phone you... A few times. It went to answerphone as per usual. I was planning to get fish and chips."

Grinding his teeth, he spat, "Fine," and walked to the door.

"I thought you'd be pleased. You love fish and chips. What's wrong?"

"Nothing's wrong. I'm tired. I'm hungry. I expected dinner, that's all. But if you're getting fish, I suppose that's fine. I might have to eat some bread and jam or something. You know how starving I get."

He wasn't in the mood for talking, she could tell that much. "I'll go then, shall I?" she said, making a show of the effort hauling her bulge took.

He glanced back and pulled a face like, 'Why are you still here?'

"Okay. Bye." Grabbing her keys and bag she fought tears and left. Pausing in the driveway, she thought about going back and confronting him. How dare he be so rude? Did he not even care what his wife and daughter might have gone through today?

Pulling the car from the drive, she headed along the road to Tenby. There might have been a time she would have cared which of the many fish and chip shops she chose. She'd read one of them had won *'Best Chip-Shop UK'* a number of times, but she couldn't remember which, so she stopped at the first one she came to—a small local chippie next to a Londis convenience store. It seemed likely to be good as the queue went out of the door.

Taking her place in the line, she realised she hadn't asked what anyone wanted. Cod and chips three times would do, or might Charlotte prefer a battered sausage or a pie. Oh look, she thought. A Saveloy. I haven't had one of those for years.

Presented with food whilst pregnant affected Annabel in one of two ways... She desired everything, salivating at every remembered taste and texture like a prisoner freed and confronted with food for the first time after being forced to eat gruel for years; or, it made her sick and the very thought caved her appetite for days. Today was a hungry day.

She regretted ordering scampi when she realised the three cod, Saveloy, chicken pie, steak pie, chips and rissole were ready and waiting in the hot cupboard while the scampi were still being fried, but it was worth it.

Virtually drooling, she rushed forwards when they called her order, dodging the amused stares following her and the huge bag of food. A chap in his seventies grinned at her. "I don't think you are pregnant. I think you just love fish and chips too much."

She chuckled at the look of horror on his face when she frowned and snapped, "I'm not pregnant! How very dare you!" Turning back when she reached the door, she put him out of his misery. "Only joking."

His shoulders slumped and his grin widened.

Wagging a finger at her he called out, "You little tease."

Still smiling as she opened the car, she carefully arranged the seatbelt to stop her lovely dinner falling over, then drove the two miles home extra slow just to be sure.

Pulling back into the drive, she smiled to herself as she removed the package with all the care she envisaged giving her new baby in a few weeks' time. "Come on, my precious," she cooed.

Frowning that the table wasn't laid, she called out, "Come and get it. Bertie. Charlotte."

Resting the bag on the worktop while she placed mats out, she grabbed a few plates and began unwrapping the food. Hearing footsteps she defended, "I ordered a bit of everything. I think my hormones got the better of me. If I serve the fish, you can help yourself to the rest."

"What's that, Mummy?" Charlotte pointed at the Saveloy.

"I don't really know. I used to have them as a kid. Some sort of spicy sausage. Try it. It's yummy."

Charlotte picked up the long pink sausage. "The skin is tough. Do I eat it?"

Annabel shrugged. "I always used to peel it, but I'm not sure you're supposed to." Head jerking from side to side, she asked, "Where's Daddy?"

"I think he went out."

Annabel dropped the rissole in her hand which broke its fall on a huge pile of chips. "What do you mean, you think?"

"I heard the front door slam."

"That must have been me going to get the food."

"No. After that. I heard it twice."

Pushing back her chair, Annabel went into the central hallway. "Bertie," she called. "BER-TIE!" Charlotte was right. He wasn't here. Stepping to the table, she tapped her fingers against the wood. How could he? Why would he leave Charlotte on her own? Picking at her dinner, the smell of it suddenly made her gag and she rushed to the toilet. When she returned, Bertie was sat snatching at food like a Neanderthal.

"Where's my cod?" Annabel stared in disbelief at her plate.

"Thought you'd finished," Bertie grunted.

Slumping in her chair, Annabel picked up the rissole again. "Is it okay if I have this," she said with more than a hint of sarcasm.

Bertie crinkled his full mouth. "I haven't tried it. Save me some."

Was this a joke? Were Ant and Dec going to jump out in disguise in a minute? She'd lost her appetite anyway now. Pushing her plate away, she coughed. "Why did you think it was okay to leave Charlotte on her own?"

"I didn't know she was here."

"What? You saw me leave. Charlotte wasn't with me. Where did you think she was?"

Bertie shrugged. "I don't know."

"Where did you go?"

His shoulders stiffened. Taking a very deliberate large mouthful, he ignored her question.

"Bertie Brimble, *where* did you go?"

Slamming a meaty fist on the table, he yelled. "To church, okay! Jesus!" Thrusting his chair back he stomped from the table.

Annabel didn't know if she was more shocked at the violent outburst or the blaspheming. She'd never seen him act this way before. "Are you okay? You seem tense."

Leaning back to glare at her from behind the fridge door, he snarled, "I'm fine! Or at least I would be if I didn't get nagged half to death the minute I walk through the door."

Hidden from view, he reached to the back of the fridge and plucked his reason for leaving Charlotte on her own from where he'd secreted the bottle behind the mayonnaise and mustard. Uncapping it he took a delicate sip before giving in and glugging from the neck.

"What's that?"

Choking on his mouthful, he turned sharply and raised his hand. Annabel flinched and leaned breathless against the cupboard. "Jesus Chriiist woman. It's water. See?" He thrust it in her face, its reddish clarity even more visible in the kitchen's artificial light. "Water." With one last defiant glug, he recapped the bottle and pushed it to the back of the fridge again. "It's mine," he said, the warning tipped with more menace than she had ever heard from her husband. Was writing a sermon really this stressful? Annabel shook her head and left to clear the table.

Expecting Bertie to be beavering away in his study, Annabel was shocked to enter the living room to find him slouched on the sofa gawping at the television.

Sitting in the armchair beside him, she eased her swollen legs onto the pouffe and sighed. Looking at what was on, she frowned. Football. Bertie never watched football. "Who's playing," she asked, hoping to glean significance from the teams, though she doubted Tenby had a team good enough to be on TV.

"Swansea. They're playing Nottingham Forest. No score yet."

"Are you interested for any particular reason?"

Bertie sat himself up on his elbows and glared at her. "I'm a bloke. Blokes like football. End of."

End of? End of what? End of discussion presumably.

"Fetch my water. You know? The bottle from the fridge."

"What about you fetching me water because I've just sat down after getting your dinner and clearing away because I thought you were busy writing your sermon. Oh, and I'm eight and a half months pregnant, in case you'd forgotten!" her eyes pricked with rage and dismay.

Bertie swung his legs round. Opening his

mouth, Annabel was already sure that what was about to come out was not to be a heartfelt apology.

"Fine!" he snorted, then abruptly his face softened. "Ah, Charlotte. Would you be an angel and get Daddy's water from the fridge? It's in a bottle at the back… behind the mayonnaise," he called after her as she left the room.

"Thank you," he said in exaggerated gratitude when she returned, glaring the while at his wife. Taking a huge swig from the bottle, he placed it on the table beside him and shot his eyes back to Annabel. "What? What are you looking at?"

"Nice water is it?" Who was he kidding? "Listen, Bertie, is there something you want to tell me? Something bothering you?"

He snorted. With an understanding chuckle, Annabel removed her crochet from her bag and began the therapeutic hooking of wool. They'd laugh about this soon. He'd clearly had a drink to calm his nerves to help him write, and because he never drank it had a peculiar effect on him.

The football finished, and Annabel was tired. She did call out, "Are you coming to bed," three times before settling for an unanswered, "Ok. I'm going up. Goodnight."

As she closed the lounge door, her husband's gentle snoring grew to Walrus volumes and she was grateful she'd get to sleep without him.

Peeping into Charlotte's room on the way past, she was sound asleep and covered neatly with the blanket, her sable hair fanned majestically around her pretty face. "Night-night, angel," she whispered before gently closing the door and padding softly to the master bedroom.

Bertie awoke with a dead arm hanging off the sofa and football on the telly. Squinting in the gloom, he remembered watching the game. He must have dropped off at half-time. Finger poised above the off button, he waited for a moment to see the score. *Swansea 0/ Notts Forrest 0.* After all that, nil-nil.

He stretched and yawned. Spying the bottle of water on the table, he debated having a last drink before bed. Why not? It must be doing him good. Holy water full of iron. It didn't matter about running out, he could get more tomorrow.

Batting the wall for the switch, the light came on and he crept up the stairs. Pausing outside his daughter's bedroom, he thought it was too late to look in on her. Resting a flat palm on the wood, he breathed her scent in deeply.

The landing light fell onto his wife's beautiful face as he pushed open the door. She looked so peaceful and alluring lying there. Flicking off the switch, she lay in darkness now, her comeliness lighting his way to bed in his mind's eye.

Pulling back the covers on his side, Bertie slunk in beside her. Her gentle breathing, in, out, in, out. Her face, full lips and freckles, a smile turning the corners of her mouth as though she could read his mind. All in his head, but he struggled to keep his thoughts as blood rushed away and only one thought remained.

With each rise and fall of her full, milk-laden chest, blood pumped to Bertie's extremities, growing him with every sigh. Prodding through his pyjama bottoms, it was becoming uncomfortable. Rubbing the swelling against his wife's round buttocks both eased and fuelled the problem.

"Annabel. Annie. Wake up. I need you."

Gradually becoming aware, Annabel roused to the prod, prod, prod. Turning, bleary-eyed, she shook her head. "Sorry, Bert. There's no way I'll get in a position where that's going to be comfy."

"We haven't done anything for months. You weren't like this with Charlotte," he seethed.

Cross that she had to justify herself, Annabel answered in a cold voice. "I wasn't sick every five minutes with Charlotte if you remember. I just don't feel like it, okay?"

Plumping her pillow, Annabel threw her head down punctuating the end of the matter.

But Bertie's matter grew ever-more unavoidable. Laying staring at the dark ceiling, he felt himself surge into his penis, becoming the throbbing, entering his wife his only thought.

Throwing back the covers, he stomped to the bathroom. Holding himself in his hand, he began to knead. Catching sight of himself in the mirror, he reflected how grotesque he looked. How undignified. He was married. He shouldn't have to feel like this. He shouldn't be denied like this.

Leaving the bathroom, he flounced round the bed. Standing over Annabel, he positioned his large frame so that he was level with her face. As she slept, or pretended to sleep, Bertie thrust himself into her mouth. Her eyes shot open and she gagged. Holding her hair, he stopped her head from leaving him. "Don't tell me this is uncomfortable too!"

She didn't have time to object as the juices which had fought their way from his thoughts through his body exploded in the back of her throat. He held her head until every last drop spilled out and he had one last thrust for good measure.

Tossing her head back on the pillow, Bertie climbed over her and got into bed.

Forcing the tears to stay in her eyes, Annabel bolted for the bathroom where she expelled the foulness from her mouth. Sitting on the toilet, she held her face in her hands and, for the countless time this month on account of her husband, she wept.

CHAPTER THIRTEEN

"Are you okay, Mummy?" Charlotte tried for the third time to get an answer from her mother who instead of making her breakfast and packing her lunch had sat in her chair staring at the wall. "Mummy?"

She'd cleared up the milk spillage when she misjudged how to pour from the giant six-pint carton, and she'd mainly swept up the cornflakes that escaped when she rolled down the bag, but all that took time and now she couldn't find her flask.

The dishwasher was full of clean dishes and cups but it wasn't in there. And she'd checked her school bag in case she'd forgotten to take it out the night before. She had no choice but to find something else.

When the bottles in the fridge were all too full to sacrifice, she remembered her dad's bottle she'd fetched last night. Running into the lounge, sure enough, there it was.

Returning to the kitchen, she debated rinsing it, but what was the point? It was only water anyway. Pouring squash into what was there already would save her time. Achieving the amber colour she liked for weak orange, she smiled, screwed on the lid and popped it into her bag along with four cheese strings, a Peperami, a packet of Monster Munch and a Mars. If she was making her own lunch, she would pack what she enjoyed.

"Mummy, is it time to go?" Those seemed to be the magic words and Annabel stirred into action.

"Oh, yes. Come on Charlotte, we're late." Stopping at the front door to grab coats, she turned to Charlotte, "I haven't made your lunch!"

"Already done," she patted her bag.

"And a drink?"

"Orange squash."

Annabel smiled. "Good girl. Sorry I haven't been with it this morning. I didn't have much sleep."

"Wriggling around was he?"

Annabel frowned and wondered if her daughter had pottered into her room in the night and seen, then she realised she meant the baby. "Yes. Something like that. Come on."

As they grew closer to school, Annabel swallowed repeatedly, aware she hadn't asked her how school was going still. Vowing to do it later she decided she was too fragile herself to offer good advice now. Nodding, she considered Charlottes gait to be one of a contented child. Maybe she should ask after all. Keeping her safe from harm wasn't enough. It was important she was happy too. "How is school, sweetheart?"

Charlotte said nothing for a few steps before answering, "S'kay. Could be better."

The truth was, whilst the 'Buzzz buzz, Charlotte Bumblebee' had stopped in the afternoon since the girl (who she now knew as Madeline) mentioned death and made everyone sad, no-one spoke to her. No-one paired up with her in lessons. No-one asked her to join in at lunch break (which they called cinio). No-one acknowledged her existence all day.

But she was resilient. "What would my daddy do," she'd wondered, hitting on the remedy promptly. "He'd pray." So she prayed. She prayed that she'd find the courage to ask to join in and not take no for an answer.

"Is anyone bullying you?" Annabel asked, recalling the teacher's comments yesterday.

Charlotte curved her lips down. If she wanted to make friends, the last thing she needed was her mum storming into the school hurling accusations. "No. I'm fine. It was awkward yesterday, but things will be different today. I'm sure. How can they resist this?" She pulled a monstrous face pulling at her cheeks with hooked fingers.

Annabel forced a laugh to be supportive, but she couldn't get Bertie's detestable behaviour out of her head. "Okay, lovely. I'll see you later," she called as Charlotte walked with purpose through the gates.

Bertie awoke to an empty bed. Memories of the night before filtered through to his consciousness. Sitting up, he cried, "What have I done?"

Flinging back the covers, he tiptoed to the bathroom and remembered it all. Holding Annabel while... well, it was abuse... Rape. He'd raped his wife.

The vomit came quick and plentiful. Most of it went in the bowl and despite the gagging it caused, he diligently wiped up the splashes before going in the shower.

It must be the stress. But there's no excuse. What might he say to one of his parish confessing that behaviour? He'd surely offer forgiveness and absolution. But he could not feel that for himself. He'd always felt guilt was a waste of time... Either a lesson had been learned, in which case guilt was no longer needed, or not, in which case you may very well commit the same sin again, so feeling guilty for it was a failure to recognise not being ready to accept your flaws and itself a sin to be absolved.

He might examine why they behaved a certain way to best advise them how not to repeat their sin. But for Bertie God's forgiveness was one thing he felt assured of, it was Annabel's that mattered. As for forgiving himself? He wasn't sure he ever would.

Drying and dressing, he took each tread of the stairs carefully. Planning to throw himself at her mercy, whatever she wanted of him, he would do. Anything.

He walked into the kitchen. She sat, staring at her hands as they lay palm down on the table. Bertie took the chair next to her and placed his own hands flat. "I am so sorry." He looked at her but she didn't look up. "I abused you… The light of my life. The only woman I've ever loved… will ever love. I don't understand why, but I promise it will never happen again."

Annabel's head raised and she regarded him with her stony stare. "If you don't know why you did it, you can't promise not to do it again. But you wouldn't do it a third time because I'd cut your fucking cock off!" A big salty tear defied her show of strength and tracked her tight jawline. Her hand flew back as Bertie leaned across the table to touch her.

"I know why you did it. You were drunk. And they reckon the drunk you is the real you… So, I'm not sure I like the real you anymore."

"I don't like me anymore, either. Not the me that did that to you. I love you. You must believe me, but I wasn't drunk. I haven't had alcohol, well, ever."

"Don't, Bertie. You said it was water, but water doesn't make people act like that."

"It was water! I promise."

Annabel narrowed her eyes. "Well, where did

you get it?"

"Exactly," he grinned, hoping humour might deflect his sin. "From the well. The Holy Well of Saint Julian. I drank the water from there. I felt so calm afterwards, the stress of writing the sermon just left me."

"And that's all you drank?"

"I promise."

"And that's what was in the bottle in the fridge?"

Bertie nodded. "I don't know, I just felt like I needed it. I didn't know Charlotte was here. I began to get agitated and remembered how calm I'd been after drinking the water so I popped back to the church to get more."

"There must be something in it. Water doesn't make you act like that unless you mix it with vodka."

"It's a Holy Well. I know people drink from it because there are shells left there for that purpose. They wouldn't drink it if it made them drunk, would they?"

Annabel shrugged. "People do all sorts."

"But not 'Church' people. What I did to you last night is unforgiveable. And I promise it won't happen again. I'll cut it off myself," he smiled, hopeful at the reception he'd got so far that she might absolve him. "I don't expect you to forgive me. I certainly won't forgive myself, but I'll pray God will have the answers. He'll show me the way never to be that person again. You do believe me, don't you?"

Annabel sighed. "I want to. Let's forget it for now. I wanted to tell you, yesterday, that the weird man was hanging around outside the school. I had to talk to Charlotte's teacher so the other mums and children had gone, but there he was. Staring at Charlotte from behind a tree."

"We have to tell the police. If they're sure they know who this person is, they need to keep Charlotte safe from him. I'll call them."

Annabel reached her hand across the table. "Thank you." She squeezed his hand and he squeezed back twice as hard.

"Thank you, my angel," and he brought her fingers to his mouth and planted the softest kiss. That was the Bertie she knew and loved: Kind, gentle, considerate Bertie.

"So, after you felt so calm, how did your sermon writing go?"

Looking away, he stammered from his blushed cheeks, "I still haven't written it. Not a word."

Pressing her lips and shaking her head, Annabel smiled. "Would you like me to help you?"

Grinning, he nodded. "Yes please."

She hadn't managed it at egwyl. Children in her class ran around playing tag and other games she didn't quite grasp, but there was always lunch break and that was much longer. She was sure to pluck up the courage then.

Before going into lessons after break, she left

the toilet and opened her locker. Opening her bag, she ate two of the cheese strings standing in the corridor, then glugged a few mouthfuls of her orange squash.

Sitting next to two girls, she frowned when she struggled to understand the maths on the board. It had all seemed so easy before break. It must be the cheese she ate. She'd heard it was a bad thing to eat before bed because it's hard to digest and can give you nightmares. It made sense it wasn't the best thing to have before trying to concentrate on trigonometry.

Craning over the other girls' books to remind herself how to do it, she flinched as one took exception and snapped, "Hey, stop copying, Bumblebee."

Without a thought, Charlotte lashed out spearing with the point of her compass. Stab, stab, stab.

The girl yowled in pain and ran to show miss the three puncture wounds in the back of her hand.

"Right, Charlotte Brimble. You will stay here and have your lunch at cinio. That's very naughty what you've done. Come and sit by me."

Charlotte gathered her things and pulled a chair across to the end of Miss Watkins desk where she sat and did nothing because she couldn't remember how.

When the other children left for lunch, Charlotte dutifully collected her bag from her locker and sat back down to eat her snacks. Miss Watkins watched in dismay as Charlotte tucked into the other cheese strings and smelly Peperami.

"Is that what you've got for lunch? Where are your vitamins? Where's your slow-release carbohydrate? No wonder you're struggling if that's the sort of rubbish you're eating." Miss Watkins stood. "Wait there. I'm going to see if I can find you some fruit. Do you like apples? What about a banana?"

Charlotte nodded. Miss Watkins walked out of the room and Charlotte opened her drink. The spiced meat and salty cheese had given her a thirst so she downed all the squash from her bottle. Throwing it on the floor, she didn't feel like waiting for miss to come back with her apple, so she left.

In the playground (she couldn't begin to get her head around what they called maes chwarae) Charlotte walked straight over to some girls running around and stood in front of one of them. "Can I play?"

"Get lost, Bumblebee," the girl jeered.

Charlotte grabbed her hair and yanked her to the ground. Her scream attracted the attention of Madeline, the girl who'd picked on her yesterday, who piled in to help getting an elbow to her mouth instead. Squealing, blood splattered over her blouse and she ran.

Charlotte chased after her. Grabbing her in both hands, she shook her and spat in her face,

"If you tell on me, I'll kill you!"

Nodding with a whimper, Madeline trembled in Charlotte's grip. Shoving her aside, she watched as the girl shuffled into the toilet to nurse her injury and her pride.

CHAPTER FOURTEEN

As planned, Annabel arrived early at the school gates. She'd checked every tree on her way; every driveway and corner, and she'd been grateful there had been no sign of the man.

Waiting, she didn't talk to the other mums who all seemed to have known each other since birth anyway. The bell rang and the children filed out. Squinting, she couldn't see Charlotte.

Each parent was called over, and sometimes their child appeared when they'd previously been out of sight from where Annabel stood. Charlotte must be behind that post, or that tree, she supposed. But when she was the last mum there and Charlotte wasn't, her heart pounded in her chest.

Spinning round, she scoured the street for the man. Had he somehow got there even before her and persuaded the school to let Charlotte go with him?

Tears streaked her face and her voice warbled as she wobbled to the teachers in the schoolyard.

"Where's Charlotte? Where's my little girl?"

"Ah, Mrs Brimble. May I have a word?"

"What? What is it? What's happened to my baby?"

A look passed between Miss Watkins and her colleague as she passed by. "Charlotte's fine. We've detained her, that's all. I need to talk to you about her behaviour today."

Following her into the school, she forced her largeness onto a ridiculously tiny chair that flexed under her weight.

"I know it's only Charlotte's second day, and she had a few problems with name-calling yesterday, but I think the way she's dealt with it... well, it's not very nice, to be honest with you."

Hearing how she'd stabbed a girl with a compass and beaten up two other girls in the playground, Annabel had to agree. "She seemed so positive this morning. So determined to make friends. What happened?"

Miss Watkins pursed her lips. "Well, to be honest, Mrs Brimble, I do find that you get out of a child what you put in."

Annabel frowned. What was that supposed to mean?

"If you feed her cheese and processed meat with no fruit and vegetables, well it's bound to affect her mood. Try to give her a more balanced diet." Glancing at Annabel's pregnant tummy, she said, "I understand it might be difficult. I can imagine preparing food might be the last thing you'll want to do in your condition. But, we do some very nice lunches here at the school. Why don't you let Charlotte have school dinners instead?"

Annabel blinked. It was hard to take in.

"Well. You have a think about it. But, we can't have a repetition of today's behaviour. If Charlotte behaves that way again, we'll have no option but to disallow her from school."

As a sheepish Charlotte was brought into the class to leave with her mother, Annabel hauled herself up and took her daughter's hand. "Come on. Let's go home."

Annabel hadn't the energy to be cross. And she felt responsible because she hadn't talked to her as she'd promised. She hadn't made a plan. Charlotte had made her own, and when backed into a corner, she'd defended herself. Annabel couldn't condone it. Not officially, but she did feel relief that her daughter wasn't going to be pushed around.

The week went by with no further sightings of the man. Bertie's phone call must have fired them into action, Annabel decided. And no further little chats after school with Miss Watkins either. It looked like Charlotte's campaign had worked and she'd won the battle and the war.

Every morning, she walked with her to the school gate and stayed until she was behind the doors, teachers waiting to check each one of the children in before the gates locked.

And every single afternoon she arrived at least half an hour early, examining each of the trees as she passed to ensure he wasn't waiting for them. The police must have spoken to him and warned him. Maybe he wasn't even guilty of killing those little girls, Annabel conceded. If he was known to the police but they didn't suspect him, it didn't seem likely, did it? Just some local weirdo.

But she wouldn't let her guard down. She detested the look of him. Maybe he wasn't guilty, but she was determined Charlotte wouldn't become the victim of a copy-cat killer.

Content with her routine and that within it, Charlotte was completely safe, Annabel began to enjoy some of what Pembrokeshire had to offer.

Gazing out at the rocky islets from the high bluff on which their tortured village sat gave hope. The tides changed every day. Each time she'd looked upon the beach in the week here, it had appeared differently: a vast wet sand shore stretching halfway around South Wales, dotted with cockle-pickers and wind-carts in the low spring tide; then the most perfect tropical paradise with dry golden sand as the moon relinquished its hold on the ocean and sent the water flooding back six hours later.

On every occasion it might seem impossible to imagine the other, and no-one could predict how it might change. Yes, the moon was as regular in its orbit around the earth as could be, but the weather varied bringing different light day to day, making Caldey Island seem sometimes within touching distance while other days as far as the moon.

Nature made it perfect. Ten-foot waves brought surfers, the expanded beach brought its cockle-pickers and wind-carts and dog-walkers, and the soft warm sandy days fetched sun-worshipers and families. Nature made it okay, and it would make this okay. Not for those unfortunate souls who lost their most precious gifts. God had tried them to their limits for reasons Annabel would never understand, but the community would heal. Slowly, they would appreciate the beauty surrounding them. And like a quarry scarring a mountainside only to be covered in time by grass and moss, the scar of Goreston's horror would heal. If only no-one dug beyond the surface. And if only no more precious lives were lost.

CHAPTER FIFTEEN

"**G**oodbye. Thanks for coming… Bye, bye, bye…"

Bertie knew from the watery eyes passing him in grateful succession that the sermon Annabel helped him write on hope had hit the right mark with his new congregation, but there was still a lot more to do.

"Thank you so much, vicar, for stepping into the breach, as it were. We're so indebted you could be here at such short notice."

For Reverend Bertie Brimble, hearing such an English accent was manna from Heaven. He'd been warned to expect some hostility to his new post, despite the circumstances of his arrival and the fact that this part of West Wales had been known since mediaeval times as '*Little England beyond Wales.*'

"I do hope you're settling in all right?" the kindly lady inquired as she clasped his hand.

Looking into her eyes betrayed her kindliness was through a stiff upper lip. He aimed to spring the balance between jovial and respectful. "Yes, thank you. It's not hard to feel blessed in such breath-taking surroundings." He nodded in the general direction of everything, which took in the magnificent historic church nestling in its wooden valley, and, in the distance, the glinting water of the Atlantic accented by the majesty of Caldey Island a mile offshore.

"Quite," said the lady with a tone of rebuke. "Why Reverend Jones should ever have wanted to leave is beyond me." His predecessor's failure to appear apparently beyond everyone. The word betrayal reached Bertie's ears during introductions when Oliver Jones' name came up, but the fact was no-one knew what had happened to him and Bertie simply wouldn't excuse anyone speaking ill of him; even if it turned out he had just upped and left as the talk of the village suggested.

There, but for the Grace of God, go I; sentiment Bertie lived his life by. He believed everyone always tries their best along their own challenging path. He was here to comfort and guide wherever he could. If things had become too much for Oliver Jones, then who was he to judge?

Awaiting a response to his return home as he stood in front of Annabel, guilt reformed quickly in his chest and he babbled as she barely looked up when he launched into his report. "It went okay. They loved my sermon,"

She nodded.

"They're hurting though. I kept hearing the word 'betrayal' bandied about. I suspect that's a little harsh. I'm sure he had good reason to leave.

Annabel nodded again. What was she to say? She was pleased. She'd written the sermon, she knew all about Reverend Jones leaving, but she felt so sick. Forcing herself to speak, just to keep Bertie upbeat, she said, "You'd think he might have talked to someone if he was feeling down. He of all people should understand the benefits."

Bertie paused, debating how to respond. Just as he normally would, he decided, knowing normalcy would wear her down as sure as a sandcastle succumbing to the tide.

"You know how I feel about the word 'should,' Annie. Maybe he did talk to someone… Just because it's not public knowledge."

Eyebrows raised to check permission, Bertie announced he was retiring to his study. "I need to prepare for the Alpha course my predecessor had planned. And no, I can't delay it until I'm settled in and got to know my parish because posters have been announcing the start date for months." Bertie shook his head as he spoke, eyes wide with importance. "If people turn up tomorrow and it's not running, we could be turning them away from the most important decision of their lives."

"I'll get on with dinner," Annabel's clipped tone declared. "Charlotte, will you come and help

Mummy cooking, please?" she called out as Bertie left the room, her voice wafting through the gaps in the century-old floorboards.

Instantly, little feet rumbled across the floor. Always helpful, the sheer size of their new kitchen compared to Hartcliffe's kitchenette delighted Charlotte to be invited to help. Picturing herself inside one of the Enid Blyton books she adored broadened her happy grin. It was all so... Ideal, she sighed.

She wouldn't think so for long.

CHAPTER SIXTEEN

"**A**h, there you are, Vicar. Thanks for coming," the same friendly lady from Sunday's service greeted as he walked into the church. He hardly recognised it with the tables laden with cakes and savouries of all description.

"When is everybody due to arrive?"

"Not for another twenty minutes, but we already have a few new faces. They're sitting round the corner in Peter's capable hands. Have you met Peter?"

Bertie rounded the pillar obscuring the crowd of half-a-dozen being entertained looking at an electric chair dangling from a man's neck. "If Jesus had been around in modern times, we may very well all be wearing these instead of crucifixes," the man explained. "But more about that later. Reverend! So nice to meet you. Cracking service yesterday, by the way. I'm Peter Constable, which is funny because I am in the police force. An Inspector now, which is confusing enough, but there was a time I was constable Constable!" he laughed and thrust out a hand.

Bertie reached out and gave a firm shake. "Nice to meet you."

"Excuse me a minute, guys," he nodded to the party of wide-eyed newcomers. "I just want a moment with our new vicar. Why don't you see if there's any food you fancy? Auria is a marvellous cook."

As the group scurried away to marvel at Auria's artistry in the kitchen, Peter spoke in hushed tones. "I usually conduct the Alpha course. This will be my fourth; Oli… Reverend Jones, was always terribly keen for me to do it. He'd take a back seat and answer questions towards the end. He said a layman made the course more accessible." Giving Bertie's arm a gentle squeeze, he added, "I thought I'd best check you had the same idea. I didn't want to step on your toes."

Bertie grinned. "Well, I have been working on what I might say,"

Peter sucked in his disappointed cheeks.

"Don't worry. I'm delighted I don't have to do it. I felt a little uncomfortable, not knowing anyone. No. I'm with Oli. You carry on and I'll field questions later on."

Peter joined Bertie in their inane grinning when a thought struck and his mouth formed the 'o' of an imminent 'oooh.' "Vicar, have you seen our well? Our Holy Well?"

Bertie's eyes fell to the floor. Before he had a

chance to answer, his host bandied on.

"Come on. We have a few minutes, I'll show you."

Bertie had no time to consider if he should say he'd seen it and drunk from it already, nor whether going out to the well so close to the start of their meeting was sensible before Peter had guided him to the back door of the church. Opening the door with the key still protruding from its ancient lock where Bertie had left it, Peter stepped onto damp earth outside. "It's just along here," he indicated beyond the copse of hedgerows which had been allowed to develop untamed.

Being careful not to slide in the mud, Bertie let himself be directed to the square cut pool as though it was his first encounter.

"There it is," Peter declared with pride. "The Holy Well of Goreston."

Although its rectangular shape told of the obvious moulding by man, the water bubbling from within was undoubtedly natural; glistening, crystal in the fading afternoon light. Flowers on the edge combined with the setting sun to imbue the pink, reddish, tinge Bertie had seen before.

"There are a couple of shells some people use to drink," Peter pointed to the chipped scallop shells at the edge. "But don't use those! You don't know how many hundreds of lips have pressed against those do you. Here, use this." He plucked a water bottle from his pocket, opened it and proceeded to empty the contents onto the grass.

Panicking that he would have to refuse to drink and cause offence, especially after the generous waste of Peter's branded water, he asked, "Is it safe?"

"Oh yes. I've been drinking it for years. It's cheaper than bottled water!"

Bottled water you just tipped away, thought Bertie. "Has it been tested though?"

"It's a holy spring. People have been partaking for centuries. We used to provide little vials of it in the nave along with a leaflet as a memento of the church. They were frequently left and we'd have to throw them away for hygiene reasons. That's when the warden put the scallop shells there instead. I ask you! Shells left out in the rain for badgers and foxes to lick, and anybody who does come to drink from the well's germ laden lips to touch! The vials were much better. Instead of replacing them, we should have promoted the water, made the Holy Well of Goreston a destination. It's mentioned in a couple of guide books, but you'd have to be a dedicated tourist to find it."

"I knew about it. It was in my guidebook."

"Well, lucky you, Reverend," he snorted. "Maybe we could discuss promotion. The more people at our little church the better, wouldn't you agree?" Before Bertie answered he added, "There's probably not much point at the moment, what with these wretched murders," he snorted, as though the damage to Goreston's tourism credentials was the biggest tragedy.

"What's happening there? Hasn't someone been arrested?"

"I'm not on the case. But I believe so. He's missing at the moment, but they'll find him, mark my words."

"Missing? You mean a wanted killer has escaped?"

"Not exactly. The Crown Prosecution wanted to make sure the charges would stick before we went all gung-ho, you know. He had an alibi so we had to let him go. For now."

"And then he killed again?"

The strain in Peter's face creased his eyes. "Like I said, I can't really talk about it. I'm not on the case." Staring at the bottle, he snapped, "You don't seem very keen, vicar. Come on, drink up."

"Oh," Bertie pushed aside his reluctance. Annabel had said 'Water doesn't make you act like that,' and she'd been right. Although he was innocent of having added anything stronger, there had to be another explanation why he'd behaved the way he had. Accepting Peter's bottle he bent to fill it then pretended to take a sip merely wetting his lips.

"It used to be a place of pilgrimage. Victorians drank gallons of the stuff declaring its health benefits." Peter nodded along to his own narration. "I've got out of the habit, what with these horrible shells they expect me to use, but I must start again. Bring my own bottle. It peps you up, no doubt about it. Full of iron, so I'm told."

"Shouldn't we be heading in," Bertie harried. It was strange, but from just the touch on his lips, he felt drawn to drink more. He understood his body craved what it needed as part of God's neat plan; a plan his rotundness suggested he struggled to listen to. Drinking more water was something he'd been advised to do many times, so why not Holy Water?

Pocketing the gifted bottle, he stopped in his stride. Visualising himself standing before Annabel and his grotesque treatment of her. Holding his breath, he clenched his fist. No. He would not be drinking more of that water.

CHAPTER SEVENTEEN

ertie had calmed and was enjoying Peter's commanding presence at the helm of the talk introducing people to the calling of Christianity, whilst he nibbled on a delicious tart of some sort.

There followed a familiar talk of Jesus's sacrifice for our sins and the electric chair pendant was thrust in the air to uncomfortable amusement. Unorthodox, perhaps, but it got the point across, Bertie nodded along.

"I'll tell you why I became a Christian, and then I will invite a few of my fellow church-goers to share their stories with you. Okay, so I have been a policeman now for over twenty-five years. I've seen a lot of bad things; people behaving in sickening ways." The group muttered as their thoughts fell to the murdered girls.

"It made me angry. How could there be a god if people acted so abhorrently?" Peter shrugged. "There couldn't, in my eyes." He let out a deep sigh. "The punishments dished out by the courts, crippled with overcrowded prisons, were far too lenient. And many times, shifty lawyers would get criminals off whom I absolutely *knew* were guilty. Everyone knew they were guilty, but they'd get away with it on some technicality…"

He took on a dark complexion and shuffled forward with his hands in his pockets. "So, I became cynical. Morose. Unpleasant. And my worst was yet to come. I almost… *Almost,* very nearly, was tempted to falsify some evidence." The room gasped. "I know. It was wrong and I didn't do it. But I was tempted. That's when I found Jesus."

Peter choked his words. "He spoke to me. In here," he thumped his heart with his fist. "If I let them get to me, they'd won. They'd have brought me down to their level. I had to see it with only love. Like Jesus. He died for their sins, and for my sins; for all our sins so we don't have to take on other's wrongs. If we can forgive, as Jesus forgives us, well… Let's just say it gives a whole new perspective. My job is to be the best policeman I can be and trust that whatever happens is part of His plan. Only he can judge because only He knows the truth."

It took a moment for the crowd to realise he'd finished. An uncomfortable ripple of applause followed before they were presented with a large black man filling their view.

"My journey is the other side of the coin," he said in a Barry White voice. "You see, I turned to crime… Violent crime to fuel a drug habit. I'm not proud. But I don't feel guilty either, because I gave my sin to Jesus and was born again. That was the me before Christ. This is the me now, and I know I'll never do those things again. I forgive the guy I used to be because he didn't know better." He left the front with tears streaming from his eyes muttering "Thank you Lord. Oh thank you, Lord."

Similar testimony followed to gasps of joy and amazement at people's reasons for turning to a better life. Peter stood and clapped a brief round of applause signalling the end of this segment of the evening. "Before we move on, a few words from our new vicar, if you wouldn't mind?" Peter nodded in Bertie's direction, head cocked in request. "I'd love to hear your story."

Cheeks burning, Bertie shuffled his way in front of the crowd. Pressing the hem of his jacket between thumb and forefinger, he opened his mouth a couple of times before words came out in a flurry. "I'm a fraud compared to the heartfelt testimonials we've heard tonight, I'm afraid," Bertie coughed. "You see, I was born into being a Christian. Not that I had the decision taken away from me, you understand—it was my choice— but my father was a vicar as well, and we were always so happy. I enjoyed a brilliant childhood. I've seen none of the horrific things poor Peter here has witnessed as a policeman, nor have I ever been faced with the choice of being involved with crime. I'm a great believer in the Grace of

God and trust His judgement entirely.

"I'm told I'm a good listener. I understand that everyone, whether they are far enough along their path to acknowledge Christ as their saviour or not; everyone is doing their best with their lot in life. That's why I'm a Christian. I always have been and I always will be." Bertie beamed, pleased his own story generated the warmth he felt pouring over him.

"Well that's lightened the mood, and shown, I think, what being a Christian is all about; and that's joy! Joy in all things, and when we see something that is not joyful, we turn God's love toward it so it can become so." Peter clapped his hands. "And on that note, I declare it's time for some coffee and more of my wonderful wife's cakes. Auria, are there any left?"

Ah, thought Bertie. He might have guessed they were married. They were a good fit,

"I haven't given my testimonial yet."

A nondescript male voice pierced the hush. Bertie wasn't familiar with the local accent; not what he'd typically considered Welsh, just the occasional twang and word here and there, but he struggled to place the man who had spoken as Welsh or English.

"Oh, sorry, Richard. You can tell us your story next week, if that's okay? We don't want to inundate our new-comers with too much all in the first session, do we?" He smiled and moved away from the front towards the cakes.

"I want to speak now," Richard's voice rose to almost shouting. Certain he had everyone's attention, he sighed "It's important."

CHAPTER EIGHTEEN

Having insisted on speaking, Richard proved surprisingly quiet. Staring into space, sunken eyes took in everything and nothing, everyone else in the church waited, breathing slowly and silently so as not to frighten off the quarry of his story.

Peter opened his mouth to speak but Richard cut him off.

"I always wanted to know God. Not in a structured way; I just wanted to believe there was something more, you know?" Nods rippled round the room. Richard's steely countenance gave the sense he would have carried on regardless.

"I had a great childhood. Just me and Mum and Dad for a while, and that was great. But then," his face broke into a glowing smile, "my favourite person in the whole world came into my life... My little sister Chloe. As soon as my parents sat me down to tell me I was going to have a brother or sister, I was so excited." Clapping his hands, he carried on with a chuckle in his throat. "I would talk to her in my mum's tummy. I remember," his laugh breached his lips, but his amusement was not infectious. It had the unmistakeable hue of craziness. "I would show her pictures I'd drawn," he chuckled more. "I'd even offer her spoonful's of my dinner. I loved her before she was even born. Like… *she* was what I'd been searching for. She gave meaning to my life in the way I'd hoped God would."

Richard shuffled in his seat and coughed. "The phone rang in my grandparents' house where I'd stayed while my mum and dad were at the hospital. They came to wake me but I was already wide awake—I hadn't slept! They rushed me into the maternity ward in the middle of the night to meet her."

He sighed, eyes glazed with a dewy sheen. "I'd chosen her name, 'Chloe'. I'm sure Mum and Dad steered me to it, but it really felt like my choice." The dew grew to a pool which the surface of Richard's eye could no longer contain and the flood resulted in a cascade of tears. He made no attempt to stem their flow as they wet his cheeks in steady streams, tumbling from his jaw and dripping onto the floor—plop, plop, plop.

"I got to hold her." His voice was a grotesque rasp now. Pausing to swallow down his ire, he forced himself on. "There's a picture on the wall in our house. I still look at it. No-one could ever look happier. Or prouder. I was a brilliant big brother, always helping with nappy changing and dressing her—I loved choosing little outfits for her to look adorable in.

"As she grew, so did my love for her. When she came to school, I looked after her. Not that she needed it, she was clever and popular, but I was there just in case and no-one would ever hurt my little sister while I was around."

Richard fell back silent again.

The tears flowed.

The crowd waited.

Finally, with a gasp of air through a face creased in agony as though emerging breathless from a dark lake, Richard croaked, "I stayed on for A-levels in sixth form. I could have gone to college. Maybe it would have served me better, career-wise. But I stayed at school—to be with Chloe."

A cry of such savagery filled the hall as Richard clutched his face in his hands. "And now she's gone!"

Minutes passed as Richard composed himself. He smiled an eerie smile. "One day she never came home from the park. You've all read about it; heard it on the radio; seen the news on television and the internet. I know you've all seen it. There's been quite the showy investigation by the police. We have conducted our own research; me, my mum and my dad, via her friends' phone contacts.

"There had been a man. The one they arrested."

Sighing at the front of the church, Peter could be heard to mumble how he wasn't part of the investigation. He answered Richard's glare with a shrug, pressing his lips together, the colour faded pushed against his teeth.

Richard continued. "This man asked her to help with his horse who was unwell. Said he needed someone to calm her while he gave her treatment."

Richard's smile remained rigid, despite the obvious aching. "I don't know how much of this you already know; I've stopped watching the news... Even Chloe's friend who told the police about the man didn't make the connection until after the event. Chloe loved horses so she made the obvious candidate. They'd suggested they all go to help, but the man said it might spook the horse, so only Chloe went."

Richard sighed. "He was stern and a bit mean, so they said. It didn't occur to them he would hurt Chloe, but they didn't trust the horse would be okay left to his care. It's what convinced my sister to go, her friend said. They were all a bit jealous that Chloe had this important job to do... But, he killed her." Tears rolled, incongruent with the smile he wore branded to his face. "He murdered my little Chloe."

Richard rocked where he stood, face hidden in hands rooted to his face. Members of the crowd nudged each other. Should they go and hug him? Should they leave him to release some of the torment racking his trembling body? Before they'd decided, he spoke again, this time in a clear voice. "Of course, it made me question even more the meaning of life and the existence of God. But, I've forgiven him; the man who killed my sister. I understand we all have our own life mapped out and Chloe's was a short journey.

"I'm pleased I had the chance to know and love her," his voice creaked as emotion leaked out in acrid bursts, "and I can't blame God for only loaning her for ten years." Richard's eyes were almost invisible behind the black pools growing in his face; his cheeks smeared as the salty water merged with dirt.

"It must have been His plan for the man to come along when he did. It must have. And I know he'll meet his own judgement one day..." his face blackened and he fell silent again.

In a sudden movement, he scurried back to his seat leaving the room in deathly silence.

Bertie was first to make a sound with a slow hand-clap as he walked to the front. "Thank you, Richard. That was very brave of you to share your story. I'm overwhelmed with your Christian kindness. I don't know if I could forgive so quickly."

Richard nodded, eyes still a blur, smile still in place. His forgiveness was unconvincing, but even saying the words would be beyond most people, Bertie thought. True forgiveness will come in time for Richard, Bertie nodded along with the suffering big brother in the front row. "We'll have those refreshments now, shall we?"

Muttering rose before everyone stood and made their way to where Auria's delicious banquet was laid out in splendid muted colour. The cakes were surely moist, but dry mouths struggled to swallow. Red-faced, half-eaten offerings returned to the table.

"Thanks for coming. We'll try to keep it a bit lighter next week," Peter implored the newcomers. "Being a Christian can be a lot of fun!"

Shuffling from the church, Bertie noticed Richard still sat in the front-facing chairs. Walking over to him, he placed a hand on his shoulder. "Are you okay, Richard? Sharing really took it out of you, didn't it?"

Richard didn't move, but answered in a monotone. "I needed to do it. To test myself. I'll be fine. This church has helped more than I can tell you."

Turning his head, a smile of some genuine warmth lit his face for a second. "And I thought my testimonial was important because everyone else found God because they wanted to change themselves, but I found him because of what someone else had done. There must be a lot of people like me."

Richard stood and turned to the door. "I look forward to next week, and another inspirational sermon, of course, vicar."

"Thank you, Richard. I meant it. I really am impressed. God will be proud of you. Chloe will be proud of you."

"Thank you," he said, and disappeared into the night.

Bertie knelt before the altar and offered a prayer for his troubled parishioner. Finishing with a breathy "Amen," he hauled himself back onto his feet. With a sigh, he heaved closed the oak door and set off home.

CHAPTER NINETEEN

"What's wrong? You look troubled," Annabel asked.

"Oh, I'm okay, thanks. Just one of the testimonials at the Alpha course was rather unpleasant. I won't go into it now." It had been hard enough persuading her to move here without bringing the whole foul business to their doorstep. Slumping beside his wife, he reached across and squeezed her hand. "How are you?"

Annabel closed her eyes and opened them slowly. "Tired. I'll be glad when this space is vacated." She circled a palm around her bump. "He's been busy tonight. I haven't got far with my crocheting."

Bertie raised his eyebrows and blew through tight lips. The crocheted scarf had barely moved on in months. It was difficult to tell if tonight's progress had been even slower.

"Shall I make us some cocoa?"

Annabel nodded and squeezed his hand back. "Thank you. We'll take it up."

As Bertie arrived at the top of the stairs with two hot mugs, Annabel stood on the landing peering into Charlotte's room. Bertie stood beside her. "Is she okay?"

"She looks so peaceful. I hope she's coping with school. I'm always so tense when I pick her up, looking out for that man, I don't let her speak in case he catches me off guard. Then when we get home, she disappears to her room and I cook. I must make the time to talk to her." She stared at the floor then brought her face up brightly. "I tell you what though, I pray this little one will sleep as well as her. She's never been a moment's trouble, has she?"

Even sleeping, Charlotte wore a contented smile.

"I wonder what she's dreaming?" Bertie whispered, "Come on. These are burning me."

Slipping their clothes off, Bertie folded his neatly on a chair on his side of the bed, while Annabel stood in pregnant glory hanging her clothes back in her wardrobe.

Bertie watched her exhausted body leaning against the headboard. He nudged her as her sleepy fingers threatened to tip scalding bedtime chocolate on sensitive places. Wresting the cup from her weak grasp, she mumbled, "Thank you," and, "Goodnight," whilst Bertie reached round to place it on the bedside table.

Glugging the last of his own, he flicked the

switch that turned off the wall lights plunging the room into darkness. Behind his eyelids, Bertie's eyes fluttered as images of Richard's tortured face flew at him from his consciousness. Harrumphing, he shuffled into a new position, but undeniable tiredness still couldn't coax his mind to oblivion.

Staring at the ceiling, the urge attacked, like it knew when to strike. What harm would it do? He had only to reach across to his trouser pocket and he could rid himself of this thirst. No! He'd just had cocoa. He wasn't thirsty.

But what about all that sugar? That *made* you thirsty. He could just swill his mouth and spit it into the cocoa mug. That couldn't do any harm.

Convinced, he pulled the chair with his hanging jacket towards him and removed the bottle. Uncapping it, he took a mouthful and swilled it around his teeth. Spitting into the cup, as he said he would, he felt pleased. See, that wasn't so bad.

Quickly, he screwed the lid tight and returned it to his pocket. He wasn't tired now. Switching the light back on and plucking the Bible from beside his bed, he flicked through the hundreds of pages and allowed himself to be guided to a passage. *Exodus 21-24:*

"… take life for life, eye for eye, tooth for tooth, hand for hand, foot for foot, burn for burn, wound for wound, bruise for bruise."

He frowned. It was a much-quoted part of the Bible, but it wasn't one that usually resonated

with Bertie. He was more in favour of Jesus saying, *"Whosoever shall smite thee on thy right cheek,
turn to him the other also."- Matthew 5:38-42*

But it resonated now. He didn't understand
why. A rage bubbled within him. It must be
Richard. How could he have gone through that
and then forgiven? Shaking his head, he tried to
understand. He'd always been a turn the other
cheek guy, but he'd never been tested. He was
big so he'd never experienced bullying. And as a
vicar, people turned *to* him, not against. He realised, he had never had anything to turn the other
cheek for. But Richard? Rage hitherto unknown
to him coursed through his body. Hands balling
into fists, he thumped his own thigh. The pain
enraged him further.

Suffering a genuine thirst now, he reached for
the bottle. It can't have been the water that made
him act the way he had towards Annabel, it had
been the recognition of his own failings. How
could he teach these poor people who are suffering their greatest loss when he'd lost nothing of
any significance?

Maybe it had even been God altering his behaviour. Because of it, he'd worried about losing
Annabel for a moment, hadn't he? She'd forgiven
him, of course, but it had given him an insight
he'd never had before.

And now, reading these Bible passages, he saw
how he truly felt: unworthy. Pursing his lips with
a dismissive shake of his head, he scoffed. Blam-

ing water! That was pathetic of him.

In a show of disgust at his feeble thinking, he yanked off the top and glugged every last drop of the bottle, finishing with a resounding "Ahhh."

Throwing his face back to the pillow, he defied sleep to deny him. As his eyes twitched under their lids, he kept them shut. With a big sigh, he turned in bed, now facing Annabel's back as she gently snored.

Her hips rolled up and down as she breathed slowly in and out. Bertie, pressed against her, began to stir. Timing his pushes in contrary motion to hers had the effect of her thrusting into him. He groaned.

He moved. She moved. It seemed so compliant, so natural. Something they'd done countless times before and had denied themselves as the physics of her biology made it more and more difficult, and nausea made her less and less willing.

"What are you doing?" Annabel stopped cold. Sitting up, she turned on her light and glared at him. "You're raping me in my sleep now are you?"

"I... I... I'm sorry, I just..."

"Turn the other way. I don't know what's got into you lately."

Bertie duly rolled over. Shame flushed his cheeks as he tried desperately to lie still, any micro movement causing unendurable twitches to his nether region flooding him with desire.

Slowly the disgrace subsided and he could

think of nothing else but his desire. How easy would it be for her to just let him? It wasn't fair to treat him like this. It was almost painful now. He didn't want to touch it, fearing he'd be set off in an unstoppable trajectory.

Gripping the sheets, he seethed at the unjustness of his suffering.

Somewhere from within, kind, understanding Bertie reached through and shook him. Bolting upright, colour fell from his face as he recognised the rage he'd felt the other night. He couldn't trust himself.

Scurrying to the en-suite bathroom, he remembered with a shudder how that had gone last time and ran for the bedroom door. He'd make a cup of tea, maybe watch a bit of telly.

Scooting along the landing in the dark he nearly reached the stairs when his foot connected with something hard. Crumpling his toes, he dropped to his knees, stifling expletives as they formed in his mind, "F.... Shiiirrrrnngg!"

Hauling himself up he squinted at what had caused his injury, hands flexed in utter rage, he recognised Charlotte's bag with a flask in it. "Why would you leave your..." Swear words filled his head but he stuffed them, fuelling the fury like a musket.

Pacing to her door, he threw it open. Standing in the doorway, he breathed hard. There she was lying peacefully in bed. Calm and serene after the pain she'd just caused him. Didn't she care?

He took a step into the room. Breathing harder, the throbbing in his pyjamas grew stronger. Taking another step, he stood at the foot of her bed.

Cherry lips, budding, pouted in and out as she breathed. She really was growing up fast. She looked so like her mother.

Deep breath in.

Deep breath out.

Deep breath in.

Out. So like her mother.

In. So pretty. Look at her.

Out.

In a sudden flash, he could be denied no more. Grabbing the corner of the bedclothes, he hauled them away, Charlotte's youthful body shivered at the rapid chill but she didn't move.

Her legs were bent and the nightie she wore just covered her thighs. So like her mother, Bertie panted.

Arm either side of his little girl, he climbed on top of her, the friction moving her nightdress higher still. Arching his head back, he knew he'd soon find satisfaction.

"Daddy! What are you doing?"

Shoving up hard with his arms, he flew backwards catching himself on the bedpost sending a jolt of agonising pain through his body as he fell to the floor. Shuffling backwards on his cheeks to the door, he whimpered. "Sorry!"

As soon as he reached it, he ran, tripping down the stairs two at a time. He kept running. Through the front door, down the lane, to the church. But arriving at the studded oak, he couldn't bring himself to go inside.

What wretchedness had overcome him now? Where would it end? Collapsing to the floor, he beat the ground with his fists. "God, help me. What is happening to me?"

Curling into the foetal position, he rocked himself fitfully to unconsciousness.

CHAPTER TWENTY

"**M**ummy. Wake up. Something's wrong with Daddy."

Annabel flapped her arm towards the light switch. "What do you mean?"

"I think he's hurt himself. He was tucking me in, and I think I made him jump. He fell over and… he was crying."

Annabel frowned. "Okay. You go back to bed. I'll check he's alright." Squeezing swollen feet into mule slippers, Annabel forced her arms through inside out dressing gown sleeves until they righted themselves then stood up. Tying the belt as she shuffled from the room, she flapped her hand at the light switch and immediately came up with a theory.

There was Charlotte's bag, evidently kicked. He must have gone to check on her and stubbed his foot on the way out. But he wasn't crying in pain. She'd felt close to tears many times since those little girls were murdered. And every time she looked at Charlotte it brought it all racing to her mind. Imagine losing her? She looked so like the other girls too. They could be sisters.

Yawning, she padded downstairs expecting to see Bertie nursing a cup of tea red-eyed, but there was no sign of him. "He'll be at the church," she sighed to herself, strolling over to fill the kettle. Feeling he'd be back soon, she placed two cups on a tray.

God answered and Bertie understood. It was a lesson. When he'd listened to Richard's testimony, he had judged, wondering how he ever managed to forgive his sister's murderer. Now, he'd been forced to walk a mile in a killer's shoes, he knew.

It was pointless to judge someone else who did something abhorrent to you; something that sickened you; something you couldn't do for all the money in the world, because they weren't seeing it the same way.

Bertie would never understand how anyone could hurt another soul, but people did every day. And if he was really the person he'd become, he would be capable of the unthinkable too.

With a confidence he'd be fine, he brushed himself off and trod the lane home. As he entered the kitchen, he jumped at Annabel sitting stirring two teas. What did she know? How could he explain?

"You okay?" she smiled.

Walking across the room, Bertie joined her at

the table and pulled out a chair. "Mmm. I think so."

Pushing his mug towards him, Annabel sipped her own. "Charlotte said you'd hurt yourself. She said you were crying, but I know the real reason."

"Really?" Bertie's dry mouth craved the hot tea, but his trembling fingers lacked the strength to pick it up.

"I've been the same. Sometimes I can't look at her without welling up."

Nodding, Bertie understood, and she wasn't so far from the truth, was she? Maybe he should tell her about Richard. That would explain things from both perspectives. "It is what you said... Seeing Charlotte after stubbing my toe on her bag brought up feelings, and... well, I had a horrific vision." Reluctant to carry on, he waited for the inevitable, 'Go on,' from Annabel. "It seemed so real. I was sure it was. But thank God, she's safe."

"Safe? Why? What happened?"

Not willing to give the unforgiveable details without some background, Bertie began, "I think it must have been that testimonial I heard yesterday. Remember? One of the Alpha coursers was determined to share his story; get it off his chest, I suppose." Gulping the grief which rose in him at the thought, he turned teary-eyed to his wife. "I didn't tell you—I guess I didn't want to upset you. *His* little sister was one of the poor girls who was brutally murdered."

He paused waiting for the 'Why didn't you tell me?' despite his feeble excuse. "I was stunned when he said he'd forgiven the killer. I have to admit to feeling judgemental. I'm not sure I could do the same. Not so quickly anyway.

"Our lovely church inspired him, he told me. That's what led him to becoming a Christian. It underlines the importance of our coming here, doesn't it?" He sighed. "Remarkable, but incredibly sad. I felt for him. That must be why I had the awful hallucination."

Annabel nodded along. "Sounds like it, but what was it, this hallucination? You still haven't told me what happened." Pushing back her chair, she eased the ever-growing bulge of burgeoning life from beneath the table. "More tea?"

Bertie shook his head. He knew he couldn't share the extent of his deviance because he didn't think he could make her understand, he sighed. "Just Charlotte, you know," he stifled a sob as he saw himself leaning over her, remembered what he had been about to do. But he never would, would he? It had been God showing him. God woke her to stop him and everything was okay. "Like I say, it must have been Richard's testimony."

Nodding in understanding of his hesitancy, she smiled. "That makes sense. Why don't you go and see him?" Fending off the look of horror growing on Bertie's face, she added, "If it's affected you so terribly after hearing it once, how do you think poor Richard feels living with it every day?"

Bertie bowed his head. She was right. "Yes. Of course. I'll go and see him tomorrow," then catching sight of the clock on the cooker he corrected it to, "today. I'll see if there's anything I can do to help." Then, in answer to his wife's raised eyebrows, he added, "More than prayer, I mean."

"Better?" Annabel asked, stifling a yawn, "Because I really could do with some sleep."

"I think so," he answered, sudden panic setting in. Would he be okay, or rather, would *they* be okay? "Yes," he decided. "I'm much better. Thank you. And I will have more tea, if that's okay. We can take it up."

CHAPTER TWENTY-ONE

Leaning in to place a kiss on his forehead, Annabel murmured, "Bye. I'm taking Charlotte to school. And I've got an antenatal appointment at Tenby Hospital after that, so I'll see you later. Charlotte; come and kiss Daddy goodbye."

Running in and squeezing him tightly, she kissed him too and skipped through the door. "Bye, Daddy. Have a good day."

A tear swelled and plopped onto his cheek.

"Don't worry," Annabel assured. "She'll be fine. Now don't forget to go and see," she frowned. "What was his name?"

"Richard."

"Don't forget to go and see Richard. Remember, that's why we came here, to support the community. And he needs it more than anyone."

"Definitely. I'll go as soon as I've showered."

Flicking his hair to one side instead of brushing it, Bertie glanced in the hall mirror but couldn't quite tolerate making eye-contact. Grabbing Richard's address from the Alpha course registration, he set off after brunch on what would normally be a fine stroll, but today painted a Pembrokeshire drizzle the Preseli Hills and sea mist sometimes conspired to create.

The little bungalow he walked towards struck him as surprisingly old-fashioned. Not what he'd expected from young Richard, although he didn't look what you might call trendy. When a lady in her fifties answered his knocking, he worried he must have the wrong house.

"Ah, good morning. I'm looking for Richard. Richard King?"

The lady frowned.

"Do I have the right house?"

She nodded. "You'd best come in." Turning her back, Bertie assumed his following her was expected. As they reached a door made from patterned glass set in a thick over-painted frame, the lady paused and pushed it open. The autumn leaf design gave way to reveal more leafyness on a mottled brown three-piece-suite which almost matched the orange-leafed curtains. Neither tried too hard to match the carpet of the type you never see any more except on television programmes about the seventies.

All lined up to face the pièce de résistance; the waffle gas-fire. It was like stepping back in time. "Are you Mrs King?" Bertie asked kindly.

The lady nodded. "That's right."

"Richard's mother?"

She nodded.

Realising she must also be the mother of poor murdered Chloe put her age at forty-something, surely. Nothing ages you more than losing a child, Bertie surmised, adding, "I'm terribly sorry for your loss."

She nodded. "Thank you, vicar." Gesturing for him to sit, she joined him opposite. Coughing, she stretched her skirt over her bulging thigh. "We're not big into religion. Why have you come to see Richard?"

As Bertie blurted how her son had enrolled on the Alpha course to open himself to the ways of our lord, he smarted at his disloyalty. He'd betrayed Richard's trust. He had every right to keep his spiritual path to himself. Perhaps Mrs King wasn't in favour of how forgiving he'd been. Bertie could understand that. Cheeks burned with relief when she put him out of his misery.

"Oh, yes. He mentioned it. I thought he'd gone off church after that last vicar."

Realising she hadn't done anything to make Richard aware he was here, it occurred to Bertie she might benefit from sharing her own grief with him. "I understand a lot of people feel very let down. I don't know what happened."

"He disappeared when we needed him; when the community needed him. Richard needed him," she sighed. "That's what." Shuffling in her seat, she carried on. "It's crushed me, losing my little girl. But it's not just us suffering. There's the other family too."

Bertie nodded.

"Identical injuries. I expect there'll be more. Serial killers don't stop at two, now do they?"

Bertie was no expert, but he had to agree it seemed unlikely. Beads of sweat crowned his brow and he stumbled over his words as Mrs King's meaning filtered in. "So they didn't catch him? I thought they had."

Mrs King shook her head. "They had a suspect. Didn't charge him for some reason. Then, within weeks of our Chloe, he killed another little girl. I don't know when the next innocent victim will lose her young life and yet another family will be devastated, but there'll be more, mark my words. The police aren't doing much. Reckon there's no connection, but it's as plain as the nose on your face…"

Bertie wasn't listening. For the first time, he could see what the move here meant; the danger he'd put his family. Peter had sidestepped the question of Terry Paige killing again, and Richard's testimony too raw to make the point, his mother's calm statement of fact hit the mark.

He had brought his own most precious gift, and soon to deliver another, to a place where a child murderer still roamed unchallenged. Last night's hideous episode, he'd called it a vision, he could hardly admit what he really, nearly was capable of, not even to himself, took on new meaning—not a lesson, but a premonition! Could

God be warning him of the danger Charlotte was in? "I have to go," Bertie blurted, pushing himself up from his chair.

"Mother," Richard interrupted, creaking open the door. "Why didn't you tell me the reverend was here?" His face was blank but for a cold smile worn with no feeling. He stared at his mum before briskly moving towards her and throwing his arms around her.

Bertie suspected that, if not for his presence, they would be in tears. Grief was a terrible pain; the very worst. "If either of you want to talk... at any time, I'm always available." Bertie's twinkling smile that everyone seemed to find comfort in failed to reach its objective under his own angst.

Torn between loyalties to his parishioner and his daughter, Bertie allowed himself to perch on the edge of his seat again as Richard sat beside him. Charlotte was safe in school, he knew that. "You must feel terribly let down by my colleague, Reverend Jones," Bertie crinkled his eyes, aware of the irony that he too would dearly love to dart from the door.

"You can say that again!" Richard spat. Hands balled into fists screwed against his knees, round and round and round.

It struck Bertie as odd how he could forgive his sister's murderer, but couldn't forgive Oliver Jones for leaving him. He felt the pressure. "I understand he's a kind man. I'm sure he must have had an important reason to disappear." He didn't know if it was right to mention, but Oli was perhaps getting a raw deal. No-one knew what had become of him and reports of his character had been previously glowing, as far as Bertie knew.

"That's what I thought. It's what we all thought. But he wasn't the man everyone believed he was, trust me!" Richard spat again.

"What do you mean?" Bertie frowned.

Wafting a hand in the air, Richard declared, "It doesn't matter anymore. What do you want?" Bertie was taken-aback at the gruff tone. "You came to see me?"

Bertie regained his thoughts. He wanted to be a comfort but he needed to go. At the same time, finding out as much as he could about the looming threat was paramount. "I've been thinking of you... What you've been through, non-stop. It must be so terrible for you." He looked at them both in turn. "Your mother mentioned the other murder. The other girl murdered after your sister."

Richard stood and stormed to the window and stared into nothing.

"The police don't believe they're connected, is that correct? That doesn't sound right, does it?" Bertie sympathised

Mrs King's voice followed, "It's obvious the same man killed both girls; my little Chloe and the poor Lilly girl."

"No. It's not, Mum."

"But they were killed in the same way, love. I know it's the same man."

"You don't! Just because they were the same, doesn't mean it was the same person who did it." He was screaming. Spittle stretching across his yawning mouth as he seethed. Catching Bertie's incredulous stare, he lowered his flailing arms to his side and added, "Necessarily."

Slumping back, he sighed. "It's still raw for us, vicar. Do you mind?" Richard tilted his head.

"Yes, of course. Sorry. I just wanted to help." As he bumbled towards the door, he turned before leaving. "Like I say, anytime you want to talk." Pulling it open, he wasn't sure how welcome his next offer would be. "I'll say a prayer for you in mass."

"Thank you, vicar," Mrs King and her son answered in unison.

CHAPTER TWENTY-TWO

They'd parked their car at their Bed and Breakfast in the charming Flemish village of Saint Florence. Using the car park was all part of the deal, but they didn't plan on returning to civilisation for a few days. Instead, they'd booked this time away on the cliff tops of Pembrokeshire to camp under the stars to get some perspective on their relationship. And it wasn't just the cheaper prices coming after the summer holidays that prompted a September deal, it was the quiet. The between seasons lull was just what they needed, as well as some discreet time away from their two sons.

They'd chatted like the old friends they were for the journey from middle England, and the first night in the B and B following a brief foray into Tenby had been ideal. Now Claire had been quiet for the last five minutes, Gareth felt awkward. "What's the matter?" he turned to his wife as she stared, dewy-eyed into the distance. "Missing the boys?"

Tilting her head in rapid bobs, she said. "We'll

phone them later, yeah?" croaking through her thick throat.

Gareth nodded, though he knew in all likelihood there would be no calls home tonight. Once they'd visited the little church they'd discovered in a guidebook, with its intriguing history and Holy well, they were off on a mighty hike on the world famous Pembrokeshire Coastal Path. They were only completing a bit of the one-hundred and eighty-six mile challenge (walking the lot meant climbing altitudes totalling the height of Everest! They'd need to work on their fitness before they tackled that.)

Along with beaches in Cuba, Vietnam and California, the beach they were headed, in a remote location reached by traversing cliff and dune, Barafundle Bay, featured in a list of the world's very best and they couldn't wait to camp and wake up to the sun rising over the turquoise ocean.

They needed it. It had been a rough time in recent months and they'd gone their separate ways when the cliché of seven monotonous years of marriage conspired with a dishy manager at Claire's work turning her head.

A bereft Gareth had soon moved his consolation prize into the former family home leaving their two sons struggling in the wake of destruction.

The arrival of the Decree nisi had finally struck them with what they should have realised from the beginning; this was bad for the kids. And they still loved each other, and they were determined to explore that before making the whole thing irreversible.

That's why Gareth had suggested this trip, but he wasn't sure if Claire had experienced the same regret for the same reason. It was one of a hundred things they never talked about. Vitriol in the back of his mouth as he glared at her across the uneven path was the creation of his suspicion it might not be their two son's she was missing.

The handsome manager of her bank had turned out to be as dull as one of his photoshoots in his part-time role modelling, where he could be found in catalogues gazing into the middle distance in wry amusement, championing anything from a natty blazer to novelty cat mugs. That's what she had told him, anyway.

Gareth had heard since that the home-wrecking swine had been offered a career advancement in Hong Kong. He didn't have all the facts, but of course relocating would have taken Claire too far from her sons. That was the real reason she came back, Gareth was sure of it.

Much as Claire's unconvincing nodding enraged him, he had to swallow it down. They were here to re-build the romance. If they could do that, then any number of gorgeous hunks could peacock in front of his wife and he'd still feel secure.

It was true Claire had been the unfaithful one (first), and her who had initiated the divorce, but Gareth accepted responsibility too. He'd been dull. He'd let romance slide. The weekly flowers became a yearly annoyance as first he forgot their wedding anniversary, and then Valentine's Day as well.

But they were here now, recouping their affection away from any distraction, and in some of the greatest scenery either of them had ever seen. And it was working.

On the first day of their break, Gareth bought a selection of touristy books from Tenby's bookshop and delighted in the holy well St Julian's little church boasted. He wasn't religious, but he was looking forward to the ceremony of drinking the water together; like it would heal their past and move them swiftly on to a cohesive future.

"I think it's down this lane," Gareth pointed to the track hidden back from a copse of trees. "Yes, look; 'St Julian's Church.'" The faded paint exclaimed. "I'm excited, are you?"

Claire smiled, more from humouring her husband than from sharing his joy. She didn't get how well-water would do anything for them. In fact, the idea Gareth thought it might, irritated her.

She hadn't said. She probably wouldn't. But if their relationship was going to make it, it wouldn't be because they drank water from a manky Victorian well. Glancing across at her husband, he was reaching his hand out to hold. In the spirit of building their future, she took it.

As the trees parted to reveal a small car-park, the church stood beyond an iron gate. "Oh, it's charming!" Claire proclaimed as the ancient stones oozed with mediaeval character.

Gareth smiled. Yanking the gate, the pair walked down the path to the large oak door studded with bolts to keep the long hinges in place. It creaked satisfyingly open to Gareth's shove to reveal a bright white-washed interior.

Oak beams crossed the vaulted ceiling and stained glass windows mottled the light giving a gentle calm. Gareth and Claire passed the altar and walked through the centre of the nave to the pulpit and transept, in one side of which sat a visitors' book which they duly signed with appropriate praise for the small church.

On the other was a door which Gareth correctly calculated from the outside view, led to the tower. A no entry sign displayed faintly on the wood. Glancing around to make sure his initial impression they were alone was correct, Gareth pulled at the door.

It was stiff. He reasoned few people ventured up the tower which made him feel more intrepid as he took the first step onto the cold, worn stone. Turning to Claire, he hissed, "Come on."

Seeing her bob her head towards the sign forbidding their entry, Gareth sighed. "What are they going to do? Damn us to Hell?"

Pursing his lips and staring at her through the whites of his eyes, Gareth poured on pressure until Claire joined him. Treading round the stairwell that lurched steeply from one side before turning an abrupt right-angle, Claire and Gareth climbed higher and higher.

"Ahhh!" Claire's scream echoed through the confines of the stone walls. "What's that?"

Gareth flinched too until he realised the air wafting past his face in the dark was a small bat. Laughing, he shook his head. "We've got bats in the belfry," he said.

"Are you all right up there?" A booming voice inquired from below. "You really shouldn't be in here. It's not safe."

Cursing his wife's feeble ability to engage with tiny wildlife, he answered her snort with a nod and turned to tread downwards again.

Dusting themselves off, they came face to face with the owner of the voice: a quintessential vicar, complete with a coy smile and ruddy cheeks.

"Good morning. I'm Reverend Brimble, but everyone calls me Bertie."

The man held out a robust hand and shook Gareth and Claire's reluctant offerings. "What brings you to our little church then?"

Sharing a quick glance with his wife, Gareth spoke for them. "It looked charming in the guide books. But it was mention of the Holy Well that grabbed me." Presuming he could confide in the vicar, Gareth mentioned their troubles. "Our marriage has been going through a rough patch. We've come to Tenby to spend some alone time rebuilding trust." He reddened at the unfinished business between himself and Claire.

Bertie beamed. "Well, you've come to the right place. It's beautiful, isn't it?"

The couple nodded.

"Would you like me to pray with you?"

They both reddened. Gareth spoke. "I don't think we've fallen that far from Grace."

Bertie knew not to force prayer on anyone. So whilst he didn't understand how anyone in trouble who had gone to the effort to come to church would refuse prayer, he'd try to help in different ways.

"We'd like to see the Holy Well. Where's that?" Gareth asked.

Bertie stammered. "I… It's around the back," then looked at his watch; he had a Christening booked at one, then gestured for them to follow.

As they stepped outside and skirted round the stone buttresses and through the ancient tombstones to the back of the church, Geraint threw out the comment, "You aren't from around here, are you? You don't sound Welsh."

Bertie laughed. "You're not wrong. I hale from Bristol originally. Before I was given the responsibility of this remarkable parish, I had the unenviable mission of caring for a community in Hartcliffe, which isn't what you might expect from that fine city… Very urban. Drugs, gangs, stabbings and burglaries all on the street we lived in. It's no place to bring up a child. They're going through a tough time right now, but we'll get through it." Reddening at the blank faces, it hadn't occurred to him that to many, the nondisclosure of the murder's precise location meant people hadn't made the connection—just as intended. "Here it is." Bertie stood before the clear pool of water glad to change the subject.

"Is the water safe to drink?" Claire asked. Gareth paused in his lurch towards the well at his wife's hesitancy. He had no doubt it was fine, but he wanted them to drink together in ceremony.

Doubts raced through his head, but to question what had happened and even consider blaming drinking Holy Water was impertinent. God had taught him a valuable lesson. If he refused to drink the water now, it would reveal he hadn't learnt it very well. Shuddering at the thought of what test might come next if he failed again, he knelt beside the pool.

Cupping water to his lips, he drank heartily, taking two further handfuls as if to say, 'See, God. I understand what you were showing me.'

"Come on Claire. Look. It's perfectly fine."

"It's a funny colour… Looks red. Water's not supposed to be red."

Bertie groaned to his feet, exhaling an exerted sigh. "I don't think it is red, really. I think the foliage reflects on the surface."

Claire puckered her lips in disgust. "You can, Gareth. But I'm not touching it. We don't need dodgy tummies when we're in the middle of nowhere camping."

Gareth's nostrils flared as he snorted his disappointment. Taking a step away from the well, he froze. No! He'd wanted to drink this water since he first read about it. And if there was any truth to the health benefits, and if it was Holy water, then if at least one of them trusted and took a drink, it could be enough. All the way through he'd sacrificed to save their marriage, and now it looked like he would have to again.

Throwing himself to the water's edge, Gareth cupped both hands and drank greedily. The taste was odd: like metal; like coins. But it was so invigorating. It had to be doing him good.

Thrusting his hands beneath the water, he splashed the elixir to his mouth until his belly hurt with the swelling.

Seeing Claire glare down at him, he reached round to his backpack, removed the canteen and emptied the contents on the ground. Holding it underwater, bubbles rippled in rapid torrents. When the final orb breached the surface, Gareth pulled the bottle out, screwed on the lid and replaced it to his bag. Scooping one more cupped hand to his lips, staring into his wife's eyes, he stood and dried himself on his shirt.

Turning to Bertie, he smarted at the shocked look on his face, "Thank you, Vicar, for showing us the well. Slapping his arm against his side as Claire refused to take his hand, Gareth stomped from the churchyard.

Claire hesitated, but determination for what they'd come here to achieve spurred her forward until the pair faded into the distance. Bertie offered a silent prayer as they disappeared, then returned to the church to make his preparations for the upcoming service.

CHAPTER TWENTY-THREE

Annabel frowned at her watch again as though it were to blame for the tardiness of her allocated midwife. She knew she was being unreasonable. There must be all sorts of reasons someone in her profession might be held up. If it went on too much longer, she'd have to consider arrangements for Charlotte's collection from school. She shuddered.

Putting her hands on her baby, she fanned her fingers to offer as much protection as she could from the world she was bringing him into. For a moment, she was glad her midwife hadn't called her in as she feared she would be unable to speak.

Wiping a tear from her cheek; and then another, until she attracted nudges and looks from others waiting in the room. She imagined what they must be thinking. Whilst losing her own baby sat at the heart of her emotion, it wasn't in the usual sense: she had every reason to expect a robustly healthy little boy. It was what gripped the entire area in a fist of fear, and of guilt that consumed her.

How could anyone enjoy the beaches and the castles and the cafés when two families were going through a trauma that would never end? Time is a great healer, so they say. And God has a plan, she heard that said more times than she could abide, but she had to admit, to herself at least, that she didn't always understand what that plan was.

Would she ever be able to look at the green hills, tumbling over sand dunes hurrying to the ocean, with a sense of joy? Or would they forever scream at her of the death of two beautiful girls just budding in their cruelly truncated lives?

She wondered if she was better off back in Hartcliffe. The looming beige of the city buildings and the tight-packed houses where everyone struggled to find a parking space; where everyone looked different to their neighbour almost said, 'Beware.' Being on-guard seemed right.

But here it was too easy to be lulled until jolted back to the grim reality asking: 'Is it you? Or you? Or You?'

The fact was no-one knew. The brutal murderer and... she couldn't stomach to consider what else he (or she, she supposed) might have done to those poor little girls, was likely to be still around... *living amongst them.*

Hugging her bulging belly, she wished she

could stick Charlotte back inside too. Keep her safe until the danger passed.

"Mrs Brimble?" a head popped round the jam of the door. "Sorry to have kept you waiting…"

CHAPTER TWENTY-FOUR

Bertie felt quite peculiar; agitated. Instead of sitting calmly at his little desk in the church's small office refreshing his memory of the names of the family he was expecting as he usually would, he'd spent the entire time since the couple had visited the Holy well pacing around the church like a madman.

He was sure he wouldn't really be able, but as he looked at the font he thought he might rip it from its resting place and hurl it at the wall.

The unspent energy sent his fingernails to his mouth; a habit he'd cracked years ago and was dismayed to revisit. He noticed the frown first, and then the disgruntled seething towards a surprising recipient—the wife of the couple.

"Why hadn't she drunk the water?" he said out loud. And it was because of her caustic glare the poor husband had declined his offer of prayer. "Stupid bitch!" he hissed, his hand flying to his mouth, his eyes saucer wide at his unexpected profanity.

It was at this unfortunate moment Bertie found himself confronted by the first member of a small family shuffling into the church.

Wearing a frown that said, 'I must have misheard,' quizzical eyebrows inquired if they had the right day, and indeed the right church, as the eyes above which they dwelt had never seen this sweaty man before.

"Yes, yes. Do come in." Red in the face, Bertie's mind raced to excuse his outburst before reeling at the realisation he still had no idea of these people's names. "Er... Mr?" He was sure they'd not been in church since he had been here.

"Cooper. Russell Cooper; my wife, Jacquie, and of course, our baby, Alice." Russell beamed at the bumbling vicar as Jacquie stood close by, expressionless perhaps due to Botox or likely to distance herself from the screaming infant in her arms.

Bertie smiled and held Russell's gaze, waiting for the recognition that Alice Cooper was a name people may have heard before. When the glint, far from being returned, transmuted into a burgeoning frown, Bertie concluded perhaps one had to be of a particular age.

"Reverend Bertie Brimble, at your service," Bertie flustered, throwing out a hand to greet them. Realising how sweaty his palm was, he drew it back and wiped it on his smock before re-offering it to a now reluctant group.

"Where's the other vicar? The one we met be-fore? Reverend Jones; Oliver Jones?"

Feeble handshakes over, Bertie answered as best he could. "He's er…" What should he say? That he was missing, presumed AWOL? That he has let down his parish? Bertie, unwilling to judge, and more unwilling to dampen proceedings opted for, "He's on leave at the moment," answering the murmurs of, 'I hope he's all right,' with non-committal nods.

"Are we expecting anyone else?" Bertie turned to the family, smiling at their shaking heads then ushered them to the pews whilst he took his place in the pulpit. "May I begin by welcoming you all, especially the parents and godparents of little baby Alice." The screams had tuned up to eleven and Bertie was raising his voice to be heard

'Shut up!' he wanted to yell, but instead thumbed through his bible. Had they asked for a particular passage? He couldn't remember. It seemed unlikely, given their infrequent attendance at church. Using his usual divine guided method of choosing, he alighted on: *2 Thessalonians 1:6, God considers it just to repay with affliction those who afflict you.*

How did that fit? He wanted something like Ephesians, about being created as God's handiwork in Jesus Christ; or even Genesis and creation. Sweating, he flipped through again.

Proverbs 25:26 'Like a muddied spring or a pol-

luted fountain is a righteous man who gives way before the wicked.'

He didn't even know what it meant. *'Let death steal over them; let them go down to Sheol alive; for evil is in their dwelling place and in their heart. Psalm 55:15'*

Slamming his hand on the page, fury burned in his eyes. How could anybody concentrate with that racket? He glared at the crowd and the shrieking child. Stomping from the pulpit he grabbed the baby from her mother and walked to the font. They could do without a bible reading; bloody heathens. They wouldn't appreciate it anyway. "Shut up, for Christ's sake!" he yelled back.

Shuffling to join Bertie, the congregation circled round, hems thumbed and glances exchanged.

Bertie's breath hissed in his ears. Gasping, he pulled at his dog-collar and rasped. Heavier and heavier he breathed, the weight of the baby aching in his arms. What came next? Oh yes. The promises. Everyone had to promise to care for baby Alice and raise her in love of God. But she wouldn't be quiet.

As he said her name, a hatred coursed through his veins. He had to get through this. It was supposed to be for her own good.

Asking for the promises in his own loud yell to overcome the baby's scream, he stopped mid-sentence. He couldn't take this anymore. "I christen thee," he bellowed, shoving her little body into the font. Splashing over the edge at the sudden displacement, the water wasn't deep enough to submerge her, but it was sufficient to bury her face. She couldn't scream then, could she?

Hands gripped his arms like claws. Screams of "Nooo!" pierced his consciousness but he couldn't be torn from his mission.

Thrusting vicious hands in rapid jerks, her little head smashed into the stone of the font floor, blood merging with the water in crimson strands obscured Bertie's view.

Angrier now, he squeezed tightly around her neck and with one final thrust as the talons gained purchase, he smiled when the last bubble popped from Alice's open crying mouth bursting forth on the surface in violent red ripples.

CHAPTER TWENTY-FIVE

Spent, he leaned back gasping, staring at the crowd

The cry of the baby in his arms brought him to his senses. What? How? A flashback of moments before wobbled him as Alice was plucked from his embrace.

"Are you okay, Vicar?" a concerned voice seeped through his reverie. "Vicar?"

Bertie swooned, seeing his hands thrusting the beautiful little girl under the water. "I, er..." he couldn't speak. Lurching towards the font, he could see the water was crystal clear and still. Not a ripple spoiled the tranquil surface. What was happening to him? "I'm so sorry. We'll have to do this another time."

What was said as the Christening party shuffled from view was muffled but he made out 'Complaints,' and 'Nutcase,' as the crowd hastened through the door, one or two pausing to scribble in the visitors' book as they glared at the hopeless vicar. Bertie hadn't the presence of mind to care. Collapsing to the floor, he clutched his face in his hands and wept.

"Stunning, isn't it?" Gareth called across the coast path to his wife who hadn't spoken a word since his petulance at the Holy well. He sufficed with her nodding. There was no answer needed and he knew he'd offended her. He was upset she wouldn't join him in the marriage mending ritual, but he knew he could have handled it better.

With the golden crescent of South Beach below, the headland in the distance promised more dramatic scenery. But when, after a mile of strident walking they were confronted with row upon row of static caravans, it was enough to silence Gareth's enthusiasm for a few minutes.

Seeing the holiday-makers relishing the private beach; couples and families frolicking in the sun brought a pang to both their chests. This time it was Claire who bridged the gap with the offer of a forgiving hand to hold.

Soon the bustling resort gave way to undiluted countryside again, punctuated by the dramatic Lydstep cliffs and caverns.

"Can't we camp here tonight? It's gorgeous."

Gareth laughed. "We've walked two miles! I think we should push on." Seeing disappointment flash on his wife's face, and with their mission statement etched in the forefront of his mind, he conceded, "But we could stop for a snack."

Laying out the blanket rolled up in Claire's rucksack, the couple set out a small selection of their provisions. With a steely glare, ready to take on the battle again, Gareth held the canteen in front of him. Shaking it, he arched his brows. "Want some?"

"No. Thank you." Claire leaned back on her hands as she smiled coyly and said, "Sorry."

With a snort of surprise, Gareth laughed. "Pardon?"

Claire laughed too. "I know you really wanted us to drink that water together, but don't worry. We'll get there. We don't need silly rituals. A night under the stars here... What could be better?"

Unscrewing the cap and taking a glug to divert from his dogmatism, Gareth vowed to let it go. She was right. What could be better?

After their early start in inclement weather, drying off after the morning's exertion made them sleepy. Taking full advantage, Gareth held his wife in his arms, fingers outstretched to play with strands of her hair, they soon nodded off to the sound of the waves crashing on the rocks below, and to the call of curlew and gull on the gentle sea breeze.

"Gareth! Gareth! You're hurting me!" Claire tugged her head from her husband's grip, but the more she pulled the more he resisted. "Gareth!"

Gasping for breath, Gareth sat bolt upright,

face drained.

Able to yank free at last, Claire tugged her head away, leapt up and ran backwards several steps. "What on earth are you doing? You bloody hurt me!"

Gareth blinked and opened and closed his mouth. "I... I..."

"What's wrong? What's the matter with you?"

Brushing himself off, he studied Claire a moment, eyes dark and difficult to read. Scowling, he looked around. Opening his mouth to speak again, Claire could almost see the cogs turning. Eventually, he uttered with a sigh, "It was a nightmare. Thank Christ for that[MC1]."

CHAPTER TWENTY-SIX

Hugging his legs to his chest, Bertie rocked to and fro muttering, "What's happening to me? What's *happening!*" Alice's little head plunging beneath the surface of the font at *his* hands! His loving, nurturing hands.

It wasn't true, of course. He'd never live with himself if it were. But it had seemed so real. The macabre scene had not been witnessed as an observer, watching horrified as he enacted those horrific... appalling... He'd been fully involved in the frenzied moment.

With a creaking cry of anguish, Bertie let his head fall back hitting the stone. Pain echoed through him, but it felt good; right; what he deserved.

Lifting his head back to upright, he let it fall again, desperate to pierce the veil of anger and free the Bertie he'd always been.

He'd never hurt a fly. Literally. They were God's creatures and warrantied only a gentle wafting towards a window should they ever prove bothersome in his home.

God was testing him, but why? He had never been one to judge even the most heinous of sins. He knew every one of God's children were only doing their best. And the most apparently evil of them clearly tried to do so without the Grace of God within them. His mission was never to judge, but to steer toward the truth that would enlighten and heal them in Jesus Christ.

So why was he being forced to empathise with a brutal killer?

The solid oak door of the church creaked open in front of him. Panic surged. He couldn't be seen this way.

As he leaned to grab the font to pull himself up, the pain in his head ripped through him bringing forth a rage like he'd never known. Why couldn't he have a bit of peace for just five minutes to con-template his thoughts? Why was he constantly at the beck and call of his parishioners?

Grimacing, he knew whoever stepped through the door was about to witness the full extent of his effervescent fury. Jingling in the smallest cor-ner of his mind he understood it was completely irrational, but it was a distant place guarded by an impenetrable maze of darkness that had sprouted in an instant.

Clinging on with desperate fingernails, he prayed he wouldn't fall from the precipice of des-pair into volcanic vehemence.

The door opened another inch.

"Daddy. What's wrong?" Charlotte stood in the doorway, head cocked to one side and framed by the muted grey of the outside light. "Why are you crying?"

Bertie stuffed the rage with tight fists and shuffled his cheeks backwards to lean against the cold stone. Shaking his head, voice quivering in his throat, he croaked a reply. "I'm okay, sweetheart."

"Well why are you crying then?" she demanded with her arms folded.

Bertie prized his lips into a curve. Holding out his arms, Charlotte ran the short distance from the door and jumped into them. Pulling away just enough to look into her daddy's eyes, she let him know she wasn't fooled.

The pressure of the truth in those little pools of love brought a great gulp of emotion to his chest which exploded from the yawning ravine of his mouth in a wailing yell. "I don't know what's happening to me!"

Charlotte shot back with a squeal.

Clutching his face in his hands, he didn't even try to hide his feelings from his daughter. He couldn't make sense of what was real and what was imagined. Had he ever been in her room? Had he treated his wife with contempt, or was it all just a nightmare? From behind his fingers he mumbled, "I've had these terrible, terrible visions... About... *you,*" his face contorted. "Terrible, awful thoughts. And then, the baby... Today... Oh my god. She wouldn't be quiet. She wouldn't. She just kept screaming and crying." Outstretched fingers tightened on his face muffling the screams he was powerless to hold back.

Abruptly he stopped. Staring at his daughter stood just out of reach, whites of her eyes framing pin-prick pupils like a dramatic celestial photograph of Saturn's rings, Bertie's mouth crinkled in distaste.

"*Why* are you here? Where is Mummy?"

Charlotte gasped. "H... Held up at the hospital... I think," she stammered.

Oh, yes. That was right, Annabel said she had an antenatal appointment, didn't she? But that was this morning. How could it take so long? That can't be the reason she left their daughter; the apple of their eye; their reason for living; that can't be the reason she left their only daughter to walk home when she knows full well there's a child-abducting murderer on the loose.

"Hang on a minute!" Jumping to his feet, he slammed a fist on the font rippling the water in restless circles. He slowly turned toward his daughter's paling face, a scowl creasing his own as bark on an ancient oak. A rigid accusing stick of a finger outstretched, twisting, gnarled by a century of ocean storms.

"At the hospital... You think?" Copying her words, he spat them back at her with biting vim. *"At the hospital, you THINK?"* he shrieked. "Well how did you get here? Walked? By yourself?!"

"Daddy. What's wrong? What's wrong, Daddy?" Charlotte shuffled back, the font blocking her retreat, she leaned away from her snarling father.

"Oh, nothing," Bertie shrugged and chuckled an unhumorous mirth. "I just can't believe your mother left you on your own." Shaking his head in ever-sharper jolts, he hissed, "And I can't believe the school just let you walk out without supervision. I honestly can't believe it." His face fell blank and his head came to a natural slowing like a spinning coin finally running out of momentum. Then he was still.

Her eyes glistened as a tear tracked from the corner, down her nose and dropped to the ground as she stared at the floor.

"Answer me, child! It's not a difficult question."

Charlotte hesitated. What question? He hadn't asked her a question.

"Did you, or did you not, walk here, alone, from school?"

Elucidated, Charlotte nodded and burst into tears.

"Oh, don't you bloody start! What are you crying for? Nothing's happened, has it?" Bertie leered. "I'm angry with the school, not you." A blackness clouded his eyes and Charlotte whimpered, scuffling away to escape her father's reach. "And your mother!" he sputtered. Standing upright, he seethed in silence punctuated only by his laboured breaths as he wheezed in and out, in and out.

Through the agonising quiet and quivering lips, Charlotte barley mouthed, "Why?"

Rage erupted from deep within and exploded in his clenched fists as he swung round. "How DARE you question me! Not everything is your business, young lady."

It was too late. Turning in such anger, he hadn't realised her proximity. His large bulk behind whitened knuckles dealt a brutal force sending her flying.

With both feet in the air, her head slammed into the sharp corner of the font.

A sickening noise reverberated and she collapsed to the floor. Blood oozed in a crimson stream and Bertie stared in shocked disbelief at the growing pool surrounding his daughter's head.

"Oh my God. Charlotte. What have I done?"

Head shaking, face contorted. "What have I done?"

"What have I done?"

CHAPTER TWENTY-SEVEN

Gareth and Claire walked in silence. He still hadn't told her what had bothered him. A nightmare was all he would commit to, and he was acting weird.

"That building isn't pretty, is it?"

The carbuncle looming into view, they knew from the map, was the Skrinkle Haven Youth Hostel. Being a former military installation barely excused the peculiar corrugated triangles that would prompt anyone to speak, but Gareth allowed only the merest curve of his lips to shape his mouth.

"Are you going to tell me what this bloody nightmare was all about?"

Gareth's hand, clammy in Claire's grip, went limp. She threw it aside. "Let me guess. It had something to do with me and Nick?"

Gareth halted. Nostrils flaring, his eyes bore into the ground with such intensity Claire expected the cliff to split and her husband float away on his own little island. He might as well have.

"We put this to bed months ago. If we're going to rebuild our marriage—which is the entire point of us coming on this trip in the first place, we have to leave it in the past." Relaxing her tone, she sighed. "We can talk about it, I suppose. If you need to get it off your chest."

"I *don't* want to talk about it. And you're right. I did dream about you… And *him*!"

Hands clenched, Claire could see Gareth's knuckles whiten and redden like a cuttlefish parading its colours to a potent threat as he tightened and released his fists.

He didn't tell her the rest of his nightmare; catching her with her lover; grabbing her hair and smashing her stupid lying face into the bluestones dotting their path.

With a grunt and rigid star hands, Gareth muttered, "Let's just get going, shall we?"

CHAPTER TWENTY-EIGHT

Anyone would describe them as nerds. Their jobs in IT fit their appearance. Despite similar heights builds and even glasses, they weren't brothers; but they often referred to themselves as such.

Their weekends were occupied re-enacting battles from a bygone age which frequently brought them to the most densely castellated country in the world—Wales, and the area with the most castles per square mile in the whole of The Principality being Pembrokeshire meant they were pretty familiar with the territory.

On Saturday there was planned an English Civil War Re-enactment at the mighty Pembroke Castle. Famed as the birthplace of the Tudor Dynasty, they were taking a more recent (historically speaking) journey back to Cromwell's Roundheads.

They had located the actual site on Golden Hill where the New Model Army had camped overlooking the battlements. It now was the garden of a rather grand Georgian House. The owners had delighted in granting permission to set up camp there for the most authentic experience, but that was days away.

In the meantime, they occupied themselves immersing in local history. Adrian had developed a fascination with Druids, and it was with this in mind they had ventured to the little church on the outskirts of Tenby in the village of Goreston.

"Gore's-ton. The town of someone called Gore, presumably?" Toby mused as they stepped through the gateway of the churchyard.

"You wait until I tell you the history of the place. It's more like 'Gory Town!'" Adrian chuckled.

Toby and Tim rolled their eyes as though a monologue of the history of The Church of Saint Julian was the last thing they'd want to hear, but really they were thrilled.

Striding up to the first wall, Adrian paused and gave the cornerstone a mighty slap. "Any idea what this is, boys?" he grinned.

Toby looked at Tim, their eyebrows dancing in incredulity that their host might expect them not to understand the basic engineering principal of a strong cornerstone. They chose to ignore him. It was obviously leading somewhere.

"Keep your voice down," Tim shushed. "There's a service going on inside… A Christening, I think." Then, in answer to the sceptical looks, he added, "Look, there's a baby in a white Christening robe and everyone's gathered around a font, so yeah, I'm pretty sure it's a Christening."

Hushing his voice to a rasping stage whisper, Adrian was pleased at the sound. It would make what he had to say even spookier. "The cornerstones were found on site. See how they differ in colour to the rest of the building?"

"Fascinating. No really," the other two teased.

"What do you think they were before?"

Blank faces. It was all part of the theatre, and Adrian was grateful for the chance to ramp up the drama. "Go on. Guess."

Crinkled lips showed a thought process, and with a shrug to indicate this was pure conjecture, Tim suggested, "From a stone circle?"

"Dating back to the Druids?" Toby interjected. Well, it made sense. It was all Adrian had gone on about on the journey down to Wales.

Face fallen, Adrian didn't hide the disappointment the pretence hadn't been longer. Then with a flash in his eyes, he enlightened them further. "You're not far off." Perching his foot on the stone, he rolled up his shirt-sleeves. With one elbow resting on a propped up knee, the other hand was free to wave in the air gesticulating here and there.

"Long before a church was built on this site; and we're talking before the twelfth century; this," he waved his free hand to point out the wooded grove where they stood, "was a Druid Temple."

Toby and Tim gasped in mock amazement.

"And you know what went on in Druid Temples, don't you?"

They both did, but didn't want to blurt it out in case the truth was less dramatic. When Adrian stamped his foot on the corner stone, turned to them with wide eyes and hissed, "*Human Sacrifice!*" they both wished they'd said.

Moving to the other end of the church, the two followed their guide as he patted that stone too. "These would have been positioned around a sacred pool or lake. One of them would have been '*the altar,*'" he said in an eerie shrill. "The pool has been resurrected as a Holy Well. Find it and we'll find where the gruesome; 'gory' if you will, sacrifices actually took place!"

Tim and Toby looked grey. There was a lot of death in the battles they play-acted, of course. But sacrifice? Human Sacrifice? That was sickening.

Reluctantly they followed the boisterous figure of Adrian as he rounded yet another corner of the mediaeval stone building. "Bingo!" he yelled. Jigging up and down; it was all his robust frame would allow in his effort to jump on the spot in excitement. "Here's our pool."

Cut square, a bubbling pool of pinkish water beckoned them forward. "The altar would have been here..." He frowned and looked around.

"Where this crypt is now, I imagine." With a giggle of alarming delight, he said, "You can almost see the blood drenching the altars and streaming away into here, can't you?"

Leaning to the water, Adrian balanced himself so he could reach a chubby palm beneath the surface. Scooping the icy liquid to his mouth, he sat back with a manic "Ahhhh! That's the stuff." Cuffing his lips he stared at the other two.

"What are you doing?" Tim whined.

"What does it look like?"

"It looks like you're drinking the blood of Human Sacrifice," Tim glared.

Toby joined Adrian in laughing at their friend and colleague. "Yes. Blood from several centuries ago has survived in this spring because...?" he scorned.

"It even looks red!" Tim flinched back as Toby tried to lead him to the water's edge.

Scooping his own cupped handful, Toby frowned as he sloshed the water around his mouth. "It tastes of blood!"

Tim shuffled back a few more steps.

"It's the iron," Adrian shook his head at his wussy compatriots. "Victorian health freaks travelled all the way from London to drink this water. Probably before submerging themselves completely, I shouldn't wonder." Spooning more water into his mouth, he swallowed it with a satisfied gulp. "It tastes of iron. Blood tastes of iron."

"But it's red!" Tim squealed.

Toby laughed along with Adrian. "It's not red. Look," he pointed. "The foliage is kind of red and it's reflecting in the water."

"Seriously, though," Adrian began. "We should fill our water bottles here before we go on our hike this afternoon.

Adrian already had the lid open from his and was holding it under the surface, a torrent of tiny bubbles attested its filling. Toby plonked his in beside and the both stared expectantly at Tim.

Removing the containers, glugging their fill and re-dunking them, Toby and Adrian frowned at their friend. "Come on. You'll soon get thirsty."

"I don't want to. It looks... dirty."

"You're scared! Ha, liddle Timofy is scared," Toby teased in a baby voice.

"I'm not scared," Tim objected. "It just doesn't look clean, that's all."

Adrian nodded. "I read about it. Don't worry. It's a Holy Well. The whole site would have been blessed before they built the church. There's no need to worry."

"I meant it doesn't look hygienic. It looks dirty."

"Well it tastes great. People pay a fortune for spring water, and here it is bubbling from the ground free. Come on. Don't be a donut."

Slowly, Tim offered his own bottle to them to fill for him. "I don't want to get my knees muddy."

"Ohh, look at our intrepid explorer. You'll do

the Roundheads proud on Saturday. 'Oh don't kill me. I don't want to get blood on my tunic.'"

They all laughed. Tim downed half the bottle before giving it back for a refill. "Fill us up, matey," he groaned, defeated.

CHAPTER TWENTY-NINE

"Richard? Come on. I've made your favourite. Shepherd's Pie."

Mrs King sighed and walked away from her son's bedroom door. She didn't understand why the vicar's visit had upset him so. Nor why he was so determined the two girls had different killers.

To her, their being unmistakably the same was almost a comfort. She felt terrible for thinking so, but for someone else to have made the same error of judgement to risk the safety of their most precious love, and to pay the same ultimate price for that misjudgement—she choked back shameful bitterness —meant she wasn't the only terrible, appalling mother in the world.

The thought offered scant comfort and she'd lingered on the notion too long. Legs buckling, the bannister was all that kept her from falling down the stairs. Gasping for breath at her near miss, she lowered herself into an ordered heap on the floor.

A crash thundered from behind Richard's door and Mrs King cried in surprise. Picturing shelves swept to the floor in rage, more banging made her flinch with every clatter and then the door flew open.

Striding along the landing, Richard paused when he reached his mother on the stairs. He crouched and stroked her face. "I'm going out," he hushed.

"But, your dinner?"

"I'm not hungry."

"It's your favourite; Shepherd's…"

"I know," he cut her off. "I'll eat it later." Clenching his jaw, he stormed down the staircase.

"Where are you going?" she called just as the front door slammed. Hauling herself back to her feet, she stuffed the tears and placed her foot on the top step. Inhaling deeply, she stepped with purpose, removed Richard's plate, took it through to the kitchen and popped it under the grill to keep warm.

As she prodded a fork through her own meal, and glanced across the table, reaching out her hand, she rested an open palm to her left. "Your brother doesn't know how to cope, Chloe, love. I'm worried about him," she said to the empty space her daughter had occupied every teatime for ten years from high-chair to a month ago. "And your dad's never home from the allotments. It's like I've lost you all." Forcing a lump of tepid minced lamb and potato past her gullet she pushed the plate away. She'd lost her appetite.

The last vicar showed concern for him too, didn't he. Richard's fists clenched on arms rigid at his side. So well-meaning. Until... He grunted as he walked. Well that was over, and now he detected something odd about this new one. What did he know? What would he do?

Flailing his arms in exaggerated marching, Richard hoped to dispel some of the disquiet building within. He vowed to spend more time with the new head of the Parish. Things turning out as they had with the 'oh so Reverend' Jones, were unthinkable. But he *was* thinking it so he had to make sure the same thing didn't happen again. He had to.

"Are you okay, Tim?" Adrian prodded his friend again. He hadn't been the same since they'd left the churchyard; he'd barely said a word.

Tim nodded a slow deliberate tilt of his head. The burial chamber they strode towards, 'Kings Quoit Cromlech,' formed by an unfeasibly large and heavy capstone balanced on equally implausible props, silhouetted against the sun as it readied turning the sky orange before hissing into the watery horizon.

In the same scene stood a magnificent castle they recognised from their youth as the location for the BBC adaptation of C. S. Lewis's 'The Lion, The Witch, and The Wardrobe.' They should have been in their element.

Tim glugged with a steely glare at his companions.

"Are you sure you're okay?"

"What is this? Have a go at Tim day? For fuck' sake!"

Toby shot a glance at Adrian. It was the first time either of them had heard a profanity from their friend's lips. "Hey! There's no need for that," He barked. "Adrian was only asking if you're all right because you're acting weird!"

Tim stopped walking. His mind whirred. He didn't want to be here. Not with these two bullies. Not anymore. With a determined stamp, he about-turned and stomped at pace in the direction they had come from.

"Tim! Tim, what are you doing? Oh come on, don't be silly!" As Tim grew further and further away, Toby yelled, "Sorry! Okay? I'm sorry."

When it had no effect, Toby wrestled with racing after his friend of twenty years, but instead, with a snarl, he turned to Adrian and hissed in unprecedented vileness, "F... him!"

The remaining pair paused for a moment and drank from their own canteens. Timothy a mere dot in the distance now, they strode in silence towards their objective. This was meant to be fun. They always found this sort of thing enjoyable. It was so far removed from the closed-in sometimes suffocating constraints of their nine-to-five. They'd be blowed if they would let that little wet-dream ruin it. What was his problem, they fumed as they marched?

He didn't feel better. What had he expected? Well, perhaps for his supposed closest (only) friends to come after him to make sure he was okay as they said they cared so much.

He could barely see them now. They weren't coming. How could their friendship move on from this?

Sighing, he pondered, what had they done to upset him anyway? He couldn't remember, but he felt they'd been doing it for years. Picking at him; mocking him. He was always the butt of their jokes. They weren't 'The Three Musketeers.' They were 'Bert and Ernie,' with 'Gonzo' tagging along. He was Gonzo. And he was sick of it.

Why, and how, he'd come to this sudden realisation, he didn't know. Maybe there was something in this Holy Water he was drinking. Perhaps that's what it did—gave you clarity of thought. Whatever it was, he knew he was better off without them.

Pausing, he took another long course of his drink, this time with the purpose of more than rehydration: sharper thinking. He might have imagined it, but he was sure he felt the effects immediately. Why was he walking? Where was he going? He had nowhere he had to be. He could just enjoy the scenery on his own terms without those two (he cocked his head in their direction) interfering.

Striding up to the highest point of the head-land, he wrapped his legs around the outcrop of rock, riding it as a stallion coursing through the violent waves two-hundred feet below. Laughing manically, he turned instinctively to share the moment with his absent friends, then screamed in anguish shaking angry fists at the sky.

With no hands to stabilise him he faltered and with a sudden surge of adrenaline he just saved himself from tumbling to his death on the jagged rocks below. Regaining his composure, he glanced behind him to see if any of the tourists who might be treading the coastal path had seen his mis-judged outburst.

Squinting, he decided the couple in the dis-tance were too pre-occupied with one-another to notice nor cared if they had. Staring at them, he imagined their conversation in his head. The man was in the doghouse, he could tell that much. Why did women never just say what they mean?

The man looked steely faced. He'd probably had enough of her answering, 'Fine,' to every in-quiry of, 'Are you all right, my love?' What was her fucking problem?

He felt like jumping from his perch, running up to them and shaking her. "You've got a man who loves you. Stop being a pain-in-the-arse and being so moody! Look at the scenery he's brought you to. You don't know you're bloody born."

Palms flat on the floor, he was on the brink of moving. "You women are all the same! Why don't you appreciate fine men?

"If your lager-lout goes to football on a Saturday then frequents the pub on the way home from work every night, you're abandoned, and when you find a nice sensitive guy like me... I mean him, you're still not bloody happy."

He could just see it now. He would run over and tell her.

"You don't understand," she'd moan back. "You don't know what *he's* like... What *I* have to put up with..."

"What you have to put up with!" he'd scream. "He's brought you here!" flailing his arms again, this time gripping extra-hard with his thighs. He'd show her how lucky she was. He'd shake her until she knew what she had. Stupid cow.

Stupid fucking bitch.

They were upon him now. What should he do? Transparently rude to her doting husband, the lady turned to Tim and greeted. "Good afternoon. Lovely weather, isn't it?"

Tim could see what the attention she gave him was doing to her husband. With a nod of understanding in his direction, he glared at her and spat, "Fuck off!"

The shock on her face amused him. For a split second, he wondered if the man might take umbrage at his outburst, but as he watched them walk away he witnessed the man's wry smile of satisfaction. He was right. She deserved it.

CHAPTER THIRTY

Bursting through the church doors, Richard stood panting. His instinct had deserted him. The Reverend Bertie Brimble was nowhere to be seen.

The atmosphere heavy; the ancient building trembled in anguish from witnessing something unspeakable. What this place must have seen in centuries passing didn't bear thinking about, Richard sighed. Kneeling, he prayed: for guidance, and for forgiveness. He prayed for the strength to do what he needed to do.

Faces flashed before his eyes. First, his sister, Chloe's, giggling and smiling knotting his heart until the tears squeezed out and down his cheeks in wreckful sobs. When he could take no more, he was granted slight reprieve with the other little girl looming at him from the darkness, swooping at him from the black of the eaves. She had been so similar to his own beloved sister, and now neither of them would ever grace this good earth with their innocence again.

Unclenching his fists, he re-clasped his hands in prayer but he couldn't feel it: the sense of peace he'd attained when he first discovered this little church. He took it as a sign.

Standing up, he strolled further into the knave and pondered where the vicar might be. Pausing at the door to the tower, he listened. Hearing no movement, he sighed and allowed the visitors' book to grab his attention. Open on the table a few feet away, new entries written in bold seemed odd. Not that he studied it generally, but the way the tome sat askew and the page lay creased struck Richard as different from the usual revered tones.

As he drew closer, he saw the dent from a pen's nib as it had been pressed far too firmly onto the paper. Flipping through the pages, Richard confirmed the indentation went through several sheets.

'*Lovely building CRAZY vicar!!!*'

'*DO NOT book a Christening here. Worst experience of my life.*'

'*I've never complained about a church, but our christening here today was a shambles.*'

There were a number of other derogatory comments along similar lines. Richard was right. The vicar had been odd this morning on his visit. How dare he enter his home and rake over their worst nightmare? And for what, his own morbid curiosity?

With a knowing nod to himself, Richard left

the church. Before turning to the gate, he headed round the building to the well. Pausing when he got there, he shrugged. He'd expected for a moment to find the Reverend there. Leaning against the catacomb next to the well, he lay a hand upon it and stroked it. Patting the cold stone, he moved away. "What have you done, Bertie Brimble? What have you done?"

The vicarage stood a short walk from the church, and that was where Richard headed now. He needed to speak to him. He couldn't let it happen again.

Through the trees the rambling house moved in and out of view in the swaying branches. Even with the fading light of late evening, there were no lights on. Muttering, he resolved to knock on the door despite there likely being no-one home, just in case.

Stepping onto the gravel path that led to the front door, no sounds emanated from behind the old rendered walls. Richard gave the knocker a hearty rap. The sound echoed in the emptiness beyond. What should he do, wait? He had no idea where they were. They may be spending the night away for all he knew.

Knotting the urges inside him, he had no choice. He would have to go home and try to rest. He would have his chat with Bertie Brimble tomorrow.

CHAPTER THIRTY-ONE

E ven the scenery couldn't breach the chasm between them. Gareth strutted, vindicated in his opinion of Claire. She too strode with a face dark and cloudy in stark contrast to the cloudless sky. The sun preparing to set in the sky seemed a perfect metaphor for the pair trying to save their marriage.

But Claire wouldn't let it fizzle out without a fight. She'd had an affair. Yes. She knew it was wrong. No-one needed telling that was wrong. But if they were to move on from it they had to put it behind them; and in all honesty, it had been justified as far as it can be.

It wasn't just that she had her head turned by a successful and handsome colleague. It was the contrast with how Gareth treated her at home. Guilt knotted inside and she batted it aside with the fury burning within.

The vows she'd made on her wedding day, she'd meant every word. 'For better, for worse...' she'd meant it. But was having an affair any worse than the abuse she'd suffered at Gareth's hands? Abuse was probably too strong a word. Perhaps neglect expressed it more.

The affair she'd had didn't breach the contract of their marriage any more than the apathy Gareth demonstrated daily for years. Perhaps her actions made things better. Sharpened her husband's senses to the threat. And because of that they were now working through their problems.

What he put her through was unendurable. An extra-marital dalliance might have been an extreme cry for help, but extreme had been required.

She had tried to hint, and then to say, and eventually to scream her objections. Promises had been attained for improvement only to be wiped away the moment Gareth felt secure again.

So now, the fact he might never feel secure could be seen as a good thing. Hypocrisy had been wrestled with, and she'd just about won. The truth was, she doubted she would forgive an affair from her husband. It wasn't the sex. Already, that was something she had to contend with after he'd moved that tart into their family home. It would be the duplicity, and perhaps worse, the justification; the 'Well *you* did it first,' attitude that would demonstrate how little responsibility he took for his own involvement in what had happened.

But, she was jumping the gun. They'd have to get back together before the opportunity for him to have an affair would even arise. Sighing, a pang of shame she couldn't assuage gripped her throat— remorse for her two boys. Allaying culpability with the belief she'd always known it would be temporary. She couldn't have foreseen the knee-jerk reaction which risked her never returning.

When she'd driven away that night, she should have taken them with her. She knew that now. But it hadn't been the promise of romance with her new lover she'd protected, it was Gareth. Foolishly, she hadn't wanted to destroy him. Taking away his wife *and* his children in one fell swoop seemed a punishment too far for the mediocrity he'd cultured.

With that in mind, she glanced at him for the first time since the awful man had been so rude to her. What was he thinking? An outsider couldn't know any of their history. If he had, perhaps it would be no surprise if 'bro code' might make them natural allies. He hadn't looked the sort of man who could keep a woman happy so he might be expected to empathise entirely with his cuckolded comrade.

But he'd been nothing but a stranger. How could Gareth get any satisfaction from what the weirdo had done? But he seemed to. The smug expression seemed to say, 'See, Claire. I told you you were a bitch!'

"I hope you're happy with yourself; your little buddy over there telling your wife to fuck off justifies your pathetic existence, does it?" She hadn't meant to be so harsh, but seeing him wince; witnessing the manly bravado slip, just for a second satisfied her immensely.

Flushed red, Gareth didn't answer, but Claire could see his mind whir, desperate to throw out a witty comeback.

"If we're going to get through this, and I do really want us to, we're going to have to be a team again," Claire interjected before he had time.

"You want me to go and beat him up?" Gareth snorted. "He was just some fat nerd."

"A nerd who was incredibly rude to your wife."

Unsure where to go with his argument, and unsure why he was so bloody angry about it, Gareth continued his moody march in silence.

Feeling better that she'd defended herself, Claire swung her arms in carefree comfort as she strolled along aware Gareth was suffering more than she.

They could set up their little tent soon, thrash out all the shit they needed to cope with, eat, and wake up to the rising sun. If things went well, maybe they could even make love under the stars! Claire felt a twinge. She hoped it would go well more than ever now. The scenery was winning and she felt amorous and romantic. They'd get through this, she was certain.

Tim stared out to sea. For the first time in his life, he had nowhere to be. He was free. And just like the institutionalised prisoner tasting liberty for the first time in years, he was afraid.

With steely determination, he willed each crashing wave to take away his stress, to fill him with new purpose like a suckling infant at its mother's breast. But more akin to a growing ache, the waves wrought tension.

Hugging his rock and forcing himself to ride the horizon of ocean, Tim closed his eyes and ordered his fears away. Under his breath he muttered, "F... off, f... off, f... off!" and it was cathartic.

With each repetition, he felt empowered. Gone was mild-mannered 'Timothy from I.T.' The Tim who answered every question with, 'I don't mind... You decide.' In his place was 'I don't give a F...! Tim. The word rolled around his tongue, a delicious gobstopper, him salivating on every crunch as it jostled in his mouth. Over and over he said it, giggling, holding the mane of his Cambrian Steed to be certain of his safety. He didn't give a f..., but he didn't want to lose this new Tim before he'd had a chance to live with him.

Screaming at the top of his lungs at the ocean, other profanities swirled around his head, but none obliged more. It wasn't just the offensiveness of the word, it was what it meant. It meant sticking it to someone; to take them and have them want you take them. And when he said 'someone', he meant a woman, a lady; reduced to putty by his mastery that in its first utterance he had instantly acquired.

He knew what women wanted. And when he said *women*, he meant *woman*. And when he said *woman*, he meant Claire.

Dismounting his rock, he uncapped his canteen and took a long drink. He must have drunk litres of the stuff. Who knew water could make you feel like this! Red Bull sales would take a hit. He was taking mineral water to work from now on. Taking a decisive step back the way he came, Tim knew they couldn't have gone far, and when he found them, he'd give her what she wanted. Whether she knew she wanted it, or not.

"Richard? Is that you?"

Richard plastered a smile on his face and tiptoed into the lounge. "Hello, Mum. Sorry. About earlier." Eyes dipped to the floor, he recalled with reddening cheeks the outburst in his room. He hoped his mum hadn't seen the mess he'd made. "The vicar calling and bringing it all up got to me. I could handle it last night, in church, in my own time. Springing it on us after breakfast was unkind and thoughtless."

Mrs King nodded. "I knew he'd upset you. Where have you been?"

"To see him. Well to *try* to see him. He wasn't at church and he wasn't at the vicarage. I'll see him tomorrow, I guess."

"I saved your dinner. It's under the grill."

Richard nodded his thanks. "I'll wash my

hands first."

Gripping the bannister with whitening knuckles, Richard swallowed down his rage. He couldn't tell his dear mum the real reason he'd gone to see Reverend Bertie. He'd upset him all right, but not for the reason he'd told her.

With a gulp of guilt, he walked into his spotless bedroom. The shelves had been put straight. The spilt cups of tea mopped up, and whatever else that had suffered as a casualty of his outburst were now without a trace. She shouldn't have had to do that. None of this was her fault. Sitting on the bed, he planted his face in his hands. He didn't know how much more of this he could cope with.

CHAPTER THIRTY-TWO

T he argument formed in Gareth's head. It didn't take long and once it gathered momentum it hurtled towards oblivion like a runaway train. "You know that bloke?" he promoted Tim from nerd no-one could be interested in to 'bloke;' an equal; a threat.

"What bloke?"

"You know *what* bloke."

Claire pondered, mystified for a moment before the penny dropped. She would have laughed if Gareth's face hadn't sucked the joy from the atmosphere like a turbocharged cooker hood. "The man who was rude to me? Oh, get real. Of course I don't know him."

"Don't lie to me, Claire. Not again."

Glaring at him, she couldn't believe her ears. Was he mad? "I'm not lying. How could I know him? You think I've come away to Wales with you to re-build our marriage and arranged a rendezvous with a weirdo in case it didn't work out!" Claire spat. "What was 'fuck off?' A code word for, 'come to my tent later'? You are seriously deranged."

"I don't think you arranged to meet him. That would be stupid. But I think you know him, yeah. Why else would he tell you to f... off, if he doesn't know you? Eh?"

"Because he's a nutter?" Claire shook her head. What had happened? This trip had begun so promisingly. One time not doing exactly as he wanted and drinking from that manky hole in the ground and he turns into a complete arsehole. They carried on putting one foot in front of the other, the scenery wafting past unnoticed.

"Did you sleep with him?"

Claire stalled. "What? You're crazy."

Grabbing her shoulders, his snarling spittle-coated lips just inches from hers, he growled his question a second time, "Have you slept with him? Look into my eyes. I'll know if you're lying."

Claire's mind whirled. She'd really damaged him, hadn't she. She would have to make him understand his responsibility for what happened, but for now she'd just try to help him through it. Looking him cleanly in the eye, she answered, "No. I have not slept with that man."

Seeing his shoulders slump with relief, she drew him in close. Voice breaking, she sobbed into his neck. "I haven't slept with anyone else you don't already know about. I promise."

Breaking free from their embrace to see his eyes and make sure he received her reassurance loud and clear, she decided he had. Leaning in, she kissed him. Round and round her lips moved on stiff unyielding counterparts. But then it came: the first stirrings. Following up with a caressing tongue, soon they were in a passionate embrace that threatened to delay the erection of their tent for some time.

When the heat got too much, yearning for privacy they paused in the darkness and fumbled the little pop-up from the rucksack. Minutes later they disappeared inside, and confident they were alone on the coast path in the dark, they consummated their trip.

The canvas dripped with condensation from their sweaty bodies and trembled in the breeze, a tortoise having a mild seizure. With final thrashings that risked tipping them prone on their back, the tortoise stilled.

Sated, but with a raging thirst, Gareth wriggled from beneath his wife and quenched it with water from the canteen. Settling to sleep in one-another's arms, Gareth fought the idea growing in his mind that he had just been monumentally played.

"You okay?" Claire asked, her hand stroking the hairs on his chest.

Why was she asking? Why wouldn't he be? That was suspicious, wasn't it? "Mmm hmm," he mumbled non-committedly. Laying back, he forced his eyes closed but they pinged open allowing a beige view of a muted night sky.

Claire shuffled closer and flinched as his side

went rigid. This was going to take a bit more work than she had anticipated.

Gasping for breath, Tim jolted from a nightmare. His hands cramped in the position of strangulation, he could still picture that woman's face screwed and contorted with her last breath, eyes pleading for mercy. He chuckled. When he found her, he wasn't going to kill her. She'd be pleading with him for something else, "If you know what I mean..." he winked at an imaginary companion and laughed.

Sleep had been surprisingly accessible on the soft grass of the cliff-tops. The dropping temperature of the darkest hour must have bitten through despite sheltering in a small gulley out of the wind. But he'd slept through that and now the warming rays of dawn lent an orange glow to his skin. He felt like an eighties Reddy Brek advert with the glowing kids waiting for their school bus.

He wondered how far ahead the couple would be... If they even still were a couple. He could tell she wasn't that into him. He'd given up trying to find them last night when darkness hid the cliff edge, but they won't have travelled in the dark either so he'd easily catch them up. Having not eaten since yesterday breakfast, for some reason he wasn't hungry. Uncapping his bottle, he took another swig of water.

He remembered reading that the body's signals

become muddled. Sometimes when we think we're hungry, we are actually thirsty. Maybe it worked in reverse, where we fool our bodies into thinking we aren't hungry by drinking plenty of water. Squeezing his chin between thumb and forefinger, Tim decided this was likely.

Not wanting food was the least of it though. He hadn't felt this good in… Shaking his head he decided he'd never felt like this ever before. Never this vibrant. Never this full of purpose; nor so confident of achieving it. Never so supportive of himself.

Pushing himself out of his hide-hole, he stretched his arms up to the rising sun, a flower positioning for a session of photo-synthesis. Six hours later he might declare in a thick Austrian accent, 'Good workout,' and kiss his leafy guns.

He was funny. What a funny guy. Strutting onwards in the direction he'd seen his prey leave him, the new improved Tim swung his arms as he walked.

He knew the scenery was stunning, but, with a sneer, he regarded it with contempt. It was just some rocks and some water—no more beautiful than anything else. He felt a worthy rival.

So when he spotted her, a few metres from what must be her little tent, standing hands-on-hips staring out to sea, he knew he'd steal her attention when he reached her.

Smiling, he noted without surprise, that the man was nowhere to be seen. Perfect.

Padding towards her, the hundreds of metres soon became ten and she didn't look round until he was only three metres from her. The soft grass and the south-easterly onshore breeze conspired in Tim's favour. Why wouldn't it? This was fate.

Eyes wide with shock took a moment to react, but Tim didn't care. He wasn't going to woo her; he was going to fuck her.

Grabbing her shoulders, he pushed her to the ground.

"What are you doing, you freak?" She yelled. Bringing her wrists up through his, she batted them away and ran for the tent.

With speed and dexterity he'd never known before, Tim threw out his leg and tripped her. Winded, she collapsed on the floor and he leapt upon her to pin her down with his thick arms, her wriggling her hardest. Discerning her tire, he opted to free one of his arms.

Yanking at his belt, he loosened it and pulled open his fly enough to release his throbbing organ. Regarding himself with a smile, he was pleased to see that every little part of him had responded well to the drinking, not eating, regime.

Waving like a proud flagpole, Tim surveyed the magnificence of his penis. He'd hated this woman hours before. Detested her. But now, as her hand reached for him, he was happy to let her gratify him. Maybe he still hated her, but like the king of the beasts, he would allow her to worship him for the sake of the species. Maybe he'd growl ferociously in her hair, perhaps even bite her to demonstrate his dominance as she pleasured him.

He knew, for the first time, what women wanted, and he was delivering.

It happened in slow-motion allowing him the opportunity to really enjoy it. Her hand was nearly at him now; fingers opened, shielded him from view. Finally in her tight grip, he groaned with delight.

"Aaargh!"

He collapsed in agony as his lioness yanked, viciously bending him downward. His busted bone pointing in a peculiar direction, twitched pathetically as pain sliced through him like a sword. "You've broken it. You fucking bitch!"

As she wriggled from beneath him, Tim staggered to his feet. The agony crippled yet mobilised him as effervescent fury at her insolence fired through him. "Come here!" he growled, throwing out a robust arm caught her in the throat.

Halted, gasping for breath, Claire was swept into his bear hug unable to shake free. "Gareth!" she croaked, not loud enough even to hear herself. "Help."

CHAPTER THIRTY-THREE

Flapping a hand from his sleeping bag, Gareth frowned. Where was she? Memories of last night flooded back. The man. Claire's denials. Making love.

It had been great until suspicions fought through the fog of her duplicity. Shaking his head in rapid jerks, he recalled with sudden disturbing clarity last night's dream.

It wasn't new. She was with *him* again. The marriage-wrecker from work. Gareth found himself watching them, an unwilling voyeur. He had pounced on her, screaming. "Why, why? Why are you doing this?"

He'd hit her, he remembered that. But as he'd turned to give Nick what for, his worst suspicion had been ratified. It hadn't been Nick after all... It was the chubby nerd from the cliff. He knew it!

Creasing his lips, he realised he knew nothing of the sort. It had just been a nightmare. Reaching for his canteen, he uncapped the lid and drank. When he was full there remained only a tiny bit. Downing the last couple of mouthfuls, he threw it to the corner of the little tent. Where was she?

With a sudden certainty she had left him, the sleeping bag zip snared in his haste to be free of the quilted confines. Jostling it when it refused to spit out the fabric, Gareth pulled with both hands bending the teeth and sending the fastener flying.

"What the hell does she think she's doing?" he snarled leaping the short distance to door-flap. Taking greater care after the sleeping bag scuppering him, Gareth paused for breath taking the tent zip in a firm grasp.

Moving it up with a satisfying zzzz, Gareth almost smiled as he crawled outside. Halting mid crunch, his eyes screwed to make out what they saw.

"I don't believe it," he growled, but he believed it all too well. His wife was in an amorous embrace with that freak from yesterday afternoon. "I bloody knew it!" he roared, pushing himself to his feet.

He could see them writhing together, his arms around her, face in the unmistakable grimace of the final throws of passion pulling her round to face him, Gareth winced as he saw the man exposed.

Right in front of him. Right in front of anyone taking an early morning walk along the path.

How could she do this to him?

With a hatred born from humiliation, Gareth stormed towards them, feet thudding on the rocks beneath the grass. An ear-to-the-ground Tonto might have reported a stampede to an expectant Lone Ranger as Gareth's anger surged through his legs with every stride providing superhuman ferocity.

Thud, thud, thud, they pounded until, breathless, he was upon them. "You dirty, lying cow!"

Heaving the man off his wife, he swung round and shoved her backwards with a two-handed pass to her bared chest. "Dirty bitch. Right in front of me!" Drawing back his fist, he failed to unleash it when chubby fingers grabbed his arm from behind.

Sharp pain bruised his spine as a large knee pressed hard into its base. Catapulted forward he knocked into Claire. Unbalanced, she tottered on her bare feet.

The edge of the cliff failed to take even her dainty weight, held together as it was by mere roots from tufts of grass, Sea Campion and Pink Thrift, the sandy soil held on with the strength of a baby and dropped her to the tumult below.

Sliding down, she yowled in pain as instinctive toes curled to slow her plummet. As her chest disappeared, her arm flew up and grabbed a handful of gorse, its woody fronds slowing her until she dangled four hundred feet above the angry savagery of the Atlantic.

Gareth fell forward from the impact, and with his wife's body no-longer there to prop him up, the momentum threw the half-naked man over Gareth's shoulder in an Olympic Judo throw.

With a cry, he flipped like a tossed coin, head clipping Claire's shoulder sent him tumbling the other way as he plummeted.

Heads or tails proved brutally apt be as he dropped towards the jagged rocks and his final fate sickeningly inevitable.

Two rocks separated by a two-foot gap that tapered to nothing where they met at their base provided a perfectly made tool for the job.

As the weird chubby stranger they'd seen together for the first time yesterday evening reached the base, his head aimed with precision between the two triangle crags of rock prizing it off like a splinter with a sickening crack as his legs and body flopped, lifeless on the other side.

Job done, the rocks relaxed as Tim's severed skull fell one way and his body the other. They would paint an interesting picture of Pembrokeshire marine wildlife when they washed up on separate beaches in a few weeks' time.

The gorse struggled to keep its tentative grip on the cliff and Claire slipped further from Gareth's view. Lunging to grab her, his balanced tipped and he fell forward.

Falling with her hand in his, the pivotal point was reached and the pair could deny gravity no longer.

As they sailed to their gruesome death, to become nothing more than food for cliff-dwelling Raven and Herring Gull, their tumbling bodies fluttered as clothing caught the thermal updraft moving them in turns closest or furthest from the frothing daggers below.

They'd witnessed what happened and knew what was to come for them. Plummeting in slow motion, during the four seconds it took to hit the rocks life's turning points revisited for them to love or regret in their last moments.

As their bodies and their lives shattered with the force they weren't allowed peace a wave plucked them from the rock and smashed them into the cliff face, repeatedly drawing them back only to throw them again and again with the full might of the ocean into the vertical rocks.

Discovering the bodies, the obligatory dog-walker or perhaps a jogger would wonder what happened. But no-one, not even those who had plunged to their deaths knew that. Not really.

CHAPTER THIRTY-FOUR

Sheets sodden with perspiration rucked in Bertie's fists. "Wha...Where am I?" Gasping, he patted the bed and recognised it as his own. Memories of what he'd done stabbed into his thoughts like right hooks. Jerking sideways, he vomited, most of it reaching the floor and only some smearing down the side of the bed.

"Oh my goodness, Bertie. Are you okay?" Annabel rushed in and stroked his clammy forehead. "I'm the one supposed to have morning sickness."

Bertie gawked, eyes wide and dry. "Are you okay?"

Annabel frowned. What was this new morning ritual? "Why are you asking? You're the one who's just been sick."

How could she act so normal? She couldn't know. "Where's Charlotte?" Bertie couldn't remember a thing since she fell. All that blood.

Jolting from the bed, he raced along the corridor to her bedroom and barged inside. "Charlotte! Charlotte!" Of course she wasn't there. She'd be in hospital, wouldn't she? "Where is she?"

"What's got into you, Bertie?" Annabel leaned against the door, arms folded. "You have one of your visions again? You're working too hard. What happened this time?"

Could it be a nightmare? Oh, please, God, let it just be a dream. Nodding, he rasped, "Where is she? Is she all right?"

"She's fine… Went to a friend's for a sleepover. I told you this. Remember? I got delayed at the antenatal appointment and asked Darcie's mum to pick her up. You know Darcie? Charlotte mentioned her. Her mum's really friendly."

Piecing the events together, Bertie couldn't make his mouth form the words. Throwing on his trousers, he left on the t-shirt he had slept in. Jumping the stairs two at a time, he threw open the front door, pausing for a second to slide his feet into his shoes, and hurtled through.

"Bertie! Bertie, where are you going?"

Arms pumping, palms flat like a ten-year-old on sports day, Bertie huffed and wheezed to the church. Squeezing past the gate ajar on creaking hinges, his shirt snagged on the latch barely slowing him as he barged his way through like a particularly hefty prop heading for the try line.

Thudding through the door, he screeched to a halt at the font breathing hard and fast.

Thank God. She wasn't there. Could she be at a friend's house like Annabel said?

"What's wrong, Vicar?"

Bertie shot round. "Ah… Richard… Everything okay?" He had to be there for his parishioners but he still wasn't one-hundred percent certain he wasn't facing his own worst nightmare. "My daughter… Charlotte, you haven't seen her have you?"

Annabel reached the door. "You!" Flying across the nave, she stood inches from Richard. "What have you done with my daughter? What have you done!" Lunging for him, Bertie caught her arm.

"Richard hasn't done anything, my love."

Annabel frowned. Clutching at the pew, her legs curtsied and the colour drained. *"Richard…* Chloe King's brother?" he nodded. Head in a swirl, Annabel couldn't make sense of it. Why was he hanging around school? Why had he been looking at Charlotte? He'd forgiven the killer. She remembered that much. Why? How could he? No. she'd been right. She didn't like him. What if the reason he'd found it so easy to forgive his sister's murderer was because it *was* him? "What have you done, Richard? Have you hurt Charlotte? Did you hurt Chloe?"

With a gasp, Richard stumbled back. Fumbling along the wall. He looked so guilty, she knew she was right. "You're the murderer!"

Shoving past, he ran to the door and pushed it

open. "After him, Bertie. We have to save Charlotte!"

"Annabel. Richard didn't hurt Charlotte."

Annabel paused and stared. "But you were so worried. You rushed down to the church. Why?" Her eyes gaped, pupils firing like arrows. "What have you done? Has something happened to Charlotte?"

Bertie stared at the floor. There was no blood. But, he had no recollection of going home. How had he woken up in bed? Had he cleaned up the tragic accident and in a daze of anguish gone home to bed?

"Bertie. You tell me now, or so help me… " She shook a fist in his face. "What have you done!?"

Falling to his knees, he collapsed in a ferocious sob. "I don't know. I don't know!"

Annabel rushed outside, as the door swung back, her voice wafted in on the breeze. "…Hello, Jacquie. It's Annabel. Is Charlotte okay?"

Bertie gripped his face in his hands. What he wouldn't give for his little girl to be safe and well. How could he not even know if she was anything but, and at his own hand?

The door clacked shut again and Annabel stood, phone poised inches from her face. "She's fine… eating pancakes for breakfast."

"Thank you, God. Thank you, thank you, thank you." Hands clasped in prayer rose above his head as he fell forward in tumultuous sobs. The worst of his fears purged, he opened his eyes and smiled at his wife. She did not smile back.

"What did you *think* had happened, Bertie? Answer carefully. I won't be lied to. I want the whole truth."

Bertie glanced at Jesus on his cross where he absolved all human sin, but he couldn't bare his soul in front of him. "I'll tell you everything, but can we do this at home? Please?"

Bertie offered his hand for Annabel to take, his chest tightening at her decline with a firm, "No! We'll go home and you can tell me what's been going on."

Tea brewed, Annabel poured with a calculated calm. "It's these visions, or whatever they are, isn't it? You haven't been entirely honest with me, have you?"

The cup jangled against the saucer as Bertie's finger trembled. He couldn't speak. He shook his head in rapid little jerks.

"Well, are you going to tell me now?" she took a sip from her own teacup, her eyes never flinching from the broken man opposite her at the kitchen table.

Her strength prompted Bertie to be brave. "I told you I'd worried Charlotte might have been..." he couldn't bear to say, and Annabel couldn't bear to hear. A deep sigh filled his lungs and expelled in defeat before he continued "But I didn't tell you what I did."

Annabel moved her cup to her saucer and

steadied it in pincer fingers.

"I don't know what came over me. I've never had those sort of feelings. Not for Charlotte, not for any child. Not for anyone but you. It's just, she looked so like you, and I was so…"

Annabel remained silent. Still.

"Nothing happened. She woke up, I realised what was happening and I jumped back catching the bedpost.

"I was so distraught, I ran to the church and God showed me. I'd been judgemental. How could Richard have forgiven? I knew I couldn't have. So God showed me… I couldn't forgive because I couldn't understand, do you see?

"I might forgive someone stealing, because reluctant as I might be to do it, if we were starving, I can imagine I might. But I couldn't hurt anyone, least of all a child… a sweet innocent little angel. I couldn't.

"And how anyone could take advantage, you know, sexually? Well the whole thing disgusts me. Yet there I was. Turned on and ready to hurt my own precious child. It was a test, you see?"

Annabel breathed in. She breathed out. She would stop from moving just long enough to hear what he had to say.

"Then there was the christening, which I'm not sure was real or a waking nightmare, but… oh my lord…"

Annabel glared, her gaze implored him to continue. He had no choice.

"Well, it began normally, and then I had this anger. The child wouldn't shut up crying. Well. She was only a baby. Anything could have been the matter. But I was furious." He glanced up at his wife and despite the disgust witnessed in her eyes, grey and regarding, he told her, just as she wanted. "I held her under the water until the last bubbles of breath popped on the surface. I held her with such force, the font filled with her blood."

Annabel's cheeks blew and she covered baby tight with her jumper.

"But, it wasn't true. Of course it wasn't true. I came out of the hallucination with her safely in my arms, but I couldn't carry on. I slumped alone by the font and cried. That's when Charlotte came in."

Annabel sat up. "Go on," she demanded.

"I was cross. I don't really know why. With you, I think. Ironically, it was because I thought you'd let her walk home alone… with the dangers we all know too much about." His eyes darted, his wife's reluctance to move here bouncing around his brain. "I was angry with the school, too," he deflected, "But it was when she defended you I lashed out.

"It was an accident. As I turned, my arm struck her and she fell and hit her head on the font." Bertie's cheeks bulged at the sickening memory. "There was blood, so much blood." His lips paused mid-word and he stared at the floor, opaque through the tears in his eyes. "The next thing," he croaked, "I woke in bed with no recollection of how I got there and you telling me you think Charlotte's at a friend's house. I thought there must have been a mistake and I might have... you know..."

"You thought you might have *killed* our daughter?"

"Well, no. I'm sure I can't have, really, I suppose, but I had to check. I had to be sure, didn't I?"

Annabel flew forward, fists flying, she pummelled Bertie's broad chest. "Get out! GET OUT!" she screeched, "I want you to leave. Now! You're not safe. I won't let anything happen to my children. You sick, sick bastard GET OUT!"

Standing defiant, she edged towards the block of knives. Bertie knew she was ready to defend herself if he objected. "I could never hurt anyone. Least of all our own child. You know that."

"I did know that. Until just now. Now it seems even you can't be certain. I'm not risking our safety; our *lives!* You have to go."

"But my parish needs me. They've been abandoned by one vicar already. It will devastate them if I go as well."

"They need you, do they? They need someone who may or may not be a paedophile bloody murderer..."

"Not! I'm definitely not."

"But two minutes ago you weren't sure, Bertie!

You had to go and check. You had to see for yourself."

Bertie stared at the floor. She was right. He was ninety-nine percent sure he'd never succumb to such fury to hurt anyone, least of all the family he adored. But he hadn't been sure. Twice, he hadn't been sure; three times including baby Alice. The floor had his full attention as he hushed, "Where should I go?"

Annabel shrugged. "I don't know. The doctor's might be a good start. You need help. These visions aren't normal."

Bertie nodded slowly. "No. I suppose they're not. And you're right. I'm no use to the church like this. I'll make an appointment."

"Do that. But you're not doing it here. I don't want you around. I knew you were acting weird. And that was before you told me all this."

"Whe... When can I come home?"

Still close to the knife block, Annabel sighed. "I don't know. We'll see what the doctor says, won't we. That's all we can do for now."

Disappearing upstairs, he re-appeared minutes later with a small holdall. Grabbing his coat from the hook, he gave a watery look at his wife who hadn't moved. "Bye," he hushed. "... See you soon." Eyes falling to the floor, Bertie left, clicking the front door closed behind him, he paused to stare at the sky, exhaling not only sorrow but relief. Annabel was right. He wasn't safe to be around. He didn't understand, and until he did, he would keep away.

CHAPTER THIRTY-FIVE

There were hundreds of campsites throughout the county boasting hill top; unspoiled scenery; views of sea, or castle or both; in the woods, on a cliff, or in the case of the recently broken Smith family, on a holiday park with amusement arcades, wave pools and entertainment from ever-smiling Fun Stars in or out of their furry character costumes that announced itself at the gate as the 'Best Holiday Park in Wales!'

Most who stayed utilised one of the hundreds of static caravans or lodges on site, but the Smiths tighter budget meant a family-sized tent had to do. And even then, the nightly rate during school holidays was beyond them.

Susanna Smith had billed it as more of an adventure than a boring old caravan, and whilst she'd said it to justify her meagre funds, ensconced under canvass, she believed it was. She could hear the waves crash and the seagulls cry and she liked it.

"Where are we going today?" Mathilda tugged at her mother's sleeve as she attempted to cook enough sausages for the family on the tiny gas ring.

It was all going well, despite the tribulations of micro-cooking meals. It had a magical quality. A real sense of adventure. "I don't know. Where do you want to go?"

Her daughter shrugged.

"How about a long walk to a secret beach?" She regretted the long walk bit. Children never liked the idea of a walk, but rarely noticed if they were heading somewhere they wanted to go.

They couldn't stay on site. Their budget would be decimated by the end of the day what with Burger King for lunch and Starbucks for a snack. Susanna hadn't realised how expensive it was here. Only ten pounds per night for their tent, but thirty pounds on ice-cream and air-hockey and grabber machines while she tried to enjoy some very loosely termed 'live music' from a gentleman who was under the severe misapprehension he resembled Tom Jones.

She planned to avoid Tenby, with its purse emptying temptations around every corner. Each street had a different gift shop, sweet shop or ice-cream parlour they hadn't yet tried. And they were all geared to a more moneyed clientele than she now found herself.

A pang of guilt at their change of fortune tightened her chest. But it wasn't her who had developed a gambling addiction. It wasn't her who had re-mortgaged their beautiful home to pay the debts. It wasn't her who had run away and abandoned her spouse and three children.

It *was* her who had been determined to keep things bright replacing her pathetic husband, Simon, with a magnificent Golden Retriever they'd named Dillon. And she felt a lot safer with him than she ever had with her estranged husband.

They'd all desperately needed a holiday, and Tenby had been a firm family favourite for as long as any of them could remember. Okay, they had to swap five-star-luxury for a tent and the dubious company of 'Bradley Bear' and his odd furry companions, but the kids loved it.

There was none of the stuffiness they'd lived with as the respectable offspring of a regional manager of a cherished household name in retail. All that was long gone, never to return. But they didn't need that; they didn't need *him* to have fun.

She still loved him. That would never stop, she supposed. Not unless she met someone else, and that seemed unlikely with the time constraints of three children a dog and a career as a supermarket cashier (taken in haste as *something* to pay the bills.)

Gulping down regret, she gazed into Mathilda's deep brown eyes. "There's a cool little church we can stop at on the way." Not a usual bribe for a ten-year-old, but since her school had visited one to perform brass-rubbings, interest in repeating the hobby had been expressed frequently.

"Yay. When can we go?"

"As soon as we're dressed, I suppose."

"I am dressed."

"Well, tell your brothers! And have you brushed your teeth?"

Mathilda shook her head. "After breakfast?"

Pausing mid-egg flip, Susanna nodded. She supposed that made sense. "Edward, Thomas. Breakfast is nearly done. Are you dressed?"

The zipper flew up on their section of the family tent and they tumbled out. Hands formed into guns, they shot each other making the sound effects with their voices as they ran around the tent.

"Careful boys! Play outside if you want to do that. Don't go far, I'm about to serve up. Oh, and take Dillon out for wee-wees."

Dillon tilted his head. He'd learned what that meant and padded towards the tent flap. Rushing out, Susanna clasped her hand to her upwardly curved lips to banish the guilt at Dillon's poor bursting bladder, and to hide her smile at the disregard he now showed their fellow campers as he cocked his leg against a neighbouring tent-pole. Susanna was grateful there was no-one else around to see it. She'd heard them all leave this morning en route to a breakfast date with 'Rory the Tiger.'

She'd kept deliberately quiet about it, but now she felt guilty for that too. Yes, it was far removed from the sophisticated tastes their leisure time usually took, but since the boys' fencing, piano lessons, and Mathilda's pony riding and cello had been shelved due to budget restraints, couldn't Rory the Tiger be just the ticket? And wasn't embracing their new non-stuffy life without their father on hand kind of the point? She'd suggest it on their walk—there was still time to meet Anxious the Elephant for pre-dinner dancing!

"Grub up!" she yelled feeling incredibly authentic, half expecting Bear Grylls to pop out of the bushes and give her a pat on the back.

As her troop sat cross legged balancing sausage, eggs, bacon, beans and buttered bread (it was going to be toast, but that would've taken another fifteen minutes with the hit-and-miss grill) on their laps, Susanna bit her lip to prevent from reprimanding for the mess they were making.

"Who fancies a picnic on a secret beach?"

The nods were instant and enthusiastic. Privacy had been taken for granted in the large detached house they'd lived in up until last year. Now, forever conscious of 'not disturbing the neighbours' surrounding them, the thought of an entire beach to themselves was bliss.

Consulting the map, Susanna had seen plenty of unnamed little bays between the more popular resorts. Without car parks or any facilities, she expected at least one of them might be empty.

Clearing away the breakfast dishes and washing up before the egg and beans had a chance to dry, Susanna then proceeded to prepare sandwiches for their alfresco lunch. They would avoid stopping at the shop on the way out of the campsite. They could only afford the essentials, maybe some sweets and fizzy pop, but no souvenir cuddly toys or whatever else the gift shop was bound to display in compelling fashion. She hoped to find a smaller, cheaper shop on their hike. Otherwise they would make do with the sandwiches and water and a couple of dubious looking apples.

Ready and washed, Susanna nodded for the tent to be zipped closed. It seemed ludicrous—what protection did that offer from any potential threat, be it thieves or wildlife? Oh well, what did it matter anyway?

Flapping the Ordnance Survey map open, she confirmed the route she'd already planned. The best way was to exit the site directly onto Tenby's magnificent South Beach and walk along past the jutting-out rocks around the bay.

Her heart raced at the thrill of it. Just her and the kids and lovely Dillon. What could be better? Not being estranged from the husband she loved and being forced to travel home to a housing association terraced house in a few days was the obvious answer, but she could put it aside for now. She'd learned, there was a lot more to life than 'things.' In fact, she nodded to herself, fairly convinced she wasn't just lying to feel better about her lot; when you're made to appreciate the little things, it turns out they're the bigger things after all.

Laughing and wondering where on earth they got their energy, she watched in awe, while she struggled on with the rucksack full of food, at her four charges, Thomas, Edward, Mathilda, and of course Dillon racing up and down the dunes, giggling and shouting, covering ten times the distance she did in her straight line.

The beach appeared already quiet, but it was at this point, she recognised from the map, they would join a privately owned beach which threatened to be full of tourists—and she thought she recalled dog restrictions too. She didn't want to be shouted at by another Simon at the head of his own family (pre-gambling debts, of course.)

That was why she'd decided upon that little church. The guidebooks promised lots of history. There was even talk of a Holy Well. That would be nice.

"Just up this track is the village called Goreston. There's bound to be a small shop where we can get an ice-cream or something" (hopefully cheaper than at the campsite or they'd all be sharing a 99), "And there's a lovely little church your sister's keen to see," she announced mainly to the boys in case there was any objection to what could be argued was a bit boring.

They grinned back at her. It struck her that they'd be happy doing anything. Just being out in this unspoiled countryside was enough. Running up the path to the small hamlet in the distance, the twins were determined to be the first to any shop that might be there, and Dillon raced beside them content to join in.

Mathilda held back and took her mother's hand. "I'm having a lovely time... But I do miss Daddy."

Susanna swallowed the lump in her throat. It wasn't enough. Of course it wasn't. Squeezing her daughter's hand, her eyes squinted in acknowledgement. It was all she could do.

"But I am having the best time," Mathilda tried to recover the situation. Regretting her comment, her hand fell limply from her mother's and they walked on in silence, before she added, "And I'm really looking forward to getting some great rubbings at the church. I've got my crayons," she thrust her hand into her pocket and retrieved a handful of thick wax crayons perfect for the job.

"Do you have paper?" Susanna inquired and laughed at the screwed-up offering Mathilda presented her with. "Don't worry. I brought more."

Mathilda threw her arms round her waist. "Thanks, Mum. You're the best."

She might be going too far, but Susanna appreciated the effort.

CHAPTER THIRTY-SIX

'Beep' another name that wasn't his displayed on the ticker display. Pulling back his sleeve, he checked his wristwatch. Nearly an hour he'd waited here. He'd been told to expect a wait as it was a same day appointment and they operated a triage system. Bertie supposed his condition was important rather than urgent.

What would he say? And what could they even do anyway? There wasn't going to be a magic pill that could make it all go away, was there. And he didn't have time to wait for whatever therapy they might insist he needed.

No, he had to find out why he was having these awful waking nightmares and persuade Annabel to allow him back into their lives.

A pang of nausea swept through him. He knew she was right. He had thought, even if it was for a split second, that he could have hurt his precious Charlotte. Twice now he'd witnessed himself act in ways he didn't recognise as being him. He couldn't be sure he wouldn't actually do it, and to assume otherwise was to risk his worst nightmare coming true.

God was testing him, he had no doubt. So, wasn't doubting that God would keep his family safe tantamount to blasphemy? Would God mind him removing himself from the lesson he was so keen for him to learn? The nausea grew in intensity and Bertie looked around for the toilet in case he needed to rush his head suddenly to the bowl.

It was the first time in his life he'd ever had a doubt. He'd always trusted God's plans for him without question. It hadn't always been through easy times, but certainty in whatever chosen course of action he'd intuited through his close relationship with The Almighty, he had felt safe.

Maybe that was the lesson.

Not everyone felt safe. He understood that, or at least, he thought he did. With the wisdom that would come from this lesson would come a greater empathy for those suffering without faith in the community. He knew God's will could only lead to that which was beneficial to all. Sighing, he let go and decided to trust again.

Like a sign, the machine beeped into life, 'Would Rev Bertie Brimble please go to consulting room 5.'

Glancing around, he soon saw signs directing him to the doctor's office. Strolling with new calm along a narrow corridor, he arrived at door number five and rapped on the wood.

"Come in," greeted a muffled voice.

When Bertie pushed open the door, the smile of a competent medic shone from a robustly healthy looking face. "Ah, Reverend. I'm Doctor Allen. Please do take a seat. What can I do for you today?"

Bertie flushed and shuffled to a chair facing the doctor. Hands restless in his lap, he moved his foot onto his knee, then returned it to the floor and hooked his ankle up to the opposite knee instead. It was so uncomfortable. Face reddening more, he planted both feet on the floor, shoved his fidgety fingers under his thighs and leaned forward. Opening his mouth to speak, he found his throat dry offering only silence.

"What's troubling you?" Eyebrows knitted in concerned bows, he smiled and Bertie knew he could confide in him.

"I've been having visions. Waking nightmares, I suppose."

The doctor nodded.

"More than nightmares really. When I've been having them, I've believed I'm awake and actually doing the things I'm seeing."

"Mmm hmm. And what things are they?"

Bertie hadn't noticed the rocking until he halted at the perfectly understandable question. Staring straight ahead, he squeezed the words through the dryness. "I'm selfish. Quick to anger. Animalistic and obsessed with, you know… sex. I even, just for a moment, well not really, but I almost abused my daughter." He hid is face in his hands. "I wouldn't have. I never…" A sob whiffled through the air from trembling lips. "Oh, God." His face fell back into his hands. Composing himself, he pulled away from his palms and sat straight. "And then another time, I saw myself hurting an innocent baby I was meant to be baptising because it wouldn't stop crying. A little baby. I love little babies. But I took her. I held her under the water; her tiny head bang, bang, bang," he motioned with his hands and arms. "I thrust her so hard I broke her skull. Oh God! I can still see it." His hand flew to his mouth. "Crimson. The water in the font was full of the baby's blood. Alice. That was her name.

"I hadn't done anything. I came out of my vision. She was fine, still crying, but fine. But I couldn't carry on. I had to cancel the Christening. I don't even know for sure if it really happened. None of it. Because after that, that's when Charlotte came. My daughter.

"I've never felt anything but love for anyone. Now… I don't know. After the baby, I dreamt, or

236

imagined or, whatever, I was angry, I knocked her. She fell." Bertie sobbed and looked straight at Doctor Allen. "I saw me killing her. Killing my own daughter! There was so much blood... so much. And then I woke up in bed, as if nothing had happened. And nothing *had* happened, but I didn't know... And now my wife thinks I'm a psychopathic pervert and has asked me to leave... Which I totally agree with. I mean, I don't know if I'm safe..."

Doctor Allen sat up in his chair. Bertie had got his attention. "I can understand why that would upset you. Nightmares occur for all sorts of reasons. Have you been under any undue stress of late?"

Bertie's lips crinkled and he shrugged loosely. "I suppose. We have moved into the area recently... to take over at St Julian's Church in Goreston. Do you know it?"

"It does sound familiar. Isn't that where the...?"

"Where the little girls were murdered? Yes. Yes it is." Bertie sighed and relaxed his posture. Just hearing it back, it sounded perfectly understandable, didn't it? The tragic murders of two girls of a similar age to Charlotte; abused and killed. And him coming here because his predecessor couldn't cope. It was natural to have bad dreams and even hallucinations, wasn't it?

"What about these nightmares or visions has worried you enough to come and see me today? Are you concerned you might act them out?"

The comfort he'd grasped onto slipped and smashed on the ground in front of him. He couldn't speak so sufficed with rapid nodding.

Dr Allen looked thoughtful typing briskly at his PC keyboard. His brief glance away relieved the piercing pressure of his gaze and rebooted Bertie's vocabulary.

"When I wake up. I think I *have* done it. I have to check to be sure... make sure she's okay. But even when I'm racing to her, I'm not convinced I won't find the... The scene of my nightmare." Face contorted into a grimace, his eyes finally rested on the glassy shock of the doctor.

"I think we need to get you to see someone. Really soon. Would you mind waiting here while I go and make a phone call?"

Bertie baulked. "What? Phone who?"

Dr Allen smiled. "I just want some advice from a colleague. Is that okay?"

Bertie smiled back. "Of course," he gestured his palms up in understanding. But as the door swung closed from the doctor's exit, he didn't understand at all.

He'd expected to be told this was all normal, maybe be given deep breathing exercises to do, or something. It seemed like that's how it was going for a moment there. But now his doctor looked shocked and set on sending him to the funny farm. Wincing at his crude description he conceded it was an attempt to distance himself.

But what if his concerns were justified? What if this wasn't normal? What if he woke up in the middle of one of his visions and it was true? He shuddered. How had this happened?

The door swung open again and a severe looking Doctor Allen strode in and retook his seat at his desk. "I'm worried about you, Bertie. You seem upset you might act out these nightmares... That you might actually kill somebody. Is that right?"

Was it? Did he really believe himself capable of hurting someone? Not him. Not the real Bertie Brimble. But it wasn't him in his hallucinations. He'd been someone else. And that person was a hideous monster capable of the most horrific violence. If he'd felt detached; if he'd watched someone else do it, maybe he could rebuff the doctor's concern. But, even recalling the feelings now, he remembered how he hadn't cared. He'd been totally self-centred. What he wanted was all that mattered. And what he'd wanted was so basic. So animal.

With a reluctant nod, he had to concede: he couldn't be certain he wouldn't become the person he saw in his nightmares. A minute in that mind-set, and goodness knows what he might do.

"Okay," the doctor sighed, resolved to his plan. "I've asked a colleague of mine, Doctor Simons, to have a chat with you. He's used to the type of phenomenon you're experiencing and is much better placed to advise you what to do about it." He paused. Placing flat palms on his thighs, he sat square on to Bertie. "Now, I want you to go straight there. Can I trust you to do that? Doctor Simons will tell me if you don't arrive."

Bertie frowned. "If that's what you think I need to do, of course I'll go straight there. Is this serious, doctor?"

Doctor Allen smiled. "I'm not the one to say. But it's serious enough for you have come in to see me, and you strike me as a man not prone to panic. And my colleague agrees. Even for your own peace of mind, you can't be having visions of hurting other people and not do something about it. That wouldn't be responsible. That's not to say it won't turn out to be nothing to worry about. Just, Doctor Simons is much more of an expert than I am." He cranked up his smile. "So I can let him know you're on your way, can I?"

"Well, you'll need to tell me where it is, but, yes; I'll go now."

CHAPTER THIRTY-SEVEN

Ice-creams dripping down fingers were keenly cleared up by Dillon to the sound of raucous giggles.

"You shouldn't let him lick you like that. Especially when there's nowhere to wash your hands," Susanna laughed along with them. "He's full of germs."

"Dogs mouths are cleaner than human mouths," Thomas and Edward chimed in unison.

Their frequent duet choruses still disconcerted her even after eight years of being their mother. "Where did you hear that?"

They shrugged and continued encouraging the licking tongue around every crevice of their fingers.

Shaking her head, a smile arcing the corners of her mouth, Susanna pointed to the steeple in the distance. "I promised your sister we'd go there."

"Yeah. You said. Boring!" the twins laughed

from their own world.

"There's a Holy Well there, apparently."

A groan turned to more giggling as Edward suggested, "We could wash our hands in it! You can't get cleaner than Holy water." He fluttered his eyelids in mock-angelicism.

"A bit disrespectful, don't you think?" But her question went ignored.

The lane offered wonderful views across the blue to Caldey Island. There were boat trips advertised on the harbour which landed on the magnificent beaches and allowed for a tour of the monastery and gift shops selling craft items and perfumes hand-made by the monks. It really was magical and Simon had loved taking them there in the past. She'd love to go there during this stay, but she hadn't realised how expensive it was—beyond the means of this single mum at any rate.

A sign hung from a post at the start of a mostly hidden lane. 'Church of Saint Julian' it directed.

"Oohh. A Secret church. You didn't tell us it was a secret church."

Pleased they had injected themselves with some enthusiasm, Susanna suggested they stop here for their lunch. As they exited a copse of trees that hid the lane, the old stone church filled their view. Mathilda was bound to love it, Susanna nodded to herself. Finding a nice spot under a tree, she laid out a little gingham blanket and proceeded to place the meagre lunch of campsite sandwiches upon it while the children explored.

Out of sight, beyond the corner of the church, she detected a commotion and shouts from her two boys, and then Mathilda's shrill tones joined in. Shoving herself up, she raced to them. Rounding the corner, she could see them laughing hysterically.

"If washing your hands is disrespectful" (Oh, they had heard), "what about this?"

Susanna took in the scene. Where was Dillon? She heard him before she saw him. Splash splash splash. His two front paws clawed at the sides of a square pool, and all she could see was his head above the water. His face straining, he was a comical sight.

"He was really thirsty," chimed Mathilda. "And then he sort of fell in!"

The laughter grew louder.

"And then he swam around. He likes Holy water. Do you think it'll make him a Holy dog?"

"It might," Susanna grinned.

"Oh, don't. My friend is a dyslexic atheist, and he doesn't believe in dogs!"

Susanna frowned, then got the joke and chuckled. "You two! You think you're soo funny, don't you?"

Edward and Thomas took bows. "We might as well wash our hands now. I mean, Dillon has kind of set the standard, hasn't he!"

Sticky fingers were plunged into the depths of the water which looked pink. I hope that's not a result of strawberry ice-cream, she thought, glancing around to see if anyone had witnessed her family's embarrassing performance. She thought she saw a face at a window near the back of the church. Straining her eyes to make it out, she pressed her lips in a downward arch. There was no-one there.

Dillon waited until he was right upon her to shake off the excess water, then bounded around the church to... Oh no! The sandwiches. Racing to beat him to them and stop him wolfing the whole lot, Susanna screamed after him. "Dillon! Dillon! Come here."

But, out of character, Dillon did not obey.

Sliding down the cupboard, Annabel allowed her bum to thud the floor. Clutching her knees as far as her size would allow, she buried her face in her thighs. Tears streamed and her body shook.

She knew moving here was a bad idea. Yes it was beautiful, there was no denying that, but she'd live in a concrete box with the only view a steaming pile of dung if it meant keeping her daughter and this little guy safe. She patted her bump, the occupant kicking hard against the attention.

It was too much. How could she care for them against an unknown foe? *Know thy enemy: Ephesians 6:11-12.* Not in the grander sense of seeing one's purpose on the larger scale of God's plans. In fact, quite the opposite. To feel safe, Annabel had to get to the heart of her fear and confront it. Who was this killer she despised?

Richard King? She thought so. But what of the man the police had targeted over him. The one they'd actually arrested. She knew nothing of him. And she'd learned a long time ago never to assume. If she was to get to know her enemy, she needed to understand every facet. It was useless guarding against Richard, and then finding the police had been right all along.

Besides. She'd been thinking about that. Maybe he hadn't killed his sister. Maybe Charlotte reminded him of her. Annabel could see the resemblance. Maybe he waited outside school to see Charlotte to be reminded of Chloe. That's why the police knew who he was. And why he hadn't been a suspect.

Everybody knew about Terry Paige. His name had been splashed on televisions and newspapers nationwide. Whilst Goreston and Tenby had been saved the spotlight, Terry had not. But he was more than a name in the newspapers.

Had they even got it right? They'd questioned him, everyone knew that. And he'd disappeared. Everyone knew that too.

Was he lurking in the bushes, fighting the urge to kill again until it became untenable and he gave up his location with another little girl lost to his desires? Was he hundreds or thousands of miles away? And, was he even guilty?

What if it was someone else? What if it was Richard? She'd changed her mind a thousand times before she decided to take action.

She would go to where the suspect's wife lived —where they both had until he'd disappeared a few weeks ago. Saliva filled her cheeks in disgust at the thought of being in her company; of sharing the same air with someone so vile they could live with a monster and not even know about it. But maybe there was nothing to know.

Hauling her hugeness from the kitchen floor, Annabel had no choice but to try to get to the bottom of it.

A scour of the local paper had reminded her with countless references to the estranged wife of the main suspect. 17 Caldey View, Goreston. And now Annabel stood in the drive deliberating her approach marvelling at the surroundings. How such a beauty spot could be home to someone so grotesque creased her forehead.

She was sure he wouldn't be here. How could he get away with hiding from the police in his own house? But the fear knotted in her stomach anyway fighting for space with her flourishing foetus. Taking a step towards the front door seemed an unattainable task. She had so many questions, but of the woman behind the door, she knew nothing.

Surely it was impossible to live with a paedo murderer and not know it? There had to be something odd about her husband. Some clue to his debauchedness. Annabel couldn't believe otherwise.

Which led her to consider the door she faced would open to reveal not just a wife but an accomplice.

"Can I help you?"

Annabel turned to greet the voice calling to her. Peering over the wood of the side gate, dark eyes contained within darker circles stared out with lifeless hatred.

Her unfriendly appearance brought first a flutter of fear, then a fresh determination to get answers. She was a mother-bear and no-one was going to hurt her cubs. "Good afternoon," she stumbled on the words, stood up straight and forced a clear tone of voice. "My name is Annabel Brimble. I'm the vicar's wife. I'd like to talk with you, if I may?"

The eyes disappeared. That went well, Annabel sighed, turning her body to walk away but unwilling to make the move into defeat. A bolt shot back and the garden gate swung open. There was no-one there but Annabel took it as an invitation. Striding towards the gateway, she hesitated before stepping into the passage beside the house to call out, "Hello? Is it okay if I come in?"

With no objection voiced, Annabel walked down the passage to an open side door which led into the kitchen. Stepping inside with more calls of, "Hello," she paused when she saw the owner of the heavily bagged eyes sitting at a table, a five-thousand piece jigsaw laid out in front of her. She wore a dirty dressing gown, beneath which tatty fluffy mule slippers encased filthy feet in two bands of matted pink fluff. Torn toenails were adorned with chipped red nail polish.

"Hello," she said again, certain this time she'd been heard.

A nicotine stained hand wafted towards another chair. Annabel moved a stack of further puzzles to the floor and sat. "I want to talk to you about your husband."

"Well I didn't think you'd come to join jigsaw club, did I?" Noticing Annabel's flitting gaze, she added, "He isn't here. He's long gone." The puzzle piece in her hand trembled in her grip. Dropping it, she shoved the picture aside destroying one leg of the Eiffel Tower. "I feel such a fool."

Head bowed, she stared at the spoilt picture. Annabel watched, not knowing what to make of the odd woman, she gripped the bottom of the chair when a sudden shriek echoed from the walls.

The woman's arms flailed sending little bits of Paris scattering over the table and tumbling to the floor. Sweeping from side to side like savage windscreen wipers, when every piece had fled for the safety of the floor, she screamed and banged the table. "Arrrrrrrrrgh! Why was I so stupid! So, so stupid!" It wasn't a question anyone could answer, but Annabel was now convinced she was either a brilliant actress or she hadn't known.

"Were there no clues?" she asked cruelly. How *could* she have been so stupid?

The woman looked away from the mess she'd made and shuffled backwards in her seat. "Oh, there were plenty. In hindsight, hundreds. At the time? I saw none. I mean, I knew he was a violent philandering pig, but a child molestor and killer? Even I didn't think he was that low. I even gave him a bloody alibi, didn't I. Swore blind he'd never left the house that day. That he couldn't have because he'd been throwing up all day and I'd had to look after him." Throwing back her head, she laughed at the ceiling. "We've moved house a dozen times. Every time it was after something like this. Every time there was a little girl murdered… And still, I didn't twig."

The brief calm gave way to squealing, legs kicking and stomping the floor as claw hands ripped at her hair and face before she broke into silent sobs and leaned, broken, towards her unexpected house-guest.

With her greasy head on her shoulder, Annabel reached a reluctant arm around the woman and squeezed her shoulder. Lips curled, she fought the fury that rose from inside. A dozen times? Twelve or more beautiful little lives wasted at the hands of her husband and she didn't see a clue? Being such a monumental fool made her partly responsible, didn't it? "Where is he now?" she asked at last.

Sitting back up straight, she stared at Annabel with dark, wide eyes. "I don't know. I honestly don't. If I did, I would have told the police and he'd be at the mercy of a judge like he deserves.

"I think he knew I wouldn't go with him this time and he'd get caught. Part of me felt something for that; not pride… Maybe relief that there was a glimmer of hope for his soul if he *wanted* to get caught. But then he disappeared, so that went out the window, didn't it?

"He didn't tell me he was going. Just never came home. I'm pleased, I suppose. I wouldn't want to see him."

Annabel nodded. There was no pause for her to add anything. Sharron Paige needed to get this off her chest. Fanned fingers guarded parted lips, her head moved in disbelieving tilts from side to side. Her lips trembled as questions she asked herself had no answer. She settled on, "Why?"

Why what? Why she wouldn't want to see him? Why he left without saying? Why he did what he did? And why didn't she know what he was doing? All those why's and more remained unanswered in the ether.

"I should have known. Stories, always similar, would break in the paper and we'd be off." She sighed. "It was never, 'Oh look, this has happened, we can't live here anymore.' It just sort of happened. New job offer. Cleaner air. Better view. Brilliant house in Pembrokeshire. Always something. I've wondered, now it's all come to light, if he didn't arrange the move, then attack the little girls knowing we would be long gone.

"Then, of course, away from the area, the news would be different and, well, out of sight, out of mind, as they say.

"It would be years in-between house moves. Decades sometimes. But then this time. Two murders so close together and the National interest. I think that's what made the difference. It surprised me there were two."

"Why?" Annabel interjected before Sharron

carried on full-flow.

"Well, Terry had been released from custody. What was he trying to say? You can't stop me? That must be it. That must be why he killed again and then disappeared."

"You're certain it was him? Both murders, I mean?"

Sharron frowned. "Both girls? Of course. A copycat in the same village is absurd. He killed them both. And another ten besides... Maybe eleven."

Annabel looked away, the disgust for the foolish woman on full display.

"I've been Googling," she defended. "Looking up news and obituaries for all the times we've moved home. I can't even remember everything, but it's ten at least. Ten more lives that bastard took to fulfil his sick wants. And the lives of their families destroyed. You can't get over something like this," she advised as though it weren't the most obvious thing. "How anyone could do that to another living thing, let alone a beautiful child, is beyond me. Well, obviously. I've got my theories though."

Sharron went silent. A knot in the pine table held her attention as her middle finger traced its outline.

"What theory?" Annabel couldn't believe she was forced to ask.

With a giant sigh, Sharron turned in her seat and looked Annabel full in the face. "He had a terrible childhood. His own sister disappeared. About the same age as these little girls. I've thought about it a lot. It's like he's trying to preserve them at that age... like his sister."

It sounded so pleasant, *'preserve them'*. Annabel shuddered.

"His mum died in childbirth and his dad absconded soon after..."

"Who brought him up then?" The *him* stuck in her throat.

Sharron shrugged. "He never liked to talk about it. There were none of his family at our wedding. But then there weren't many of anyone. Not everyone can afford flights to The Bahamas, can they?"

She looked set to give a wistful recount of their happy day, but then her face clouded again. "I should have seen it coming. I almost don't blame him. But I do blame myself. I blame myself for not noticing the clues... for not saving those poor angels..." she broke again in wracking sobs.

Annabel couldn't bring herself to comfort her this time. With no further information seemingly forthcoming, she slid back her chair and walked silently from the house.

CHAPTER THIRTY-EIGHT

The soft homely décor was out of place. Homely from a by-gone era of tasteless eighties chintz. Even the silent television was a huge box. Bertie stared at it. Why was a muted screen so compelling?

The room next door was visible through Georgian wired glass. Chairs were set out in a circle as though awaiting the regulars at Alcoholics Anonymous. In reality, Bertie supposed, they were there for group counselling. He shuddered. The piano in the corner gave it the touch of school assemblies where the designated teacher might murder well-known songs and hymns.

Flickering from the television took his attention again. The local news mouthed silently by a girl with bad hair. He'd missed the headlines and reading the subtitles under the girl's face proved dull. He wasn't interested in what a disgraced councillor had been up to.

Instead, his gaze fell to a poster about the

dangers of alcopops which looked like it might have filled its space on the wall since 1986. It sat next to another which noted with regret how the Bro Cerwyn Centre for Psychiatric care was unable to provide tea and coffee facilities for safety reasons. Bertie pictured crazed lunatics running round scolding themselves with boiling hot water whilst laughing maniacally.

The subtitles flickered for attention promising the weather would follow the sport, both of which Bertie had little interest in; concerns with Britain's climate reserved for those with more settled minds.

The door creaked open and a man walked in clutching his hand. It seemed the wrong waiting room for him—but there was no way anyone might mistake this building for an A and E department. Despite several free seats, he plonked himself next to Bertie with a sigh.

An obviously troubled soul would normally prompt Bertie to offer help and prayer. Today he didn't feel of service. He didn't feel worthy. After the third pointed sigh, he gave in. He had no choice. "Are you okay?" he inquired with a gentle smile.

The man shook his head. "They keep sending me here to these jokers. I'm not crazy. It's well documented, what I've been saying. Professor Schwartz from Arizona published a paper years ago. Of course, loads of people say it's nonsense, but this guy is a professor of many things so he's a smart individual." He nodded along to his own argument. "Even those who believe him say it's major organs only, but *he* says muscles can produce the phenomenon too… And he's written over four-hundred scientific papers…"

Bertie frowned. "I'm sorry. I don't know what we're talking about?"

"This!" The man thrust his right hand in the air. Bertie flinched at the terribly scarred forearm. When the man put his hands next to one-another, they were clearly quite different.

The gasp from Bertie's lips flushed his cheeks red at his insensitivity.

"Watch." The man stood and walked out appearing seconds later in the therapy room next door. Striding with purpose towards the piano, he pulled the stool back and sat.

Lifting the keyboard lid he placed his hands to the keys and proceeded to play a very poor left-handed 'chopsticks' muted but perfectly audible through the glass. Bertie smiled. He didn't understand what he was expected to glean from this display. The man stopped playing, grinned at Bertie, and raised his donated right hand. Placing it to the piano keyboard, he paused before the fingers raced up and down the keys with all the skill and precision of a concert pianist.

With a flourish, he struck the final key closing the lid only when the last note's reverberation faded.

Walking back to the waiting room he flumped next to Bertie. "What do you think of that, Vicar?"

"I… I…" Bertie didn't know.

"Never had a lesson in my life. A month after this," he waved his hand some more, "I could do that. My left hand is learning too. Like it's remembering motor-skills it's never been taught."

Bertie was sceptical. Why would you come to the doctor with a sudden ability to play Rachmaninoff?

"It's not all good news though. Amusing enough at first… A sudden taste for camomile tea; that took a while to realise what I was craving, I can tell you! But that's when the nightmares started. Always the same." He took a deep breath. Bertie was surprised to see his eyes moisten. "I'm dying. Every night. Every single night. The steering wheel in my hand…" Pupils like pinpricks, Bertie could tell it was a struggle to say. "I turn and, I know what's coming but there's nothing I can do. Cyclists… dozens of them. I have to swerve or I'll hit them, but there isn't room. Coming towards us is a bus going way too fast. I try to squeeze into the gap between it and the bridge and then everything goes black. I wake up gasping convinced I'm dead, but there's always something dragging me back to reality. I can't close my eyes. It's intolerable.

"So, of course, I did some research and I'm not the only one. Far from it. One in ten transplant recipients report similar phenomenon. It wouldn't surprise me if the true figure is much higher. If my nightmares weren't so awful, I certainly wouldn't have mentioned them. Not with how ridiculed I've been made to feel. But I've got to get rid of this. I'll have a prosthetic, or a bloody hook! Anything but this." He jerked his arm in a savage movement. His hatred of the limb unmistakable. "And they won't cut it off until I've been evaluated by these clowns." He nodded his head to the corridor where psychiatrists and counsellors where likely doing their thing.

Lines creased Bertie's forehead. "You're having the person whose hand you now have's nightmares?"

"Yes. See, you get it straight away. I knew a vicar would understand! I'm having their memory of dying and it's terrible. Unbearable. Along with all the other stuff. I'm not crazy! Look it up. Professor Schwartz."

Bertie couldn't believe it but he seemed so sincere. He was sure he'd heard of people having limbs amputated because they didn't feel 'right.' Having one hand different to the other would definitely seem odd, but he doubted he was really having the memory of its donor. Bertie held firm with his faith that life went on in Heaven, or the other place, when we pass away... not hanging around in bits of our bodies which are reused by someone else. No. That couldn't be true.

A door swung open and a pleasant bespectacled female face peered out. "Bertie Brimble?" When she saw him, she beamed. "Come this way, Reverend."

Following her along a corridor, she paused to open a solid wooden door about half-way. "Take a seat."

Bertie wondered if anything would be concluded by which of the three seats a patient chose from nearest to farthest the psychiatrist's own chair. He sat on the closest one to show he was ready to take her advice.

"Hello, Bertie... May I call you Bertie?"

"Yes, of course," Bertie smiled.

"Great. Thanks. My name is Doctor Simons."

What? No first name for you? Maybe I should revert to Reverend Brimble, Bertie thought petulantly.

"Your G.P.'s worried about you. Do you know why?"

Bertie nodded. "I've had waking nightmares; more, hallucinations perhaps... I don't know the definitions... about killing my lovely little girl,

Charlotte." In telling, it seemed so distant; so pre-posterous. "He asked me if I worried I might act them out, and honestly? They're so real I can't be sure."

Doctor Simons regarded him with a smile. "I see from your note you live in Goreston. Is that right?"

Bertie nodded.

"Where those terrible murders happened?"

She must know, Bertie thought, but accommo-dated her with another nod.

"When you have these nightmares or hallucin-ations, where do you wake up?"

Bertie frowned in consideration. "In bed. But I'm surprised to be there. I don't remember how I got there."

"You mean, you fall asleep somewhere else and wake up in bed?"

"Well, not the first time, after Richard's tes-timonial... He's one of the victim's... Chloe's brother. He comes to the church where I'm the vicar and he shared his story with us."

"And you had a nightmare about hurting your daughter the same night? Is that right?"

"Yes. It was so real I ran away to church to pray. I'd woken her up and she'd woken my wife up. We talked it through, kind of. I guess I held back, but I thought I knew. I thought it was okay..." No more words could fight through his grief.

"And the next time, you weren't at home... But then you woke up at home?"

Regaining his voice, Bertie rasped, "I wasn't even asleep. I had conducted the most awful Christening where I thought I'd murdered the baby. And then later, Charlotte came to see me and I killed her... By accident this time; kind of."

"Is it possible you were asleep? That you dreamt the Christening but have muddled it up in your head?" Not awaiting a response, Doctor Simons continued. "Moving house is very stressful. A lot of people suffer nightmares and hallucinations after a move."

Bertie shook his head. "It was easy. The church provides the house and we only had a tiny flat in Hartcliffe to move from. It all went well."

"But you've come here, presumably because of the terrible murders? And then you met the victim's brother? It all makes perfect sense. Honestly. All perfectly normal."

Bertie's shoulders sagged and he exhaled through circled lips. He stuffed his relief for fear of crying, but Doctor Simons knew. Leaving a pause, she let the emotion catch up with Bertie and watched detached as he sobbed his deliverance away.

"Normal?" he queried through tear-drenched eyes that just managed to discern the doctor's emphatic nodding.

"Under the circumstances, I'd be surprised if you didn't experience something like this. You did the right thing coming to us though. It can be a worry if you're not used to what to expect."

Rising from his chair, Bertie thrust grateful hands at his saviour.

"Before you go, I have to ask so don't be alarmed, I'd ask anyone the same. It's my duty: Do you have any notion to hurt anybody or yourself?"

Bertie considered the question. No. Of course he didn't.

He left the room smiling. With a clean bill of health he could go back home. '*We'll see what the doctor says*' Annabel had ordered. Well the doctor had said he had nothing to worry about. He'd be surprised if he had another hallucination after that, he thought with a grin.

But as he prepared to exit through the waiting room, the grin slipped and crashed at what he saw...

CHAPTER THIRTY-NINE

H e'd killed again, according to his wife, just to spite the police. 'You can't stop me' his motivation, and she should know, Annabel considered. *Should* know. But she'd missed all the clues for decades. Could she really be treated as an expert now?

If he had murdered another little girl just to show he could, what's to stop him coming back and doing it again? Wouldn't that show his power even more?

But what if he hadn't? What if there had been a copycat? Wasn't that common? What if he hadn't done it? What if Sharron was getting it wrong now he'd left her?

Whatever the truth, it didn't make it safe; from him, or Richard King, or whomever else and Annabel was left with a hunger to find out more —to find out all she could about her enemy, to keep her loved ones safe.

Wobbling back to her kitchen table, she threw

open her laptop, digits drumming while the intermittent Wi-Fi found its signal. With a deep breath, her fingers hovered. What should she type?

She couldn't just research child murders. That would be horrific and she'd have no reference as to whether Terry Paige was involved or not. The local papers where he lived might have the stories, but she had no idea where to start.

Typing his name brought the usual Facebook and social media results, and not surprisingly, his profile was scant with only a handful of pictures and almost as few friends. She sent out message requests to the ones who were there. Maybe they'd message back and she'd have some locations to work with.

Tapping an index finger to pressed lips she had an idea. He'd never been caught. That meant that unless someone else had been wrongfully convicted, the murders would be classified as unsolved. With a list of unsolved murders she'd stand a chance of correlating the evidence to Terry.

Not relishing the thought of countless names flashing onto the screen, with tentative prods of the keys she entered '*unsolved murders, UK*' into Google's search bar. What would she find? Was a list confidential and open only to the relevant authorities? Perhaps a blog of well-known cases that was anything but comprehensive? Bang. She hit return, stunned with the ease every unsolved crime in British history popped up courtesy of Wikipedia.

Beginning in the eighteen-hundreds, she scrolled through to the nineteen-eighties and nineties. There were hundreds of unsolved murders, but infanticide was thankfully lower in number. It still made sickening reading.

A fourteen-year-old dragged into the woods in Norfolk in 1997... Another in Norfolk in the same year, this time an eleven-year-old. Bodies found but cases closed until further evidence was uncovered.

Annabel's cheeks grew and she rushed to the bathroom as morning-sickness combined with disgust.

Returning to the keyboard dabbing her acid lips, she stared at the screen. They were older than the recent victims, but maybe he was an opportunist. Maybe the similarity of the recent victims in age and appearance was more of a coincidence than she'd assumed.

Bringing up reports from Norfolk newspapers in another tab didn't name Terry as a suspect, but if Sharron could be trusted, they had probably already moved from the area when the bodies were discovered. Had he always planned to leave Goreston without his wife, or was it as she suggested… he was repenting and wanted to get caught then changed his mind?

There were no other murders that fit for a few years, but early 2000 provided very familiar reading in Liverpool. Just the one poor girl, nine this time, abused and dumped in a similar way. The distance between the crimes must have failed to alert the police to their similarities, but with Annabel's insider knowledge it was fuel to the fire.

Again in 2004 and 2006 then 2010. That was it until now.

Newspaper reports did nothing but fill in some of the gaps, including angelic smiling faces of the victims. Annabel winced and knew they would forever haunt her.

It was as she'd been told—spasmodic and spaced out by years, even decades. That might mean he wouldn't return and the girls of Goreston were no longer at risk. But they'd never arrested him before. Now, his name was all over the papers; it was how she'd known his address. That made this time different, which meant how he would react was unpredictable.

The thought of him smugly safe a hundred miles away plotting his next attack wasn't something Annabel could let go. She'd go to the police. Sharron might have already told them what she told her, but she had to be sure. And she would demand to know what they were doing about it!

Before closing the laptop, she found herself scrolling back to the seventies. Sharron wasn't much older than her, so presumably Terry would have been a child of not more than ten or eleven then, but something drew her to look. And when she did, she couldn't look away.

Scanning the lines of text, a shiver rattled her spine as she became more and more certain. It was him. Two crimes shared a similarity that shook Annabel in her chair. She gulped and forced herself to read on.

Ten-year-old Lisa Paige, found sexually abused and dumped in the Castle Grounds on Hartom Common, Hertford in 1979. With no witnesses, police reluctantly closed the case. *Lisa Paige... Terry Paige...* Sharron had said his sister had disappeared. Could that be what led him to the revolting life he chose? It wasn't an excuse, nothing could excuse it. But maybe it could help her understand. Typing Lisa Paige into the search bar changed her mind. One little press of a keyboard and everything made sense.

An old school photo smiled out at her, it even featured her brother smiling behind. It was the face of evil. How could she think that of a child who must have been what? Eleven? Twelve?

It wasn't that entry that convinced what must have happened all those years ago. It was an entry on the same page. Another murder. Not infanticide this time. This time it was someone much older and Annabel had to rush to the toilet again before reading. No wonder the police were sure it was him.

Sitting back at the table, dabbing her delicate lips, Annabel stared at the screen and read on. This murder, two years later, was also Paige. Eleanor Paige. Found electrocuted in the bath by an electric heater in the water. After finding no possible suspects other than her thirteen-year-old son, Terry, whom police were reluctant to entertain as a suspect on account of his age and lack of motive, they eventually ruled the case as suicide. Critics questioned this logic as the calculated trajectory of the bar heater hitting the water didn't fit with her having done so herself so the case remains unsolved.

The boy, Terry, was taken into care when his father had a mental breakdown having lost his daughter and his wife, and was ruled unfit to care for a child...

Oh my god! Annabel gasped. He didn't lose his sister, and his mum didn't die in childbirth... He killed them both! Struggling for breath, Annabel was sure of it.

CHAPTER FORTY

The half-hourly news channel had come full circle and was showing the tale-end of the weather forecast he missed before when piano-prodigy had taken his attention. But it wasn't the weather that stopped him dead. It was as innocuous and average as ever, predicting sunshine with the chance of rain—like any other early autumn day.

It was what they showed after the weather that gripped Bertie in a fist of fear: a recap of today's headlines; the leading one for Wales being the bodies washed up on a beach in South Pembrokeshire… Bodies Bertie recognised.

Identified as Gareth and Claire Proctor from Cambridgeshire along with remains of a third body that were 'difficult to distinguish.'

Legs swaying, Bertie winced and grabbed onto the nearest chair for support. What had he done after he met them at the well? Supposedly conducted the Christening from Hell and murdered his daughter, both things which he had just agreed with an expert in mental health hadn't even happened and never would.

But here, two more people he'd come into contact with *were* dead. Had his guilty mind concocted the Christening fiasco to cover for what he'd really done?

One thing was sure. Recognising the couple meant he must have gone to the church. He must have been there or how else could he have met them at the well? Somehow he'd made it to bed with no knowledge of how he'd got there and a lot of time to account for.

Colour drained and his head spun.

"Are you okay?"

It was piano-man again.

Bertie shook his head. "I feel sick," he warbled. "That's all."

He had to get out of here. If the doctor came out and asked him what was wrong, he'd crumble. Goodness knows where he'd end up. He had to go, but he couldn't return home as he'd so delighted in moments before. He wasn't safe. He couldn't be trusted. Until he clawed his way back to reality, how could he be?

Battling through his mind-fog to remove himself from the chair and the building, when he made it outside, he slumped against the wall.

The only place he could go was the church.

He'd have to stay in his office away from everybody until he'd worked out what was going on.

Fairly sprinting, when he arrived at the bus stop, panting, he was dismayed but not surprised there was a queue of people. With a concerted effort, he ignored them for fear of what a conversation with him might lead to. Barely speaking to the driver, he threw what he hoped was the correct money into the receptacle and sat down at the first empty row of seats.

Eyes fixed on the window, scenery flew by indiscernibly until they passed through Tenby and he knew his stop came next. As soon as the bus waited at the Goreston stop, Bertie rushed out and shot head down for the church.

About to retreat to the confines of his little office, he became overcome by a feeling of grubbiness. He wanted to wash himself; clean away the confused Bertie to perhaps reveal the friend-to-everyone pillar of the community he'd always felt he was. At home he could have showered, but here there was but one option.

Shaking his head, he couldn't. It would be freezing, but the desire to go to the well and bathe would not abate.

Throwing closed the door to his office and bolting it he hoped would quell the ridiculous notion, but far from it, the compulsion intensified to insufferable extents.

Yanking back the bolt, he stormed from the room, disappointed at this new compulsive, impulsive side to his personality that defied all logic. He only hoped now that after bathing in the well, he would at least remember it and not wake back in bed mystified.

Stood at the edge of the pool, he couldn't imagine why he hadn't immersed himself in its depths every day. Had he not felt fantastic when he'd drunk a little?

Scooping handfuls of the odd tasting water to his lips, he glugged away before falling forward and sinking fully beneath the surface.

CHAPTER FORTY-ONE

Richard left home yet again with the purpose of a face to face with Bertie Brimble. Was he avoiding him? Probably.

Marching down the hill, he knew the church would soon be in sight. Should he rehearse what to say? No. He'd done that the previous times and had been frustrated in his attempt. The truth was, he didn't know what he wanted to say. He just needed to be there.

That first time he'd seen her, just a glimpse, when he'd gone to speak with his vicar. Her sunny little face skipping into the room. Just like Chloe. For a second he could almost believe she was still here.

Since then, she'd not left his mind. She was so like Chloe. It was like it was all happening again. That's why he had to be prepared.

Holding his hands out in front of him, he examined them with wide eyes. Thrusting them into pockets as though holstering a pair of lethal pistols, he jutted out his jaw and soldiered on.

Grabbing Charlotte's hand, she marched down the hill from the school.

"Where are we going?"

"I have to go and tell the police something, sweetheart. It shouldn't take long." She wasn't clear what she wanted to say apart from demanding answers. Why did they let Terry Paige out of their sight when his own wife is convinced he's guilty? Surely her alibi couldn't count for much? And why were they so sure Richard King was innocent?

Charlotte scowled. "Can't I wait at home? I'm tired. I've had a busy day today; we had a maths test and a science test."

"Sorry, angel. I can't leave you at home on your own," she said and immediately regretted it.

"On my own? Where's Daddy?"

Sighing, Annabel stumbled on her answer, "Daddy's very busy with work at the moment. He might not be home for a little while."

Charlotte stared at the floor. She'd noticed the tension. She'd heard the raised voices and words hissed whenever she came near. It had happened to other children at school, here and in Hartcliffe. The kids were always the last to know.

"Where is he? In case I need to ask him something."

"I told you. He's busy with work. What do you want to ask him?"

Charlotte shrugged. "I don't know. Something. Where can I find him?"

"You'll have to ask me. He can't be disturbed at the moment. Very busy. He told me not to let anyone bother him."

She was lying. Anyone could tell that. Why were they going to the police? Was Mummy going to say nasty things about Daddy? Pouting, she asked, "What do you need to say to the police? Has Daddy done something?"

Annabel stuffed a tear and her unconvincing, "No, don't be silly," did not fool Charlotte for a minute.

They walked in silence pausing intermittently for Annabel to grasp her belly to take the strain. The police station wasn't far now. Annabel was sure she could make it.

Baby had other ideas. A huge splash cascaded down Annabel's legs, ran over the pavement then streamed along the curb in an ever receding river giving into the porous ground below.

"Wow, Mummy? Have you wee'd yourself?"

"No, darling," Annabel gasped. That's your brother coming. Call an ambulance.

They were prompt. Annabel barely had enough

time to call Darcie's mum and ask her to have Charlotte.

Jacquie arrived in minutes, even before the ambulance having only left school herself moments before.

"My goodness, look at you! Bertie on his way, is he?" when she didn't get an answer she assumed he too would be at the hospital, a birthing partner to bring their son into the world. It's what they'd planned. But Annabel hadn't even tried to phone him. He never answered his phone anyway, but she didn't want him there. Whether she would after the birth remained to be seen. She understood he was stressed, but until she knew exactly who she could trust, Bertie Brimble would have to keep away.

"Don't worry, Annabel," she said as the ambulance crested the hill into view. "I'll look after this one."

"Thanks," Annabel smiled.

"Come on. What do you want for tea?" Holding Charlotte and Darcie's hands, she led them to the car where they joined Darcie's baby brother, George cooing in his car-seat. Charlotte said nothing.

"Isn't it exciting," Jacquie grinned at Charlotte in the rear-view mirror. "Are you hoping for a little brother or a little sister?" she cooed.

Charlotte shrugged.

The green-eyed monster rearing its ugly head, Jacquie nodded to herself. "I bet you'll be a big help, won't you?" she encouraged.

Charlotte shrugged with even less enthusiasm.

Definitely jealous. She'd seen it with her own two. She'd get her and Darcie playing nicely, and before Charlotte would know it she'd be a big sister and sibling love would take over.

"Who wants to go to McDonald's?" she cried. Lips askew, she was sure the cheering from the back came from Darcie and George and none from Charlotte. This was going to be harder than she thought.

She wasn't jealous. She couldn't wait for her little brother to make an appearance. Her poor mummy had gone through it, being sick every morning and getting bigger and bigger by the minute.

But that was no excuse to shut her daddy out. A tear tracked down her grubby cheek. He'd be mortified if he missed his son being born. And she loved the story of how he'd rushed across Bristol for her birth only just making it.

Blowing out her cheeks, she mumbled, "Mrs Owen… Jacquie… I think I'm going to be sick."

Glancing at her charge in the rear-view mirror, she did look pale. "Hold it in, sweetheart," she smiled, pressing her lips hard to block the eruption of cursing which threatened to follow. This was a new car as well. "Hold on. I'm pulling over now."

The click-click of the indicator preceded the slowing and halting of the Owen family car. Charlotte threw open her door and rushed for the bushes.

Making revolting noises to keep anyone from following, she edged away from the bush into the field behind. Checking she couldn't be seen from the road, she let rip with one more tirade of spewing and retching before bolting for the horizon.

From a safe distance, she ducked behind a tree. Smiling, she congratulated herself on a job well done as neither Darcie, her mum nor her little brother even looked in her direction or where she'd pretended to be sick in the hedge.

She'd find her daddy and tell him the new arrival was on his way. Then they could go to the hospital together.

CHAPTER FORTY-TWO

He'd walked past the school on the way to the vicarage. The police had warned him of the distress he was causing Mrs Brimble, but he wanted to see her. Not to speak to, just to get a glimpse little Charlotte and be reminded of his sister.

When they'd walked in the opposite direction of the vicarage, he'd rightly calculated they might be going to the police. After her accusations yesterday, he was reluctant to let that happen.

But when her waters broke and the ambulance came, he no longer needed to and a further opportunity arose.

He watched as the paramedics left and Charlotte disappeared in that other family's car. But then they stopped.

Too far away, he couldn't see her now, but he'd witnessed her escape through the hedge. He didn't know where she was but he thought he knew where she was headed… to a date with destiny.

Richard had been right all along. It was a good job he'd been watching and waiting. He knew the time would come to kill again.

Jacquie was frantic. She'd lost Charlotte within minutes of her being left in her care. What if something terrible had happened? What if she had perished to the same fate as those other poor little girls?

Terrified for Darcie and George, she ushered them to the safety of the car and locked them inside. Calling and yelling, "Charlotte! Charlotte! Charlotte!" brought no reply, and she was certain… The Goreston murderer had struck again.

Racing to her car, she shot behind the wheel, re-locked the door and phoned the police. As she hit the red 'End Call' button, she prayed it wouldn't be too late to save Charlotte.

Richard waited before following through the gap in the hedge. He saw the other mum freaking out and couldn't risk her detaining him. Time was of the essence.

The track of small footprints was easy to follow in the long grass of the field. She had a head-start but he was confident he'd catch her.

Where did ten-year-olds get their energy? As he raced up the hill he panted with the exertion. Light was fading fast tonight after a heavily clouded day. He couldn't risk losing his quarry but he knew she wouldn't be far and he was sure he knew where she was going.

Pausing at the summit, he leaned against the thick trunk of a tree to get his breath shaking his head. He didn't want this to happen, but he'd known it would. He'd known from the very start.

CHAPTER FORTY-THREE

Floating in his clothes Bertie experienced something akin to bliss, but it wasn't a feeling he was used to. In the past, he'd felt the hand of God take all his troubles away; leaving them at his door and considering them dealt with. This was not that.

He'd drunk from the well before descending into the water because his grubby presence wouldn't make it more appetising and he was determined to have his fill. From where the determination came he didn't like to contemplate.

The water had been cold but he'd waded in without a care. Fully clothed treading deeper until the gully closed over his head.

Giddily he allowed the rose liquid to glug into his throat until it threatened to drown him and he burst spluttering to the surface.

He heard them before he saw them. Children giggling, and then a dog bounding around the corner.

"Dillon. Wait up!" two voices cried in unison.

Hauling his sodden frame from the pool, he scrambled across the churchyard to the back door which led to his little office. Panting, he leaned against the door, water pooling at his feet from his dripping clothes.

Peeping through the lead-light window, he could just make out the figures of three children. Two boys and a girl. A pretty girl.

They were drinking from the well. No. They were washing their hands! In his Holy well. He continued watching as the boys bent down, and then the girl. Squinting, he wondered why they were laughing. Then he saw the splashing. Some-one was in the pool. Bertie gasped. It was their bloody dog! Fists clenched ready to pound into their stupid faces, he'd show them some bloody respect.

He stopped dead. There it was again. He felt like a different person. Grabbing the key from the hook, he thrust it into the lock and turned it clockwise with a firm clunk. Hearing the bolts shoot into place, he yanked the key back out and threw it along the nave. It clinked and clattered on the chequered tiles to land underneath a pew near the vestibule.

With a wail he fled toward his office, the water falling from him in rivers left a slippery stream which his sodden shod feet adhered to like oil on ice. Groin splitting, the pain as his legs went in two different directions brought forth an all-too-familiar rage.

Clinging to a curtain behind the pulpit, he dragged himself from the floor. Teeth grinding, he strode with purpose to the back door and glared unseen through the opaque glass.

The mother was there now. Look at them laughing. Laughing! While he locked himself in his own church for their safety. Why? He owed them nothing. Coming here to wash in his well. Now that was disrespectful.

Grabbing the handle, he twisted it, rattling the knob from side to side but it wouldn't move. Of course, his brain-fug allowed him to recall, he'd locked it. What had he done with the key?

Spinning around, he glared at the inside of his church. "Where is the God-forsaken key!" he boomed. Remembering the clatter as it tumbled down the nave. "Aha!" he squealed.

Sprinting from the door, he made it two steps before the slippery stone felled him again. Collapsing to his knees, his attempts to right himself sent him flying forward and his forehead collided with the buttress of the cross.

With slurred expletives, he crashed to the floor, his skull bouncing from the stone.

"Dillon, don't you dare eat our sandwiches,"

Susanna cried after the disobedient mutt, giggling as she rallied behind him. But giggles changed to screams as she turned the corner to find him biting at everything on the mat in a frenzy.

"Dillon! What do you think you're doing?" She was furious now as she marched to the Golden Retriever, arms out to grab him.

Hackles raised and teeth gnashing, Dillon's drooling fangs snapped viscously at the hands coming his way.

Jerking them back, she watched as her faithful hound devoured everything she'd lovingly prepared that morning. With a snarl of contempt, he cocked his leg on the blanket before running off into the woods.

She collapsed to the ground and wept. She'd never trust a male again.

CHAPTER FORTY-FOUR

The pain was immense. It was difficult to tell where he ended and the floor began. Stretching a cramping arm, he wriggled it from under his torso and brought it to his head. Prodding the worst of the throbbing, he flinched as it worsened but it didn't appear life-threatening. Just a big bruise.

What had he been doing? He couldn't remember.

He was thirsty. Pushing himself up to his knees he noticed the wetness. Why? There was nothing to drink in his office but he had the spring water bubbling through the well. Hauling to his knees, he stepped to the back door. Twisting the knob, he frowned to find it locked. "Strange," he said.

The key wasn't on its hook. How irritating. Marching as fast as his aching limbs would accommodate, he soon reached the vestibule. Heaving the huge oak door he stepped outside.

Hurrying along the outside buttresses, keen to

drink, he stopped dead in his tracks. "Oh, God. Oh god oh god oh god…" he faded into silence.

His instinct to help stalled as he drew closer. Gasping, hands covering his mouth, he stumbled from side to side shrieking "No. What have I done?"

Falling to his knees, the answer was obvious. He'd struck again. He'd come here from the hospital, blacked out and then? He could remember none of it but the death surrounding him was testimony. He clasped his hands in rapid prayer. "Our Father, who art in Heaven…"

Repeating the Lord's Prayer, Bertie fell into a tight ball hugging his knees to his chest. God had tested him and he'd failed. He'd failed in the worst possible way. There could be no way back from this.

"Well there it is," Adrian stated the obvious as Toby rested a foot at the huge capstone on its three pillars of rock. "King's Quoit."

"Yeah. We're here," Toby sighed. Tim's sulky outburst had really put a damper on things despite their assertion it shouldn't. Opening his canteen, he took a mighty glug. "Ahhh."

As the water hit his stomach it quenched a thirst more than his body's need for rehydration. "We'll have to get more of this, I reckon," he pointed the spout at the sky setting the plan in motion.

Adrian nodded. "It's delicious. A bit weird at first, but I'm barely noticing that iron, blood taste. You can feel it melding with your body, can't you? It's beyond isotonic."

"We may as well head back now, Toby agreed. "We can be at the church in a couple of hours and refill our canteens."

"I'm coming back with a bigger container. I want to take this stuff home."

"Yeah!"

"Yeah!" they both cheered.

In comforting knowledge they would soon be replenished, they drained their bottles.

"The energy is amazing. Do you think it's got weird Druid mumbo-jumbo in it?" Toby gazed in wonder at his empty container.

"No. I don't." Adrian shook his head. "It will be a complex mixture of minerals. That's all. There had to be a reason the Victorians flocked there."

"Yeah, but that could have been because of what the Druids did to the water though, couldn't it?"

Adrian's lips curled so much they touched his nose in distaste of the notion. "I doubt the stuff the Druids did had any real effect. No. It'll just be the minerals. Maybe we could send it off some-where when we get back to Cambridge? Have it analysed?"

They strode at such a pace it was almost trotting.

"It really is good stuff," Toby enthused. "I feel amazing."

In the distance, two joggers ran towards them. Both looked incredibly fit; a tanned shirtless man and a girl in tight Lycra. Adrian was the first to react. Stopping in his tracks, he let them run to him. Sharing a knowing smile with the man, he stared at the woman's breasts as they bounced up and down.

"Alright, darlin'" he sleazed. "Give us a squeeze."

Toby was shocked. He'd never heard his friend talk like that. He was always pitifully shy with girls. The grimace on the woman's face made him laugh. "Yeah! Show us your tits!" he squealed in delight.

"Fuck off!" she spat as she jogged by without a pause.

"Fuck you, more like!" Adrian grinned at Toby.

"Yeah, fuck you anytime," Toby chided along.

The man stopped and ran towards them. "You two fat bums need to learn how to treat a lady."

"Leave it, Troy. They're not worth it," the pretty girl called behind her.

"Yeah. Leave it, Troy." Adrian mocked, shoving him.

Receiving a perfectly aimed right-hook in

reply, furled from the very muscular taut chest of the jogger, his eyes crossed and he fell to one knee.

"Bastard!" Toby cried. As the man stood over his friend, he scoured his surroundings for a weapon. Selecting a hand-sized stone from the floor, he held it above his head.

"Troy! Look out!"

Troy side stepped in time to miss the full force of the blow. Catching the side of his head he staggered forward.

"Run Troy. Quick. He's a psycho!"

Troy's legs were well-programmed for running and they responded impeccably to the threat.

Toby swung the stone with less conviction this time, baying the couple with cries of, "You better walk away. That's right. Jog on…"

Adrian sat up laughing. "Jog on. Good one, mate."

Toby laughed too. "Yeah, I know."

The pair strode with a new arrogance. No-one was going to mess with them.

"I tell you what, Toby, mate."

"What?"

"I'd have given her one. She was fit."

The swelling in Toby's trousers as he pictured himself on the tight body of the cute girl made it difficult to walk. His lips turned down as saliva filled his mouth and dribbled from the corners of his lips.

The cliff-top, the sky and the sea blended into one grey soup as Toby waded his way through with one purpose. He wouldn't let an opportunity like that pass him again. He would not be disrespected by some dumb bitch. Ever.

Adrian's mood dropped too. Okay, they'd stuck it to the arrogant moron with the super-fit body, but they hadn't had any female contact. The number of times either of them had ever seen any action wasn't something they talked about, but estimates ranged in the low zeros.

It was no surprise, was it, with the way women treated them. It wasn't fair. Don't wear skin-tight clothes dripping in sweat if you don't want attention, they leered. That was obvious. Adrian had jogging bottoms. He wore them all the time at weekends when he wasn't re-enacting a battle somewhere. He'd never tried, but the name suggested they'd be just the job for running in.

So choosing to jog in sexy clothes had to be deliberate. They might have handled her better; maybe wooing rather than cat-calling, but it wasn't their fault.

Previous inexpertise could be linked to lack of confidence. But this trip, and almost certainly the amazing water from Goreston, had released new confident versions of themselves. Adrian didn't know how, but he was determined to make the most of it before it wore off. This was too good. It was bound to fade at some point. Feeling the panic he quickened his pace. "Come on, Toby. Let's get back to the well."

From the fuddle in his head, Toby hastened also. Like a drunk going with the flow, he hobbled along in a morose trot.

They'd never walked so far in one day. Legs aching, lungs burning, it was with relief they rounded a hill and saw the church spire in the distance. Only about a mile to go.

Stumbling up the path like sumo-suited marathon runners on the final stretch, they each grasped a gatepost and gasped for breath. Too exhausted to remain upright, they leaned, hands on thighs, and wheezed themselves back to health.

"Thirsty…" Toby croaked. Plucking his water bottled form his bag, he unscrewed the lid and tipped it to his dry lips… empty.

Stumbling down the path, he ran towards the well. Collapsing inches from the edge, he flopped his arm into the cool ruby water and cupping his hand, brought a full scoop to his mouth.

He drank greedily looking up when Adrian collapsed beside him and performed the same ritual.

"Dillon…. Dillon, where are you?"

It was a gentle young voice. From the echo on the breeze, it sounded like it came from the edge of the churchyard. "Dillon, Dillon, Dillonnn!"

Glimpsing her through the trees, a new stirring flushed through the chubby comrades. It was a girl. Young, they weren't sure how old, but sexy as hell.

Her nubile legs ran in little streaks as she careered from one side of the graveyard to the other. Who was Dillon? Probably her boyfriend teasing her. Withholding his cock. Clever bastard. That's the sort of control they needed to learn. Leave them gagging for it.

Hauling their still exhausted bodies from the ground, they knew if they called out the girl would run. Misguided loyalty to her lover, no doubt. Well they could show her some real love from real men.

She came closer. "Excuse me. Have you seen my dog?"

Dog? It was obviously a chat-up line. Girls were so forward nowadays. "Yeah. He's over here," Adrian lied.

Toby considered correcting him but cottoned on quickly. "Over here, he is," 'You sexy bitch,' he added in his mind.

Ten-year-old Mathilda was thrilled. Thank goodness. She'd been so worried about lovely Dillon. Mummy wasn't being much help. It was upsetting, but sitting and crying wouldn't find him. And her brothers were no use. They were too easily distracted.

So, it had been left to her to find him, and now she had.

"Just round the corner…"

Of course. He loved that little pool. It made sense he'd head back there. She frowned as Dillon failed to appear at the water's edge. Oh no! He must have scurried off again. "Dillon! Dillon!"

"Shhh!" Adrian hissed. "You don't want to frighten him."

Why would he be scared? Tears sprung to her eyes. Unless he was hurt. "Oh, no. Poor Dillon." That's why he'd run away. He was in pain.

Dashing to the pool, she halted, arms falling to her sides, breath blowing over her lips. He was gone. Turning, she was shocked to see one of the men with his trousers down. Ugh, she thought. He should go behind a tree or something if he needed the toilet.

"Want some of this?" he asked, flapping his willy around.

Why? It made no sense. Want some of what?

The other man thrust his hand over her mouth at the same time she tried to scream.

"Shut up! Don't start that old shit. You know you want it."

Her little body racked as the man wobbled towards her pulling ever quicker at his willy.

"Get away from her!" The scream accompanied Susanna rushing at the two men three times her size. Shoving with all her might, she unbalanced Adrian.

Mathilda loosed her mouth enough to bite hard the man holding her.

"Oww! Little bitch!"

Scrabbling from the dip in the ground, Mathilda sprawled from the man's grasp writhing this way and that until she was free from his breathy plodding.

His cry was pure fury. Throwing a hand out, he caught Susanna's hair and yanked it down. She fell to the floor with a thud. "I'm getting me some action. I won't be put off any more!" he shrieked in her face.

Gripping her wrists with one chubby hand, he used his free one to wriggle free from his trousers. The sight of himself hanging limply angered him further. "Look! You've lost the mood now."

Flinching from the thrusting sausage as it waggled towards her mouth, Susanna was determined to bite the bloody thing off if it came anywhere near her.

"Get off me you sick pervert!" she snarled.

Why did they always say that? Fucking little prick teases

The sound shocked them all. Then the sight of a small yellow Kujo as he flew around the corner. Bounding towards them like near-death Woundwort in Watership Down, Dillon's foaming jaws had their full attention.

Snarling teeth snapped at anything that moved; an unfortunate situation for Toby whose shrivelling maggot grabbed his interest first.

Two hundred pounds per square inch is average in dog-bite terms. A German Shepherd's is higher, and the Turkish Kangal is getting on for nearly one thousand: almost as powerful as a lion. But the ferocious bite of a large adult Golden Retriever is, as one might expect, more than sufficient to relieve a Human male of its reproductive appendage.

The scream echoed through the valley as Dillon's canines sunk through gristle and cartilage. Blood sent to keep Toby erect now fountained in crimson spurts over the dogs face.

Adrian, infuriated with his friend's treatment as a result of a dalliance with yet another ungrateful frigid woman, leapt for the dog. "Come here, you vicious bastard."

It was the last thing he would ever say, as Dillon, in what he must have known would be a fatal move, sunk his teeth (still clogged with parts of Toby's anatomy) into Adrian's jugular.

Blood spewed as he rasped threats in his death-throws of what he would do to them all.

As he collapsed in a bloodied heap, Susanna shuffled frantically away.

Dillon turned to her and with a whimper, scarpered through the bushes. Before he disappeared, Susanna was sure she saw the real, loving Dillon in his eyes. What was wrong with him? Was he rabid?

"Mathilda? Edward? Thomas? Are you okay?"

Tear-streaked, the three of them gazed down at her and nodded in quick jerks.

"Come on. Let's go."

"But what about Dillon? He saved us," Mathilda croaked.

Susanna nodded. "I think he's not very well. Maybe we should call the RSPCA. They can get him to the vets. What do you think?"

The nodding continued and the bruised little family shuffled from the church. "We'll call the RSPCA and the police."

"No! We can't," cried the twins. "They'll take Dillon away from us!"

Susanna choked back the tears. Of course they were right. He'd killed two men. He couldn't come home. They couldn't not tell, could they?

They'd returned to Tenby and back to the safety of the holiday park when Susanna decided on her course of action. The children were watching with staring unseeing eyes, the antics of Bradley Bear and his furry chums on stage as they sang excruciating original songs whilst waving their arms in lieu of moving their lips.

It had been a day they would never forget. Sitting with all the jolly families after what they'd seen. After what they'd left behind…

"Wait here," Susanna whispered in their ears. "Don't leave the theatre. I'm just popping out for a while." With a stern stare, she was certain of the children's obedience. She didn't want them to witness what she was about to do. When Mathilda's eyes wet at the idea of being alone, she held her hand. "Don't worry, Tillie. You're safe here with all these people. I might be able to get Dillon back."

She'd convinced herself that Dillon had acted the way he had towards her when she'd tried to stop him eating the sandwiches because he'd sensed the threat. Somehow, he'd known those awful men were coming.

She owed him her life. She wasn't going to let what happened keep them apart. Fumbling keys from her pocket, she started the car and edged quietly from the campsite. Pausing to let some exuberant holiday makers cross the road, she pulled out and straight over the crossroads to Goreston. It was less than a mile to go via the roads. Soon she pulled along the lane to the old church.

Slamming shut the car door, she raced around the church. With a frown, she was sure she heard voices from inside. A girl calling for her daddy. What should she do? Susanna determined she was in no danger. Dillon had already dealt with the threat and she had to be quick.

If she was going to find Dillon, she had to have time to get him home, hundreds of miles from his crime. To buy that time, she had an awful job to do. But he'd saved her life. She owed him this.

As she rounded the corner of the church, she stepped to the well. Kicking at the body nearest her, she jumped back. She'd seen the movies where the supposedly dead killer unexpectedly grabs an unsuspecting ankle, and she wasn't about to be so foolish.

Bending over, she rested flat hands on the man's round torso and heaved. He rolled first one arm, then the other, tumbling into the crimson pool and dropping out of sight to the bottom.

The other body proved harder, but she had no choice. Glaring at his cold eyes, she fought the urge to spit on him from a sudden misguided panic about leaving traceable DNA at this crime scene. Grasping both his wrists, she hauled him an inch at a time. He was heavy.

Gathering momentum with every heave, suddenly he slid on the remains of his anatomy to the edge of the water coming to a stop in a steaming heap. Susanna lifted her leg and rested her foot on his back to shove him in.

"Don't... Please," Toby pleaded.

Susanna gasped. He wasn't dead. With a furtive glance at his ruined nether region, Susanna didn't pause. Shoving him with all her weight, he flopped into the pool and sank as his friend before him.

Susanna waited. Three bubbles burst on the surface, and then it was still.

Staring at the water, daring it to ripple... for the hideous man to reach out to grab her. She was prepared. He wouldn't get out, she was determined.

CHAPTER FORTY-FIVE

Shivering, curled on the floor, Bertie was roused by the distant timbre of Charlotte calling him.

"Daddy! There you are. Are you okay?"

No! He couldn't let her near him. He didn't know what he was capable of. The dreams? They must have been premonitions? Last time he recalled Charlotte visiting him here, he'd killed her.

He was convinced he'd brutally murdered the two men by the well even though he had no memory of it other than seeing someone at the Holy water and being angry about it.

Pushing up from the floor, he allowed a glance back to Charlotte. Damn! She'd seen him. He had to get away.

Sprinting for the church, he threw the oak doors closed behind him and rattled the bolts home. Trotting along the nave, he passed the cross and the door to the tower and reached the door that led to the well and the scene of the grotesque murder scene.

Could he escape here, re-lock the door before Charlotte would think where to look? What if she heard him and saw the bodies?

Banging from the vestibule convinced him to get out. Grasping the handle, he turned it but it wouldn't budge. Was it locked? Where was the key?

Clever girl. He could see Charlotte's small fingers wiggling the bolts free as she reached under the gap in the centuries old oak door. Where could he go? She'd find him in the tower or the office, but the tower had the added danger she might fall. He would lock himself in his office and stay silent.

With quick thought, he removed one of his shoes and left it by the locked door. Charlotte might spot it and work out he must have escaped and re-locked the door behind him. She'd find the bodies, but at least she wouldn't find him. At least she'd be safe.

Flying into his little office, he bolted the door and hid behind his desk.

"Daddy? Daddy, where are you?"

Trembling, he controlled his breathing. He couldn't let her find him.

It was from a distance, but understanding where she was going made following her easy for

Richard. It was a scene he'd been forced to play before. He didn't relish it now, but he knew what he had to do... What God needed him to do.

She was at the front of the church now. It seemed locked but he could see her bend down and wriggle the bolts free. He'd done the same thing himself weeks before. He took it as a sign.

The empty church echoed to the sound of her breath. Taking a tentative step, she didn't know why he was trying to get away from her, but it wasn't a game.

Her mummy going to the police; her daddy not being home and running: it made no sense but she knew it was serious. "Daddy? What's wrong? What have you done?"

From behind the desk, Bertie prayed she'd find the shoe and be wrong-footed. His love for her twisted in his heart, but at the same time the new familiar rage built within him. She must know he didn't want to see her, yet she'd gone against his wishes. Why would she do that? Grinding his fist into his thigh, kneading pain into himself, he stared at the door and willed her away.

Walking slowly, listening for tell-tale breathing, Charlotte moved along the nave. At each pew she paused and stared. He wasn't there, but wait... What was that? Plucking the key from the floor, she clutched it tight and continued along the aisle to the cross.

The curtain behind the pulpit hung oddly, several rings snapped from their pole. "Daddy. I know you're behind the curtain. Please don't hide from me. I don't care what you've done. I love you."

Behind the desk, Bertie's heart broke. He wanted desperately to believe her, but couldn't. If she saw what he'd done, she could never love him.

Reaching the curtain, Charlotte knew her daddy couldn't remain so silent. Knowing he wouldn't be there, she still flapped it open to reveal nothing, just as she expected. Then she saw it.

By the back door, her daddy's shoe. He must have been in such a hurry to escape seeing her, his shoe came off and he didn't stop to put it back on.

Reaching the door, she picked up the shoe and turned the handle. It was locked. He must have run out and locked it behind him. Unless…

Offering the key in her hand to the keyhole, it opened the door. Stepping outside, she called briefly before her logic caught up with her. He couldn't have locked it from the outside and the key be inside. There could be another key, but she didn't imagine there was. From where she found this one, it had most likely been thrown. He *wanted* her to believe he'd gone through the door. I mean, whose shoe falls off by a door? Too convenient. So where was he really?

She considered the tower. It wouldn't take much effort to see if he was there. Opening the door, she peered up. It was pitch black, but she'd been up before. It led to the turrets on the top. Maybe he was there, but if he was in the only other place he could be—his office, then if she was preoccupied climbing the steps in the dark, he might run away again.

Re-closing the door, she stepped towards the only other door. With both doors in sight, she tried the handle. It too was locked. "Daddy, I know you're in there. You must be to have slid the bolt. Please talk to me."

Knowing he'd been outsmarted, Bertie cried, "Charlotte, please. Leave me alone. I can't talk to you. You don't understand!"

"No, I don't," Charlotte's voice trilled with a sob caught in her throat. "I don't care what you've done. I just wanted to tell you the baby's coming!"

Bertie gasped. The baby. Was that good? Could he be trusted? Images of baby Alice swirled in his mind… the blood, the gurgling…

The door rattled. "Daddy, please let me in. We can go to the hospital together."

Tap, tap, tap. Tap, tap, tap. Rattle, rattle.

"Oh for God's sake leave me alone!" Bertie screamed. Scrambling from behind the desk, he shot to the door threw back the bolt and yanked it open. Her little face gazed up at him, tears in her eyes. He'd never shouted at her before.

Part of him wanted to clutch her to him, but he didn't trust himself. What if killing her was the final test from his Lord? *Genesis 22:1-2 Abraham and Isaac*

Bertie wasn't prepared to make the same sacrifice. He wasn't even convinced Abraham should have done deciding instead it was a big misunderstanding and God finally got through to him before it was too late and he killed his own son.

He would gladly defy God if it meant keeping Charlotte safe. That was something new he'd learnt. The anger was just at bay beneath the surface. Allowing enough through to be sufficiently terrifying to frighten his daughter away, Bertie growled, "Just leave me in peace. I can't be bothered at the moment!"

"But, Daddy. Why don't we go and see Mummy? We might have a new baby by now!"

"Do as you are bloody told, young lady." Calculated but firm, Bertie grasped her shoulders. Shaking her he was sure to get her attention. But then, he couldn't stop. The shaking grew more and more severe and her little head flew back and forth, screams echoing through the mediaeval rafters.

"Daddy, don't! You're hurting me. Stop!"

Thwack!

Bertie fell to the ground. Charlotte gasping for breath scrambled free. Free from her daddy and free from the man who stood over him.

"Wait. Charlotte. It's all right. I won't hurt you."

Ducking the man's grasp, she swerved through the pews and out through the vestibule. Throwing open the door, she ran up the lane and away from the church, tears streaming down her little face.

Richard stood and contemplated his work. That made three people he'd killed. He'd had no choice. Well, perhaps the first time. He chose not to let Terry Paige die a normal death and face judgement day in his own sweet time. He couldn't allow that. And if he had his time over again, apart from never letting Chloe out of his sight, he would smash the life out of the evil bastard, gleefully watching his evil soul slip from his eyes as he sent him to his maker.

Bending with a sigh, Richard grabbed the ankles of his latest victim. As he heaved him the few feet to the door, he realised this would be a greater task than he would want. Bertie Brimble was heavy.

Leaning his full weight he shifted the body a metre at a time. Not far to go.

Reaching the back door, he rattled the handle and the door opened. From there it was only a few feet to the well and another few to his final destination.

Walking backwards, an ankle gripped in each hand, Richard towed the sprawling Bertie one metre after another, Bertie's arms swinging behind him over his head through the dirt.

They paused at the well. Why people had such a fascination with it, Richard would never know. It was only water. You wouldn't catch him drinking from it. Not after what he'd seen. Peering in now, he couldn't even see the bottom, so much sediment floated around.

Reaching behind a slab of granite at the Cawdor Family Crypt, Richard heaved it open. It took force but he'd done it before. "I shouldn't have had to do this," Richard muttered to the silent Bertie. "You're supposed to be men of God. There's no God in you!"

Flinching back at the smell, he stepped in and re-grabbed Bertie's ankles. "I liked you. You seemed so nice. But then, I liked Reverend Jones too. That's what made me suspicious. You started acting weird just like he did." Richard sighed. "What was it? Did you join the church to cover the monster you are? That makes sense. At the Alpha course, everyone turned to Christianity to improve who they were. What if who you were was a monster? Well, maybe you'd be tempted to go all the way and join the clergy. Is that right? Is that why you ordained?" Of course no answer came.

"And then you come here where my beautiful sister…" he still couldn't say the words. "I couldn't believe it. I found them… Oliver Jones and the other poor little girl, Lilly. My mind whirled. I'd dealt with whom I thought was my sister's killer. Had I got it wrong?

"But as Oliver Jones begged for his life; said he'd done nothing like this before; said he'd been taken over, I knew.

"It seemed only right that his last resting place should be with the very scum he admired so much. And then you came along. Thank God that I was in time. Maybe you didn't deserve to die. I mean, technically you haven't killed Charlotte. But only because I stopped you." Richard frowned. "No. You were going to kill her. I can't start doubting myself now. The synchronicity of seeing Charlotte hop out of that car. No, I can't question it now. If I hadn't stopped you, you would have murdered her."

With one final shove, he rolled Bertie inside the small stone room. Hand over his mouth to stop from gagging, he pushed the rock back and listened for the clunk as it fell into place. "I told you this church helped me more than I could tell you. Now, in death, you'll understand why."

Shaking his head he walked away up the lane. Glancing back at the church, he stifled the emotion it wrought. Was God here? So much evil had happened. But he'd been called to counteract it, hadn't he?

Coming to church after Chloe, well, that made sense. Finding the opening to the crypt? Well that smacked of more than coincidence; especially when he came face to face with Terry Paige... his sister's killer.

It wasn't peace it gave him, but purpose. Wasn't it just like Chloe to put other people first? She'd sacrificed herself so that Richard could rid the world of her killer and those who followed. How many lives had they saved together? Nodding to the sky, he rasped, "I love you Chloe."

Shuffling along the road, he'd soon be in bed where he'd sleep it off as he had before. He needed his rest to be ready for the next threat when it came.

CHAPTER FORTY-SIX

Bertie's eyes fluttered but his mouth wouldn't connect to his brain. Maybe it was just as well. If Richard knew he wasn't dead, would he try to finish the job?

The smell was the most terrible he'd ever experienced. It was pitch black in the tomb, but Bertie knew what was in there with him. And he knew why.

Holding out little hope, he moved his numb arm to his pocket and removed his phone. It couldn't work, could it? Not after its soaking in the well? Pressing the button on the side, Bertie cried with relief as the little screen illuminated with the phone brand and a cheery welcome.

At first, he stared at it to ascertain bars of signal. Only when there were none did his eyes leave the screen.

From the tiny illumination what it lit was horrific. Lying beside him, a look of terror on his sallow face, were the remains of who Bertie now knew to be Oliver Jones. He still wore his smock and dog-collar, under his mauve face. The crypt had preserved him well.

With a whimper, Bertie turned on the torch function of his phone and shone it beyond Oliver to the other body.

Slumped in the corner, the bloodied corpse of Terry Paige lay with a self-satisfied smirk on his face. How had he felt, confronted with the brother of his victim? Was he even guilty? Wouldn't the police have kept him in custody if he were?

Beyond Terry, something caught Bertie's attention. What was that sound? The light glistened from something and lit the inside of the crypt with eerie ripples. Water!

Revulsion sprung to Bertie's lips as his mind whirled. He couldn't quite piece it together, but a theory was forming rapidly in his mind.

Rachmaninoff tinkled through his thoughts. He shook his head. Come on, Bertie. Don't be distracted. You have to get out of here. You aren't a monster. Like Richard. God has been steering you too.

Still the macabre violence of his chords and racing fingers flurried through Bertie's thoughts until, breathless, the concerto brought him crashing to the truth.

The water! Terry Paige. That was it! Murdering

paedophile, Terry Paige had been 'donating' his bloody remains to anyone who drank at the well. And just as the piano playing prodigy had received the hand of a concert pianist along with new desires and abilities to play, he and Oliver Jones had been filled with the disgusting desires of this aberration.

Images of Claire and Gareth from this evening's News fought their way into his mind. Of course! Gareth had drunk the water too. Bertie had seen him. And now they were dead. It wasn't difficult to imagine what might have led up to that.

And the bodies by the pool? A similar murderous fate no doubt. Everyone said it tasted of blood. It did. Richard thought he was saving lives, but people were dying as his sister's killer murdered beyond the grave.

The rage the donor water still in his body brought forth erupted. In the confines of the crypt, violence was contained, but Bertie's thrashing limbs struck Oliver as he aimed for Terry. His shod foot made contact. He was going to knock that smug smile off his face. Kicking and kicking, he couldn't see, but could feel the flesh loosening from his skull. He'd been in here for weeks and he was rotting. The smell confirmed that. Exhausted. Bertie shone his torch. There was no sanctimony now. It can't have been true, but it looked as though Terry had felt every kick.

"Dillon. Here boy." Susanna had retraced her steps and avoided looking at the well. The gap in the hedge where Dillon disappeared was hard to find in the fading light, but she forced her way through into the field beyond.

"Dillon. Good boy. Where are you?"

Walking the perimeter of the field, the sea twinkled in the orange of the setting sun. The spike of Lydstep rock fluttered her heart. He'd torn off in such a hurry, what if he'd flown straight off the cliff? Remembering passing the same spot earlier, she tried not to picture his broken body on the rocks below.

The awful men who had attacked her and her family, Dillon had despatched in such spectacular style, flitted in her mind, batted away by conscious thought determined to remain on task.

"Dillon! Where are you?"

Before she even reached the coast she heard his whimper. The hazy sunlight was enough to illuminate his dark eyes in the shrubbery. "Dillon?" Edging towards him, she held out her hand. "It's okay. I forgive you. You must have sensed those nasty men. That's why you were aggressive. I know. I understand. I'm not going to leave you here so you might as well come out now."

With a whine and a wag, Dillon shambled from his hiding place, the shame dripping from him with sagging ears and creased eyes.

"Come on, boy. It's okay."

Leaping for her, Dillon smothered his owner with licking kisses, still unsure if her mercy was for real.

"Thank you. Thank you for saving us, Dillon. You're a good boy."

Wagging in full motion now, the reunited pair fairly skipped back along the field to the church-yard.

No sooner had they ducked through the hedge than Dillon was growling again.

"It's okay, boy. They aren't there anymore. You did a good job," the words stuck in her throat at the grotesque memories.

Dillon persisted. Jolting away from her, he ran for the well. Susanna gazed on, half expecting the zombie apocalypse and the two men crawling from the water she'd dumped them in like creatures from the swamp.

But Dillon didn't run to the water. He stopped at a vault a few feet from it. Sniffing, he barked and scratched at the stone.

"Come away, Dillon. Come on!" Susanna couldn't endure more death. Her children needed to see their dog again. They needed to get back to normal.

But he wouldn't budge, growling and barking.

"My dad's in there." Charlotte shuffled from behind a tree. Quivering, she wiped her eye with her sleeve.

"Oh, sweetie, I'm so sorry to hear that. When did he... leave us?"

Charlotte squinted trying to work out what the lady meant. Shaking her head, she whispered, "He's not dead. A man put him in there."

"What man?"

"I don't know his name. He's been to our house and waited for me outside my school. He hurt my daddy."

Susanna's eyes bulged. Had she walked into the twilight zone? Was everyone in this village a murdering psychopath? Gulping down her own guilt at the man pleading for his life who she'd shoved under the water, she said, "Well, we have to get him out."

Charlotte pointed to where she'd seen the tomb open. "I've been trying to open it. Something here clicks and it slides to reveal a big hole, but I can't make it work," she squealed, desperate to make this lady understand. "That's where the man put him." She hid her face in her hands. Youthful optimism coursed hope through her veins, but there was doubt too.

Susanna felt around the base. Nothing obvious protruded. Patting her hands all over, she became increasingly certain there was no way to open the crypt. Closing her eyes, she began to feel a fool. She'd get back to her car and find it vandalised, or missing altogether.

"What are you doing?"

"Look out, It's him!" Charlotte blurted as she jumped out of reach, scurrying out of sight. Dillon bared his teeth and Richard thought better of making a grab for Susanna.

Lowering his arms, he glared. "You can't open that. It wouldn't be a good idea."

Gripping Dillon's collar, Susanna struggled to hold on. "This girl says her dad is in there."

Richard shook his head. "That's ridiculous isn't it? She's obviously making it up. Now come away. Please." Taking a step towards Susanna, Dillon growled and jumped up. Susanna creased her eyes. Dillon was a good judge and this man was creepy.

"Come away. Please. It's not a good idea to open it up."

He was afraid. She could see that now, and looking beyond the grubbiness of his face and clothes, she saw how young he was. Not more than twenty.

"The little girl says her dad's in there and I believe her. You don't want him to die, so help me open this," appealing to his better nature, Susanna hoped.

"He's dead." Turning to where he'd last seen Charlotte, he cried, "He was going to kill you. Trust me, I've seen it before." Crazy eyes falling back to Susanna, he went on, "They join the church to hide the monsters they are you see? I couldn't believe it. I thought I'd killed the wrong man at first when I found Terry Paige. But then Reverend Jones became weird. Cocky, aggressive. I should have known what he was capable of. I'd seen the same cockiness in Terry. But I didn't and he murdered poor Lilly because I was too late. I hadn't worked it out, you see."

"What did you do?" Keeping an even tone to gain his trust, she hoped he would open the tomb.

"I stopped him hurting anyone else."

"And did you put him in here?"

He nodded. "That's why I can't let you open it. I'll be in trouble, and then me and Chloe can't stop the next one, you see? No-one else is looking out for them like I am. For the safety of all the beautiful young girls. I saw it in the new vicar too. I knew this day would come and I caught him shaking Charlotte like a rag doll. I couldn't let him hurt her, could I? So I hit him, and, well, you can't open the crypt."

"Who's Chloe?"

"She was my sister. Still is, but now she talks to me from here." He patted his heart. "Stopping more murdering scum is the only good thing that's come from her death… So like her to be so selfless. Sacrificing herself so we can save the rest together. But if you open it and I'm found out, don't you see. She'll have died for no reason… Do you see?"

"Listen. You have to. The poor girl's dad is trapped inside."

"He's a murderer too! Or he would have been if I hadn't stopped him. He was going to kill his own daughter. He doesn't deserve to be alive does he?"

The man she'd pushed under the water filled her thoughts. She knew exactly what he meant. He must have seen what she'd seen. To him, this tomb was as incriminating as the pool was for her and Dillon. What good would it be if the law avenged the abominations she'd seen disposed of there? All that would achieve is they'd both go to prison, lovely Dillon would be destroyed, and her children, who had gone through quite enough, would end up in care because their gambling addict father would be no use.

"Okay," she said. "I believe you. I understand. I think you did the right thing and I won't tell. But what about the girl? If she tells the police about her dad in the tomb…"

Richard clenched his fist and hit himself hard in the forehead. What should he do? How could he stop her from telling? He couldn't hurt her, could he? He'd be as bad as all the others? He would find her; talk to her; make her understand.

"Chloe," he called, then shaking his head in rapid jerks to clear his mind, he yelled, "Charlotte. Come here. It's about your daddy."

"Dillon will find her." With a nod of agreement from her new partner in crime, Susanna released him. Rushing into the hedges, he shot out of sight. "Quick. Don't let her get away."

It swirled in Susanna's head. The girl might describe her, or her car, and, of course, Dillon was another identifying feature. She hoped they'd find her fast and persuade her to keep quiet. Biting her cheek, she couldn't believe how she was thinking.

But she wouldn't risk being associated with a scene of how many murders? She'd lost count.

The man tore after Dillon, "Good boy. Good dog," he yelled as the Golden Retriever hurtled across the field towards the cliff. In the distance, a tiny figure, displaced by the commotion, ran as fast as she could away from the church.

She was no match for the dog. Bounding up to her he jumped and brought her to the ground in one bound. Licking her face and wagging, Charlotte patted him. "You have to let me get away, dog. They want to hurt me. Please let me go."

Plucking a stick from the ground, she hurled it far but he showed no interest and the man was gaining fast. "Get away, dog. Let me go." As Charlotte sprinted, Dillon ran beside, leaping and grabbing her hand in play.

Almost reaching the cliff edge, Charlotte tried calculating a route she might make that the man couldn't because of his size. But it was all in her mind. She'd never walked this way before.

Closing her eyes just for a second, she prayed. "Please, God, help me escape." With a surge of confidence, she rushed as fast as her legs would take her towards the edge of the cliff.

Thump, thump, thump, the man's feet were nearly on her. The dog slowed her, but she weaved in and out of his playful bounds.

She could see the cliff edge now, and she could hear the water below crashing into the rocks. "Please God, please, God, please God," she repeated.

Closing her eyes one last time, she took a leap of faith.

Richard was almost upon her, he couldn't believe what he was seeing. "Stop. I only want to talk to you!" Watching, open mouthed as she soared into the air, he threw out his arms to catch her. Stumbling over Dillon as he weaved in and out where Charlotte jumped, he tipped forwards tumbling in a somersault over Charlotte as her course fell closer to the cliff.

As the gorse caught her school tie and slammed her onto a rocky ledge where she disturbed a roosting pigeon, she winced in horror as the man fell head over feet over head, vanishing into the crashing waves beneath.

Above her, the dog's barking echoed from the rocks into the night.

CHAPTER FORTY-SEVEN

The churchyard flashed intermittent blue and red. Officers searched every corner with torches. "She was last seen followed by a male suspect in the field to the right. You can cut across to the school from there. Her dad's the new vicar and we're presuming she was coming to see him."

"Should we get the dogs?"

"If they're in the area, I think we should, yes," DC Griffiths agreed. "And the helicopter too."

The hive of activity went unnoticed by Dillon and Charlotte, and Susanna.

Charlotte thanked God. She had leapt and he had caught her. But now, the school tie threatened to tear and let her fall, or strangle her. Reaching up trembling hands, she gripped onto the gorse, but the dry twig in her grasp snapped at once.

Eyes searching for anything to grab in the dusky light, she gasped as a face peered over the edge. It was the dog lady.

"Good boy, Dillon. Oh my goodness!" she cried seeing Charlotte. "I thought you were a goner." Stretching down her arm, her reach wasn't long enough and Charlotte couldn't move for forcing her tearing tie to make its choice.

The woman disappeared before reappearing moments later with something in her hand. The clatter of a chain tumbling towards her was manna.

As the dog lead came within reach, Charlotte gave a silent prayer of thanks, and regarded the chain. She was sure she could reach it but she'd have to swing to one side to touch a jutting out rock to propel her the few centimetres she needed to grab it. If she missed, her school tie wouldn't save her.

Swinging across on bouncing feet, her toe caught the rock and she sprang up. Mid-air, nothing to prevent her falling but grabbing the lead, that's when the thought occurred. Could she trust this woman?

Arm outstretched, her fingers grazed the collar, as her tie snapped and hung on the gorse bush.

In the last second, the chain dropped enough for her to grab tight.

"Hold on!" Susanna cried needlessly. "I don't have much of a hold."

White teeth gripped the handle below where Susanna tugged. Leaning back with a mighty growl, Dillon hunkered for the job in hand, or mouth. As Charlotte's fingers reached over the cliff, followed by her arm, then shoulders, Susanna rushed to grab her.

"Come on honey, come on. Take my hands."

Charlotte looked into her eyes. She'd wanted to leave her daddy in the tomb. She had sent the man chasing after her.

The grass in her grip tore as the tuft gave in and her weight swung backwards.

With a primaeval cry, Susanna leapt forward and grabbed both her wrists. Hauling her to safety, she threw her arms around her.

As they trembled in the fading light, they became aware of the police lights for the first time. Holding Charlotte's shoulders, Susanna gazed into her eyes. "Please don't tell them you saw me. Please. Dillon did a bad thing and he could be in a lot of trouble. Do you understand? And if it wasn't for him…" She didn't need to add, 'You'd be dead at the bottom of the cliff.'

"But you could have helped my dad and you didn't. You sent that man to catch me."

"To talk to you, that's all. I didn't know you'd run. I'm sorry. I really am. Go now and tell the police to open that crypt. But please don't mention me. They'll take Dillon and he saved my life. And now he's just saved yours too."

There was too much to consider. Charlotte loved the dog. And if saving him meant saving her too, then she would. If she didn't promise, she didn't trust that the lady would let her go anyway. "I won't say anything. I promise."

"Good girl. I'm going to take Dillon now before before he ends up in trouble. Will you be okay?"

Charlotte didn't have time for foolish questions. Before the woman demanded any more from her she ran towards the blue flashing lights and to safety.

Discovering her will keep them busy, Susanna thought as she found the steps down to the beach which led along to the holiday park. She could report her car stolen, and no-one need ever know about Dillon and what he did.

"Over here." The police lady hugged Charlotte to her. "Charlotte Brimble? Lots of people have been very worried about you! Are you okay? Did anybody hurt you?"

"They tried to, but God wouldn't let them."

CHAPTER FORTY-EIGHT

Bertie filtered the putrid air from his mouth. He'd cried out until he was hoarse but despite hearing a commotion outside, there had been no response.

Everything was crystal clear now, and it was another lesson. Deuteronomy *32:35–'It is mine to avenge; I will repay. In due time their foot will slip; their day of disaster is near and their doom rushes upon them.'*

Richard King had avenged his sister, and who wouldn't if faced with the same? But in so doing, he added to the evil and it multiplied. Bertie sighed. Reverend Oliver Jones, the good man everyone had said, turned into a monster by the donated remains of a killer.

Bertie knew.

There was no coincidence. Going to the doctor, being sent to Doctor Simons the very same day as the man with the newly found pianist skills and nightmares of his donor's death. He'd dismissed it because it hadn't fitted into his faith. But true faith should always be questioned, because the truth never changes. It is not afraid of questions. It welcomes them.

And now he knew himself how it changed you. Someone else's perspective; a shift in desire; in empathy; in rationale, and he was no better than anyone else.

What would have happened if Richard King hadn't stopped him? She was already screaming, 'Daddy stop. Daddy, you're hurting me.' But he hadn't stopped, and he had hurt her.

So better this. Better his last memory be a clarity in understanding of his Lord, than to have caused harm to his little angel, Charlotte.

Richard was on an unstoppable path. And just because he knew why he'd taken the first step didn't make the destination any nobler. How many times would he kill because he felt justified? Carrying on was all that gave meaning to what had happened to his sister. But he'd created that which he sought to destroy. Without Terry Paige, Oliver Jones would never have hurt Lilly. So in avenging one life, he cost two.

And Bertie had seen the men dead by the pool. And he'd seen the three bodies washing ashore on the television. That made eight people who had died as a result of his act of vengeance. Eight. Soon to be nine, he knew, as his breathing became more and more laboured.

Bertie saw the good in him. He would never have done it if he'd known where it could end. But God makes it clear: *Romans 12:17-21 'Repay no one evil for evil, but give thought to do what is honourable in the sight of all... Never avenge yourselves, but leave it to the wrath of God, for it is written, "Vengeance is mine, I will repay," says the Lord...*

"If your enemy is hungry, feed him; if he is thirsty, give him something to drink...

Do not be overcome by evil, but overcome evil with good.'

All the times he'd allowed the Bible to open where it wanted had led him here. He hadn't listened, but looking back it could hardly have been clearer.

The effect of Richard's vengeance was undeniable, but, Bertie acknowledged, he was about to pay the price for his own. It wasn't the pain he'd inflicted on another; Terry Paige surely hadn't felt a thing as Bertie kicked and kicked his bones from his body, but Bertie had. He'd suffered all the rage and venom for the evil the man had wrought, and now he was to pay the ultimate price.

It's funny how when you're forced to appreciate the little things, it turns out they're the bigger things. And the littlest thing of all, the thing we take for granted every breath we take is the air that gives us life. Air that Bertie now valued for the first time. Because it was that air, and the oxygen within, already depleted in its role decaying the remains of Oliver Jones and Terry Paige that now finally threatened to disappear forever. With every breath, Bertie transformed the composition of his limited supply.

It was an odd thought to have as he closed his eyes for the final time, so he tried to change it, filling his mind with happy things: His faultless, tolerant, forgiving wife. His beautiful girl whom he'd adored even before her birth, and now... And now a new little life, created in love to carry forth the Brimble name. Love. That was all that mattered.

Love.

Love.

Love.

CHAPTER FORTY-NINE

I t took a while to find the way to open the crypt, but access to the right kind of experts meant it was only a matter of time.

"Hello. Is there anybody in here?"

As the torchlight fell on the butchery and the smell filled the nose of the fireman as he peered into the vault, Bertie prized open slits of eyes and pulled apart his dry lips.

"I am," the sound like wind through reeds caught the air as it rushed to fill every hole.

"She was right! There is someone alive in here. Come on, help me!"

As the crew forced themselves in and stretchered the heavyweight vicar from his grave, Bertie smiled. Love had saved him. And as he let his gaze run free, he saw her. His little girl.

Visions of all that he'd done, and all he'd nearly done filled his head and tightened his heart. He didn't deserve saving. He should have resisted the evil that had threatened. If he was unable, how could he ask it of anyone else?

But then she came closer. "Daddy. I knew you'd be all right," she smiled down at him with the innocence of the heavens.

Grasping hold of the sides of the stretcher, Bertie displaced his weight and threw himself to the ground.

"Whoa. Careful there. We need to take you to the ambulance; get you checked out."

Pushing the help aside, he crawled on hands and knees to Charlotte's feet. Kneeling up, he prayed she'd want to hug him. When her arms enveloped him, love flooded in and conquered all else. Snuffling into her hair he cried, "Charlotte, my angel. I'm so sorry."

Charlotte broke free from his embrace to stare into his ruddy face. "What for?"

Bertie frowned. "For... For..." he stammered. So much had happened it was pointless holding on. He owed it to his family to forgive himself and move on. Eyes twinkling, he smiled. "I don't know. I just love you."

"I love you too," she smiled back and threw her arms back around him. Clutching her hard, he knew he'd never let her go.

EPILOGUE

They advised him to go to hospital, but when he said he was going there anyway to meet his new son and that he'd be in the right place if he needed help, they had no choice but to agree.

Promising the police he'd make whatever statements they needed tomorrow, they agreed as well. He was a victim not a suspect.

And so, paying the taxi as it pulled into the drop-off point at Withybush General Hospital, Bertie and Charlotte hurried along the corridor.

'*Physiotherapy/Ffisiotherapi,*' '*Maternity/Mamo-laeth,*' the sign directed, taking twice as long to read in two languages. "Down here."

They reached the lift. The two flights of stairs would be too much, Charlotte had insisted. "You've been through a lot, Dad." *Dad* now. Not *Daddy.* That was reserved for babies perhaps. And she was a life-saving heroine and possible big-sister.

Approaching the double doors, Bertie's heart beat wildly.

"You took your time!" a voice from a side room bellowed.

"Grandad Tom!" Charlotte squealed."

"Reverend Richards. What are you doing here?" Bertie gasped.

"Well, that's not much of a welcome for your father-in-law, now is it? Annie called me. Said she wasn't sure you'd make it in time."

"And you drove all the way from Bristol?"

"It's not that far. Only a couple of hours. Your lot are here from Hereford. I'd say that's more impressive."

Tears filled Bertie's eyes and he could barely speak. "And Annabel?"

"Doing brilliantly. I was there at the birth! I never thought I'd see my daughter in such a position, but I tell you what. It's a humbling experience. She's my new hero." He grinned, knowing full well his daughter's opinion of him and understanding Bertie's confusion. "I always just wanted the best for her. And now, well, she *is* the best. I'm so proud. Her mum would have been proud too," his gaze fell to the floor while he regained his composure. "Come on. There's someone who wants to meet you."

Bertie followed his father-in-law to a room beyond the double doors where they were buzzed in by a smiling midwife. It was a knowing smile. A proud smile.

Holding Charlotte's hand, he joined his mum, dad and sister beside the bed and let his eyes fall on what they were gazing at.

"What's he doing here?" Annabel shuffled in the bed.

"Mum. Stop." Charlotte eased between them. "It's alright. Daddy's okay now."

"is she right, Bertie," Annabel's eyes bore into him.

He had no voice to speak but his nods were earnest. He understood now. He'd succumbed to evil and he'd been rescued by overwhelming love.

Recognising the truth, she accepted. "Meet your son," he next words.

Passing the little bundle who objected immediately with open mouthed hunting for milk, he happily gripped his daddy's finger instead. "Look, Charlotte. It's your baby brother."

Charlotte beamed at him. "What's his name?"

They hadn't decided. He could join the long line of Bertie's from the Brimbles or, "What about Thomas?" Annabel gushed, turning to her dad. "You were brilliant, Dad. I couldn't have done it without you and I'm so pleased you're here. What do you think? Thomas? After my dad?"

With moist eyes and a thick throat, Reverend

Richards nodded. "I'd be absolutely delighted."

"Thomas it is!" Bertie exclaimed.

"Hello, Thomas." Charlotte beamed. "Croeso I Gymru."

Two weeks later…

With Thomas bouncing on her knee, Annabel watched the News. "Mummy doesn't like the News, sweetheart, but Daddy and Grandad do," she cooed, smiling at Bertie and her dad who was enjoying his time away from the city. She was sure she'd revert to her head-in-the-sand ways again before long, but it was a relief to not have to watch every stranger behind every tree.

There was still the matter of Lilly's mum and dad being tortured with their faces on TV disclosing how they'd always remember their daughter, but they had a peace knowing her killer was no more.

The police and the press had not drawn the same conclusions as Bertie. They weren't about to agree the essence of Terry Paige afflicted anyone who drank the well water, so assumed he killed Lilly, which in a way he did. It wasn't worth arguing the point. Certainly not to Bertie Brimble.

But they still closed the well after finding the two bodies of Adrian and Toby whom they stated to the press appeared to have been attacked by a wild animal, maybe a rabid fox or badger, their deaths ruled as 'misadventure.'

They didn't seem that keen on uncovering the truth. Any version of it that allowed them to declare the Goreston Massacre in the past not the present sufficed. And so, as is often the case, the matter disappeared from television to be forgotten within months by the public at large, and never spoken of again by the parish of the Church of Saint Julian and its Holy Well.

Three hundred miles away in Hertfordshire, Susanna Smith reached out and ruffled Dillon's ears in both hands. "A badger, eh? Or a rabid fox? No mention of a crazy Golden Retriever, was there, boy?"

"So this is my replacement, is it?" Simon grinned, holding Mathilda's hand as they came in from the garden where he'd been putting the finishing touches to the Wendy-House he bought her for her birthday.

"Maybe he's an embellishment, not a replacement," Susanna's hooded eyes blinked slowly. Simon had devoted all his time since their split in therapy and promised he'd never so much as look at a lottery ticket, let alone a bookies or online gambling, and Susanna was willing to give him another try.

Goreston had given her a new perspective.

They'd never share their finances like they had, but there was more to life than money. There was love.

'Tis better to have loved and lost
than never to have loved at all.'

Tennyson's famous line, a comfort and now an epitaph for the graves of Chloe King, Richard King and Lilly Jones.

In time, the devastated parents might agree. They would go through a hundred days of pain to have but one day of the love they'd lost.

The grief would last a lifetime. They already knew that.

The spaces at the dinner table never to feel less empty, nor would the birthdays and Christmases missed ever fail to fuel that agony of if-only.

But through their loss, they may learn appreciation for the little things and greet them with a deeper gratitude because of what they know.

The love they share cannot and will not be destroyed. It will forever endure.

Being parents of the lights of their lives is the greatest of all gifts. And not even death can take that away

I'D LOVE TO HEAR FROM YOU ABOUT ABSOLUTELY ANYTHING...

You can get in touch with me here: mccarterauthor@gmail.com, and, www.facebook.com/ michaelchristophercarter and, www.michaelchristopher-carter.co.uk

ABOUT THE AUTHOR

Michael grew up in the leafy suburbs of Hertfordshire in the eighties. His earliest school memories from his first parent's evening were being told "You have to be a writer"; advice Michael didn't take for another thirty-five years, despite a burning desire.

Instead, he forged a career in direct sales, travelling the length and breadth of Southern England selling fitted kitchens, bedrooms, double-glazing and conservatories, before running his own water-filter business (with an army of over four hundred water filter salesmen and women) and then a conservatory sales and building company.

Unusually for someone at the cutting edge of sales, Michael explored his spiritual side and qualified as a Reiki Master in 1999, and soon after left the workd of sales behind and became a carer for a family member and moved to Wales, where he finally found the time and inspiration to write.

Michael now indulges his passion in the beautiful Pembrokeshire Coast National Park where he lives, walks and works with his wife, four children and Golden Retriever.

BOOKS BY THIS AUTHOR

Paranormal Tales From Wales Series

This title is part of Carter's series of standalone novels: Paranormal Tales from Wales
Each story, set in the beautiful principality, features different supernatural elements; from psychic powers to unusual hauntings, from deadly dreams to parallel realities, from other-worldly visitors to surprising monsters, and much more. If you like a twist in your paranormal tale you can check out Michael's other titles on Amazon. Simply search 'Michael Christopher Carter'

Printed in Great Britain
by Amazon